RAINBOW VALLEY

RAINBOW VALLEY

BY

L. M. MONTGOMERY

WITH FRONTISPIECE
BY M. L. Kirk

GYAN

Published by

Gyan Publishing House
5, Ansari Road
Daryaganj, New Delhi-110002
Phone: 011-47034999, 9811692060
E-mail: books@gyanbooks.com

Distribution Network
gyanbooks.com
India, USA, Canada, UK, Australia

ISBN: 978-93-6208-339-5 (PB)
First Published, 1919

2nd Impression 2024

Printed at: Gyan Press, Delhi.

RAINBOW VALLEY
Author: L. M. MONTGOMERY

"ROSEMARY WEST STEPPED ASIDE FROM THE BY-PATH AND STOOD IN THAT SPELL-WEAVING PLACE"

Page 131

RAINBOW VALLEY

BY

L. M. MONTGOMERY

Author of "Anne of Green Gables," "Anne of the Island,"
"Anne's House of Dreams," "The Story Girl,"
"The Watchman," etc.

"The thoughts of youth are long,
long thoughts."
—*Longfellow*

WITH FRONTISPIECE IN
BY M. L. KIRK

NEW YORK
FREDERICK A. STOKES COMPANY
PUBLISHERS

To

THE MEMORY OF

GOLDWIN LAPP, ROBERT BROOKES
AND MORLEY SHIER

WHO MADE THE SUPREME SACRIFICE
THAT THE HAPPY VALLEYS OF THEIR HOME LAND
MIGHT BE KEPT SACRED FROM
THE RAVAGE OF THE INVADER

CONTENTS

RAINBOW VALLEY

RAINBOW VALLEY

CHAPTER I

Home Again

IT was a clear, apple-green evening in May, and Four Winds Harbour was mirroring back the clouds of the golden west between its softly dark shores. The sea moaned eerily on the sand-bar, sorrowful even in spring, but a sly, jovial wind came piping down the red harbour road along which Miss Cornelia's comfortable, matronly figure was making its way towards the village of Glen St. Mary. Miss Cornelia was rightfully Mrs. Marshall Elliott, and had been Mrs. Marshall Elliott for thirteen years, but even yet more people referred to her as Miss Cornelia than as Mrs. Elliott. The old name was dear to her old friends; only one of them contemptuously dropped it. Susan Baker, the gray and grim and faithful handmaiden of the Blythe family at Ingleside, never lost an opportunity of calling her "Mrs. Marshall Elliott," with the most killing and pointed emphasis, as if to say "You wanted to be Mrs. and Mrs. you shall be with a vengeance as far as I am concerned."

Miss Cornelia was going up to Ingleside to see Dr. and Mrs. Blythe, who were just home from Europe.

They had been away for three months, having left in February to attend a famous medical congress in London; and certain things, which Miss Cornelia was anxious to discuss, had taken place in the Glen during their absence. For one thing, there was a new family in the manse. And such a family! Miss Cornelia shook her head over them several times as she walked briskly along.

Susan Baker and the Anne Shirley of other days saw her coming, as they sat on the big veranda at Ingleside, enjoying the charm of the cat's light, the sweetness of sleepy robins whistling among the twilit maples, and the dance of a gusty group of daffodils blowing against the old, mellow, red brick wall of the lawn.

Anne was sitting on the steps, her hands clasped over her knee, looking, in the kind dusk, as girlish as a mother of many has any right to be; and the beautiful gray-green eyes, gazing down the harbour road, were as full of unquenchable sparkle and dream as ever. Behind her, in the hammock, Rilla Blythe was curled up, a fat, roly-poly little creature of six years, the youngest of the Ingleside children. She had curly red hair and hazel eyes that were now buttoned up after the funny, wrinkled fashion in which Rilla always went to sleep.

Shirley, "the little brown boy," as he was known in the family "Who's Who," was asleep in Susan's arms. He was brown-haired, brown-eyed and brown-skinned, with very rosy cheeks, and he was Susan's especial love. After his birth Anne had been very ill for a long time, and Susan "mothered" the baby with a passionate tenderness which none of the other children, dear as they were to her, had ever called out. Dr. Blythe had said that but for her he would never have lived.

"I gave him life just as much as you did, Mrs. Dr. dear," Susan was wont to say. "He is just as much my baby as he is yours." And, indeed, it was always to Susan that Shirley ran, to be kissed for bumps, and rocked to sleep, and protected from well-deserved spankings. Susan had conscientiously spanked all the other Blythe children when she thought they needed it for their souls' good, but she would not spank Shirley nor allow his mother to do it. Once, Dr. Blythe had spanked him and Susan had been stormily indignant.

"That man would spank an angel, Mrs. Dr. dear, that he would," she had declared bitterly; and she would not make the poor doctor a pie for weeks.

She had taken Shirley with her to her brother's home during his parents' absence, while all the other children had gone to Avonlea, and she had three blessed months of him all to herself. Nevertheless, Susan was very glad to find herself back at Ingleside, with all her darlings around her again. Ingleside was her world and in it she reigned supreme. Even Anne seldom questioned her decisions, much to the disgust of Mrs. Rachel Lynde of Green Gables, who gloomily told Anne, whenever she visited Four Winds, that she was letting Susan get to be entirely too much of a boss and would live to rue it.

"Here is Cornelia Bryant coming up the harbour road, Mrs. Dr. dear," said Susan. "She will be coming to unload three months' gossip on us."

"I hope so," said Anne, hugging her knees. "I'm starving for Glen St. Mary gossip, Susan. I hope Miss Cornelia can tell me everything that has happened while we've been away—*everything*—who has got born, or married, or drunk; who has died, or gone away, or come, or fought, or lost a cow, or found a beau. It's so delightful to be home again with all the dear Glen folks, and I want to know all about them. Why, I remember wondering, as I walked through Westminster Abbey which of her two especial beaus Millicent Drew would finally marry. Do you know, Susan, I have a dreadful suspicion that I love gossip."

"Well, of course, Mrs. Dr. dear," admitted Susan, "every proper woman likes to hear the news. I am rather interested in Millicent Drew's case myself. I never had a beau, much less two, and I do not mind now, for being an old maid does not hurt when you get used to it. Millicent's hair always looks to me as if she had swept it up with a broom. But the men do not seem to mind that."

"They see only her pretty, piquant, mocking, little face, Susan."

"That may very well be, Mrs. Dr. dear. The Good Book says that favour is deceitful and beauty is vain, but I should not have minded finding that out for myself, if it had been so ordained. I have no doubt we will all be beautiful when we are angels, but what good will it do us then? Speaking of gossip, however, they do say that poor Mrs. Harrison Miller over harbour tried to hang herself last week."

"Oh, Susan!"

"Calm yourself, Mrs. Dr. dear. She did not succeed. But I really do not blame her for trying, for her husband is a terrible man. But she was very foolish to think of hanging herself and leaving the way clear for him to marry some other woman. If I had been in her shoes, Mrs. Dr. dear, I would have gone to work to worry him so that he would try to hang himself instead of me. Not that I hold with people hanging themselves under any circumstances, Mrs. Dr. dear."

"What is the matter with Harrison Miller, anyway?" said Anne impatiently. "He is always driving some one to extremes."

"Well, some people call it religion and some call it cussedness, begging your pardon, Mrs. Dr. dear, for using such a word. It seems they cannot make out which it is in Harrison's case. There are days when he growls at everybody because he thinks he is foreordained to eternal punishment. And then there are days when he says he does not care and goes and gets drunk. My own opinion is that he is not sound in his intellect, for none of that branch of the Millers were. His grandfather went out of his mind. He thought he was surrounded by big black spiders. They crawled over him and floated in the air about him. I hope I shall never go insane, Mrs. Dr. dear, and I do not think I will, because it is not a habit of the Bakers. But, if an all-wise Providence should decree it, I hope it will not take the form of big black spiders, for I loathe the animals. As for Mrs. Miller, I do not know whether she really deserves pity or not. There are some who say she just married Harrison to spite Richard Taylor, which seems to me a very peculiar reason for getting married. But then, of course, *I* am no judge of things matrimonial, Mrs. Dr. dear. And there is Cornelia Bryant at the gate, so I will put this blessed brown baby on his bed and get my knitting."

CHAPTER II

Sheer Gossip

"WHERE are the other children?" asked Miss Cornelia, when the first greetings—cordial on her side, rapturous on Anne's, and dignified on Susan's—were over.

"Shirley is in bed and Jem and Walter and the twins are down in their beloved Rainbow Valley," said Anne. "They just came home this afternoon, you know, and they could hardly wait until supper was over before rushing down to the valley. They love it above every spot on earth. Even the maple grove doesn't rival it in their affections."

"I am afraid they love it too well," said Susan gloomily. "Little Jem said once he would rather go to Rainbow Valley than to heaven when he died, and that was not a proper remark."

"I suppose they had a great time in Avonlea?" said Miss Cornelia.

"Enormous. Marilla does spoil them terribly. Jem, in particular, can do no wrong in her eyes."

"Miss Cuthbert must be an old lady now," said Miss Cornelia, getting out her knitting, so that she could hold her own with Susan. Miss Cornelia held that the woman whose hands were employed always had the advantage over the woman whose hands were not.

"Marilla is eighty-five," said Anne with a sigh. "Her hair is snow-white. But, strange to say, her eyesight is better than it was when she was sixty."

"Well, dearie, I'm real glad you're all back. I've been dreadful lonesome. But we haven't been dull in the Glen, believe *me*. There hasn't been such an exciting spring in my time, as far as church matters go. We've got settled with a minister at last, Anne, dearie."

"The Reverend John Knox Meredith, Mrs. Dr. dear," said Susan, resolved not to let Miss Cornelia tell all the news.

"Is he nice?" asked Anne interestedly.

Miss Cornelia sighed and Susan groaned.

"Yes, he's nice enough if that was all," said the former. "He is *very* nice—and very learned—and very spiritual. But, oh Anne, dearie, he has no common sense!"

"How was it you called him, then?"

"Well, there's no doubt he is by far the best preacher we ever had in Glen St. Mary church," said Miss Cornelia, veering a tack or two. "I suppose it is because he is so moony and absent minded that he never got a town call. His trial sermon was simply wonderful, believe *me*. Every one went mad about it—and his looks."

"He is *very* comely, Mrs. Dr. dear, and when all is said and done, I *do* like to see a well-looking man in the pulpit," broke in Susan, thinking it was time she asserted herself again.

"Besides," said Miss Cornelia, "we were anxious to get settled. And Mr. Meredith was the first candidate we were all agreed on. Somebody had some objection to all the others. There was some talk of calling Mr. Folsom. He was a good preacher, too, but somehow people didn't care for his appearance. He was too dark and sleek."

"He looked exactly like a great black tom-cat, that he did, Mrs. Dr. dear," said Susan. "I never could abide such a man in the pulpit every Sunday."

"Then Mr. Rogers came and he was like a chip in porridge—neither harm nor good," resumed Miss Cornelia. "But if he had preached like Peter and Paul it would have profited him nothing, for that was the day old Caleb Ramsay's sheep strayed into church and gave a loud 'ba-a-a' just as he announced his text. Everybody laughed, and poor Rogers had no chance after that. Some thought we ought to call Mr. Stewart, because he was so well educated. He could read the New Testament in five languages."

"But I do not think he was any surer than other men of getting to heaven because of that," interjected Susan.

"Most of us didn't like his delivery," said Miss Cornelia, ignoring Susan. "He talked in grunts, so to speak. And Mr. Arnett couldn't preach *at all.* And he picked about the worst candidating text there is in the Bible—'Curse ye, Meroz.'"

"Whenever he got stuck for an idea, he would bang

the Bible and shout very bitterly, 'Curse ye, Meroz.' Poor Meroz got thoroughly cursed that day, whoever he was, Mrs. Dr. dear," said Susan.

"The minister who is candidating can't be too careful what text he chooses," said Miss Cornelia solemnly. "I believe Mr. Pierson would have got the call if he had picked a different text. But when he announced 'I will lift my eyes to the hills' *he* was done for. Every one grinned, for every one knew that those two Hill girls from the Harbour Head have been setting their caps for every single minister who came to the Glen for the last fifteen years. And Mr. Newman had too large a family."

"He stayed with my brother-in-law, James Clow," said Susan. "'How many children have you got?' I asked him. 'Nine boys and a sister for each of them,' he said. 'Eighteen!' said I. 'Dear me, what a family!' And then he laughed and laughed. But I do not know why, Mrs. Dr. dear, and I am certain that eighteen children would be too many for any manse."

"He had only ten children, Susan," explained Miss Cornelia, with contemptuous patience. "And ten good children would not be much worse for the manse and congregation than the four who are there now. Though I wouldn't say, Anne dearie, that they are so bad, either. I like them—everybody likes them. It's impossible to help liking them. They would be real nice little souls if there was any one to look after their manners and teach them what is right and proper.

For instance, at school the teacher says they are model children. But at home they simply run wild."

"What about Mrs. Meredith?" asked Anne.

"There's *no* Mrs. Meredith. That is just the trouble. Mr. Meredith is a widower. His wife died four years ago. If we had known that I don't suppose we would have called him, for a widower is even worse in a congregation than a single man. But he was heard to speak of his children and we all supposed there was a mother, too. And when they came there was nobody but old Aunt Martha, as they call her. She's a cousin of Mr. Meredith's mother, I believe, and he took her in to save her from the poorhouse. She is seventy-five years old, half blind, and very deaf and very cranky."

"And a very poor cook, Mrs. Dr. dear."

"The worst possible manager for a manse," said Miss Cornelia bitterly. "Mr. Meredith won't get any other housekeeper because he says it would hurt Aunt Martha's feelings. Anne dearie, believe me, the state of that manse is something terrible. Everything is thick with dust and nothing is ever in its place. And we had painted and papered it all so nice before they came."

"There are four children, you say?" asked Anne, beginning to mother them already in her heart.

"Yes. They run up just like the steps of a stair. Gerald's the oldest. He's twelve and they call him Jerry. He's a clever boy. Faith is eleven. She is a regular tom-boy but pretty as a picture, I must say."

"She looks like an angel but she is a holy terror for mischief, Mrs. Dr. dear," said Susan solemnly. "I was at the manse one night last week and Mrs. James Millison was there, too. She had brought them up a dozen eggs and a little pail of milk—a *very* little pail, Mrs. Dr. dear. Faith took them and whisked down cellar with them. Near the bottom of the stairs she caught her toe and fell the rest of the way, milk and eggs and all. You can imagine the result, Mrs. Dr. dear. But that child came up laughing. 'I don't know whether I'm myself or a custard pie,' she said. And Mrs. James Millison was very angry. She said she would never take another thing to the manse if it was to be wasted and destroyed in that fashion."

"Maria Millison never hurt herself taking things to the manse," sniffed Miss Cornelia. "She just took them that night as an excuse for curiosity. But poor Faith is always getting into scrapes. She is so heedless and impulsive."

"Just like me. I'm going to like your Faith," said Anne decidedly.

"She is full of spunk—and I do like spunk, Mrs. Dr. dear," admitted Susan.

"There's something taking about her," conceded Miss Cornelia. "You never see her but she's laughing, and somehow it always makes you want to laugh too. She can't even keep a straight face in church. Una is ten—she's a sweet little thing—not pretty, but sweet. And Thomas Carlyle is nine. They call him Carl, and he has a regular mania for collecting toads and bugs and frogs and bringing them into the house."

"I suppose he was responsible for the dead rat that was lying on a chair in the parlour the afternoon Mrs. Grant called. It gave her a turn," said Susan, "and I do not wonder, for manse parlours are no places for dead rats. To be sure it may have been the cat who left it there. *He* is as full of the old Nick as he can be stuffed, Mrs. Dr. dear. A manse cat should at least *look* respectable, in my opinion, whatever he really is. But I never saw such a rakish-looking beast. And he walks along the ridge pole of the manse almost every evening at sunset, Mrs. Dr. dear, and waves his tail, and that is not becoming."

"The worst of it is, they are *never* decently dressed," sighed Miss Cornelia. "And since the snow went they go to school barefooted. Now, you know Anne dearie, that isn't the right thing for manse children—especially when the Methodist minister's little girl always wears such nice buttoned boots. And I *do* wish they wouldn't play in the old Methodist graveyard."

"It's very tempting, when it's right beside the manse," said Anne. "I've always thought graveyards must be delightful places to play in."

"Oh, no, you did not, Mrs. Dr. dear," said loyal Susan, determined to protect Anne from herself. "You have too much good sense and decorum."

"Why did they ever build that manse beside the

graveyard in the first place," asked Anne. "Their lawn is so small there is no place for them to play except in the graveyard."

"It *was* a mistake," admitted Miss Cornelia. "But they got the lot cheap. And no other manse children ever thought of playing there. Mr. Meredith shouldn't allow it. But he has always got his nose buried in a book, when he is home. He reads and reads, or walks about in his study in a day-dream. So far he hasn't forgotten to be in church on Sundays, but twice he has forgotten about the prayer meeting and one of the elders had to go over to the manse and remind him. And he forgot about Fanny Cooper's wedding. They rung him up on the 'phone and then he rushed right over, just as he was, carpet slippers and all. One wouldn't mind if the Methodists didn't laugh so about it. But there's one comfort—they can't criticize his sermons. He wakes up when he's in the pulpit, believe *me*. And the Methodist minister can't preach at all—so they tell me. *I* have never heard him, thank goodness."

Miss Cornelia's scorn of men had abated somewhat since her marriage, but her scorn of Methodists remained untinged of charity. Susan smiled slyly.

"They do say, Mrs. Marshall Elliott, that the Methodists and Presbyterians are talking of uniting," she said.

"Well, all I hope is that I'll be under the sod if that ever comes to pass," retorted Miss Cornelia. "I shall never have truck or trade with Methodists, and Mr. Meredith will find that he'd better steer clear of them, too. He is entirely too sociable with them, believe *me*. Why, he went to the Jacob Drew's silver wedding supper and got into a nice scrape as a result."

"What was it?"

"Mrs. Drew asked him to carve the roast goose—for Jacob Drew never did or could carve. Well, Mr. Meredith tackled it, and in the process he knocked it clean off the platter into Mrs. Reese's lap, who was sitting next him. And he just said dreamily, 'Mrs. Reese, will you kindly return me that goose?' Mrs. Reese 'returned' it, as meek as Moses, but she must have been furious, for she had on her new silk dress. The worst of it is, she was a Methodist."

"But I think that is better than if she was a Presbyterian," interjected Susan. "If she had been a Presbyterian she would most likely have left the church and we cannot afford to lose our members. And Mrs. Reese is not liked in her own church, because she gives herself such great airs, so that the Methodists would be rather pleased that Mr. Meredith spoiled her dress."

"The point is, he made himself ridiculous, and *I*, for one, do not like to see my minister made ridiculous in the eyes of the Methodists," said Miss Cornelia stiffly. "If he had had a wife it would not have happened."

"I do not see if he had a dozen wives how they could have prevented Mrs. Drew from using up her tough old gander for the wedding feast," said Susan stubbornly.

"They say that was her husband's doing," said Miss Cornelia. "Jacob Drew is a conceited, stingy, domineering creature."

"And they do say he and his wife detest each other—which does not seem to me the proper way for married folks to get along. But then, of course, I have had no experience along that line," said Susan, tossing her head. "And *I* am not one to blame everything on the men. Mrs. Drew is mean enough herself. They say that the only thing she was ever known to give away was a crock of butter made out of cream a rat had fell into. She contributed it to a church social. Nobody found out about the rat until afterwards."

"Fortunately, all the people the Merediths have offended so far are Methodists," said Miss Cornelia. "That Jerry went to the Methodist prayer meeting one night about a fortnight ago and sat beside old William Marsh who got up as usual and testified with fearful groans. 'Do you feel any better now?' whispered Jerry when William sat down. Poor Jerry meant to be sympathetic, but Mr. Marsh thought he was impertinent and is furious at him. Of course, Jerry had no business to be in a Methodist prayer meeting at all. But they go where they like."

"I hope they will not offend Mrs. Alec Davis of the Harbour Head," said Susan. "She is a very touchy woman, I understand, but she is very well off and pays the most of any one to the salary. I have heard that she says the Merediths are the worst brought up children she ever saw."

"Every word you say convinces me more and more that the Merediths belong to the race that knows Joseph," said Mistress Anne decidedly.

"When all is said and done, they *do,*" admitted Miss Cornelia. "And that balances everything. Anyway, we've got them now and we must just do the best we can by them and stick up for them to the Methodists. Well, I suppose I must be getting down harbour. Marshall will soon be home—he went over-harbour to-day—and wanting his supper, man-like. I'm sorry I haven't seen the other children. And where's the doctor?"

"Up at the Harbour Head. We've only been home three days and in that time he has spent three hours in his own bed and eaten two meals in his own house."

"Well, everybody who has been sick for the last six weeks has been waiting for him to come home—and I don't blame them. When that over-harbour doctor married the undertaker's daughter at Lowbridge people felt suspicious of him. It didn't look well. You and the doctor must come down soon and tell us all about your trip. I suppose you've had a splendid time."

"We had," agreed Anne. "It was the fulfilment of years of dreams. The old world is very lovely and very wonderful. But we have come back very well satisfied with our own land. Canada is the finest country in the world, Miss Cornelia."

"Nobody ever doubted that," said Miss Cornelia, complacently.

"And old P. E. I. is the loveliest province in it and Four Winds the loveliest spot in P. E. I.," laughed Anne, looking adoringly out over the sunset splendour of glen and harbour and gulf. She waved her hand at it. "I saw nothing more beautiful than that in Europe, Miss Cornelia. Must you go? The children will be sorry to have missed you."

"They must come and see me soon. Tell them the doughnut jar is always full."

"Oh, at supper they were planning a descent on you. They'll go soon; but they must settle down to school again now. And the twins are going to take music lessons."

"Not from the Methodist minister's wife, I hope?" said Miss Cornelia anxiously.

"No,—from Rosemary West. I was up last evening to arrange it with her. What a pretty girl she is!"

"Rosemary holds her own well. She isn't as young as she once was."

"I thought her very charming. I've never had any real acquaintance with her, you know. Their house is so out of the way, and I've seldom ever seen her except at church."

"People always have liked Rosemary West, though they don't understand her," said Miss Cornelia, quite unconscious of the high tribute she was paying to Rosemary's charm. "Ellen has always kept her down, so to speak. She has tyrannized over her, and yet she has always indulged her in a good many ways. Rosemary was engaged once, you know,—to young Martin Crawford. His ship was wrecked on the Magdalens and all the crew were drowned. Rosemary was just a child—only seventeen. But she was never the same afterwards. She and Ellen have stayed very close at home since their mother's death. They don't often get to their own church at Lowbridge and I understand Ellen doesn't approve of going too often to a Presbyterian church. To the Methodist she *never* goes, I'll say that much for her. That family of Wests have always been strong Episcopalians. Rosemary and Ellen are pretty well off. Rosemary doesn't really need to give music lessons. She does it because she likes to. They are distantly related to Leslie, you know. Are the Fords coming to the harbour this summer?"

"No. They are going on a trip to Japan and will probably be away for a year. Owen's new novel is to have a Japanese setting. This will be the first summer that the dear old house of dreams will be empty since we left it."

"I should think Owen Ford might find enough to write about in Canada without dragging his wife and his innocent children off to a heathen country like Japan," grumbled Miss Cornelia. "*The Life Book* was the best book he's ever written and he got the material for that right here in Four Winds."

"Captain Jim gave him the most of that, you know. And he collected it all over the world. But Owen's books are all delightful, I think."

"Oh, they're well enough as far as they go. I make it a point to read every one he writes, though I've always held, Anne dearie, that reading novels is a sinful waste of time. I shall write and tell him my opinion of this Japanese business, believe *me*. Does he want Kenneth and Persis to be converted into pagans?"

With which unanswerable conundrum Miss Cornelia took her departure. Susan proceeded to put Rilla in bed and Anne sat on the veranda steps under the early stars and dreamed her incorrigible dreams and learned all over again for the hundredth happy time what a moonrise splendour and sheen could be on Four Winds Harbour.

CHAPTER III

The Ingleside Children

IN daytime the Blythe children liked very well to play in the rich, soft greens and glooms of the big maple grove between Ingleside and the Glen St. Mary pond; but for evening revels there was no place like the little valley behind the maple grove. It was a fairy realm of romance to them. Once, looking from the attic windows of Ingleside, through the mist and aftermath of a summer thunderstorm, they had seen the beloved spot arched by a glorious rainbow, one end of which seemed to dip straight down to where a corner of the pond ran up into the lower end of the valley.

"Let us call it Rainbow Valley," said Walter delightedly, and Rainbow Valley thenceforth it was.

Outside of Rainbow Valley the wind might be rollicking and boisterous. Here it always went gently. Little, winding, fairy paths ran here and there over spruce roots cushioned with moss. Wild cherry trees, that in blossom time would be misty white, were scattered all over the valley, mingling with the dark spruces. A little brook with amber waters ran through it from the Glen village. The houses of the village were comfortably far away; only at the upper end of the valley was a little tumble-down, deserted cottage, referred to as "the old Bailey house." It had not been occupied for many years, but a grass-grown dyke surrounded it and inside was an ancient garden where the Ingleside children could find violets and daisies and June lilies still blooming in season. For the rest, the garden was overgrown with caraway that swayed and foamed in the moonshine of summer eves like seas of silver.

To the south lay the pond and beyond it the ripened distance lost itself in purple woods, save where, on a high hill, a solitary old gray homestead looked down on Glen and harbour. There was a certain wild woodsiness and solitude about Rainbow Valley, in spite of its nearness to the village, which endeared it to the children of Ingleside.

The valley was full of dear, friendly hollows and the largest of these was their favourite stamping ground. Here they were assembled on this particular evening. There was a grove of young spruces in this hollow, with a tiny, grassy glade in its heart, opening on the bank of the brook. By the brook grew a silver birch tree, a young, incredibly straight thing which Walter had named the "White Lady." In this glade, too, were the "Tree Lovers," as Walter called a spruce and maple which grew so closely together that their boughs were inextricably intertwined. Jem had hung an old string of sleigh bells, given him by the Glen blacksmith, on the Tree Lovers, and every visitant breeze called out sudden fairy tinkles from it.

"How nice it is to be back!" said Nan. "After all, none of the Avonlea places are quite as nice as Rainbow Valley."

But they were very fond of the Avonlea places for all that. A visit to Green Gables was always considered a great treat. Aunt Marilla was very good to them, and so was Mrs. Rachel Lynde, who was spending the leisure of her old age in knitting cotton-warp quilts against the day when Anne's daughters should need a "setting-out." There were jolly playmates there, too—"Uncle" Davy's children and "Aunt" Diana's children. They knew all the spots their mother had loved so well in her girlhood at old Green Gables—the long Lover's Lane, that was pink-hedged in wild-rose time, the always neat yard, with its willows and poplars, the Dryad's Bubble, lucent and lovely as of yore, the Lake of Shining Waters, and Willowmere. The twins had their mother's old porch-gable room, and Aunt Marilla used to come in at night, when she thought they were asleep, to gloat over them. But they all knew she loved Jem the best.

Jem was at present busily occupied in frying a mess of small trout which he had just caught in the pond. His stove consisted of a circle of red stones, with a fire kindled in it, and his culinary utensils were an old tin can, hammered out flat, and a fork with only one tine left. Nevertheless, ripping good meals had before now been thus prepared.

Jem was the child of the House of Dreams. All

the others had been born at Ingleside. He had curly red hair, like his mother's, and frank hazel eyes, like his father's; he had his mother's fine nose and his father's steady, humorous mouth. And he was the only one of the family who had ears nice enough to please Susan. But he had a standing feud with Susan because she would not give up calling him Little Jem. It was outrageous, thought thirteen year old Jem. Mother had more sense.

"I'm *not* little any more, mother," he had cried indignantly, on his eighth birthday. "I'm *awful* big."

Mother had sighed and laughed and sighed again; and she never called him Little Jem again—in his hearing at least.

He was and always had been a sturdy, reliable little chap. He never broke a promise. He was not a great talker. His teachers did not think him brilliant, but he was a good, all-round student. He never took things on faith; he always liked to investigate the truth of a statement for himself. Once Susan had told him that if he touched his tongue to a frosty latch all the skin would tear off it. Jem had promptly done it, "just to see if it was so." He found it was "so," at the cost of a very sore tongue for several days. But Jem did not grudge suffering in the interests of science. By constant experiment and observation he learned a great deal and his brothers and sisters thought his extensive knowledge of their little world quite wonderful. Jem always knew where the first and ripest berries grew, where the first pale violets shyly wakened from their winter's sleep, and how many blue eggs were in a given robin's nest in the maple grove. He could tell fortunes from daisy petals and suck honey from red clovers, and grub up all sorts of edible roots on the banks of the pond, while Susan went in daily fear that they would all be poisoned. He knew where the finest spruce gum was to be found, in pale amber knots on the lichened bark, he knew where the nuts grew thickest in the beech woods around the Harbour Head, and where the best trouting places up the brooks were. He could mimic the call of any wild bird or beast in Four Winds and he knew the haunt of every wild flower from spring to autumn.

Walter Blythe was sitting under the White Lady, with a volume of poems lying beside him, but he was not reading. He was gazing now at the emerald-misted willows by the pond, and now at a flock of clouds, like little silver sheep, herded by the wind, that were drifting over Rainbow Valley, with rapture in his wide splendid eyes. Walter's eyes were very wonderful. All the joy and sorrow and laughter and loyalty and aspiration of many generations lying under the sod looked out of their dark gray depths.

Walter was a "hop out of kin," as far as looks went. He did not resemble any known relative. He was quite the handsomest of the Ingleside children, with straight black hair and finely modelled features. But he had all his mother's vivid imagination and passionate love of beauty. Frost of winter, invitation of spring, dream of summer and glamour of autumn, all meant much to Walter.

In school, where Jem was a chieftain, Walter was not thought highly of. He was supposed to be "girly" and milk-soppish, because he never fought and seldom joined in the school sports, preferring to herd by himself in out of the way corners and read books—especially "po'try books." Walter loved the poets and pored over their pages from the time he could first read. Their music was woven into his growing soul—the music of the immortals. Walter cherished the ambition to be a poet himself some day. The thing could be done. A certain Uncle Paul—so called of courtesy—who lived now in that mysterious realm called "the States," was Walter's model. Uncle Paul had once been a little school boy in Avonlea and now his poetry was read everywhere. But the Glen schoolboys did not know of Walter's dreams and would not have been greatly impressed if they had. In spite of his lack of physical prowess, however, he commanded a certain unwilling respect because of his power of "talking book talk." Nobody in Glen St. Mary school could talk like him. He "sounded like a preacher," one boy said; and for this reason he was generally left alone and not persecuted, as most boys were who were suspected of disliking or fearing fisticuffs.

The ten year old Ingleside twins violated twin tradition by not looking in the least alike. Anne, who was always called Nan, was very pretty, with velvety nut-brown eyes and silky nut-brown hair. She was a very blithe and dainty little maiden—Blythe by name and blithe by nature, one of her teachers had said. Her complexion was quite faultless, much to her mother's satisfaction.

"I'm so glad I have one daughter who can wear pink," Mrs. Blythe was wont to say jubilantly.

Diana Blythe, known as Di, was very like her mother, with gray-green eyes that always shone with a peculiar lustre and brilliancy in the dusk, and red hair. Perhaps this was why she was her father's favourite. She and Walter were especial chums; Di was the only one to whom he would ever read the verses he wrote himself—the only one who knew that he was secretly hard at work on an epic, strikingly resembling "Marmion" in some things, if not in others. She kept all his secrets, even from Nan, and told him all hers.

"Won't you soon have those fish ready, Jem?" said Nan, sniffing with her dainty nose. "The smell makes me awfully hungry."

"They're nearly ready," said Jem, giving one a dexterous turn. "Get out the bread and the plates, girls. Walter, wake up."

"How the air shines to-night," said Walter dreamily. Not that he despised fried trout either, by any means; but with Walter food for the soul always took first place. "The flower angel has been walking over the world to-day, calling to the flowers. I can see his blue wings on that hill by the woods."

"Any angels' wings I ever saw were white," said Nan.

"The flower angel's aren't. They are a pale misty blue, just like the haze in the valley. Oh, how I wish I could fly. It must be just glorious."

"One does fly in dreams sometimes," said Di.

"I never dream that I'm flying exactly," said Walter. "But I often dream that I just rise up from the ground and float over the fences and the trees. It's delightful—and I always think, 'This *isn't* a dream like it's always been before. *This* is real'—and then I wake up after all, and it's heart-breaking."

"Hurry up, Nan," ordered Jem.

Nan had produced the banquet board—a board literally as well as figuratively—from which many a feast, seasoned as no viands were elsewhere, had been eaten in Rainbow Valley. It was converted into a table by propping it on two large, mossy stones. Newspapers served as tablecloth, and broken plates and handleless cups from Susan's discard furnished the dishes. From a tin box secreted at the root of a spruce tree Nan brought forth bread and salt. The brook gave Adam's ale of unsurpassed crystal. For the rest, there was a certain sauce, compounded of fresh air and appetite of youth, which gave to everything a divine flavour. To sit in Rainbow Valley, steeped in a twilight half gold, half amethyst, rife with the odours of balsam-fir and woodsy growing things in their springtime prime, with the pale stars of wild strawberry blossoms all around you, and with the sough of the wind and tinkle of bells in the shaking tree tops, and eat fried trout and dry bread, was something which the mighty of earth might have envied them.

"Sit in," invited Nan, as Jem placed his sizzling tin platter of trout on the table. "It's your turn to say grace, Jem."

"I've done my part frying the trout," protested Jem, who hated saying grace. "Let Walter say it. He *likes* saying grace. And cut it short, too, Walt. I'm starving."

But Walter said no grace, short or long, just then. An interruption occurred.

"Who's coming down from the manse hill?" said Di.

CHAPTER IV

The Manse Children

AUNT MARTHA might be, and was, a very poor housekeeper; the Rev. John Knox Meredith might be, and was, a very absent-minded, indulgent man. But it could not be denied that there was something very homelike and lovable about the Glen St. Mary manse in spite of its untidiness. Even the critical housewives of the Glen felt it, and were unconsciously mellowed in judgment because of it. Perhaps its charm was in part due to accidental circumstances—the luxuriant vines clustering over its gray, clapboarded walls, the friendly acacias and balm-of-gileads that crowded about it with the freedom of old acquaintance, and the beautiful views of harbour and sand-dunes from its front windows. But these things had been there in the reign of Mr. Meredith's predecessor, when the manse had been the primmest, neatest, and dreariest house in the Glen. So much of the credit must be given to the personality of its new inmates. There was an atmosphere of laughter and comradeship about it; the doors were always open; the inner and outer worlds joined hands. Love was the only law in Glen St. Mary manse.

The people of his congregation said that Mr. Meredith spoiled his children. Very likely he did. It is certain that he could not bear to scold them. "They have no mother," he used to say to himself, with a sigh, when some unusually glaring peccadillo forced itself upon his notice. But he did not know half of their goings-on. He belonged to the sect of dreamers. The windows of his study looked out on the graveyard but, as he paced up and down the room, reflecting deeply on the immortality of the soul, he was quite unaware that Jerry and Carl were playing leap-frog hilariously over the flat stones in that abode of dead Methodists. Mr. Meredith had occasional acute realizations that his children were not so well looked after, physically or morally, as they had been before his wife died, and he had always a dim sub-consciousness that house and meals were very different under Aunt Martha's management from what they had been under Cecilia's. For the rest, he lived in a world of books and abstractions; and, therefore, although his clothes were seldom brushed, and although the Glen housewives concluded, from the ivory-like pallor of his clear-cut features and slender hands, that he never got enough to eat, he was not an unhappy man.

If ever a graveyard could be called a cheerful place, the old Methodist graveyard at Glen St. Mary might be so called. The new graveyard, at the other side of the Methodist church, was a neat and proper and doleful spot; but the old one had been left so long to Nature's kindly and gracious ministries that it had become very pleasant.

It was surrounded on three sides by a dyke of stones and sod, topped by a gray and uncertain paling. Outside the dyke grew a row of tall fir trees with thick, balsamic boughs. The dyke, which had been built by the first settlers of the Glen, was old enough to be beautiful, with mosses and green things growing out of its crevices, violets purpling at its base in the early spring days, and asters and golden-rod making an autumnal glory in its corners. Little ferns clustered companionably between its stones, and here and there a big bracken grew.

On the eastern side there was neither fence nor dyke. The graveyard there straggled off into a young fir plantation, ever pushing nearer to the graves and deepening eastward into a thick wood. The air was always full of the harp-like voices of the sea, and the music of gray old trees, and in the spring mornings the choruses of birds in the elms around the two churches sang of life and not of death. The Meredith children loved the old graveyard.

Blue-eyed ivy, "garden-spruce," and mint ran riot over the sunken graves. Blueberry bushes grew lavishly in the sandy corner next to the fir wood. The varying fashions of tombstones for three generations were to be found there, from the flat, oblong, red sandstone slabs of old settlers, down through the days of weeping willows and clasped hands, to the latest monstrosities of tall "monuments" and draped urns. One of the latter, the biggest and ugliest in the graveyard, was sacred to the memory of a certain Alec Davis who had been born a Methodist but had taken to himself a Presbyterian bride of the Douglas clan. She had made him turn Presbyterian and kept him toeing the Presbyterian mark all his life. But when he died she did not dare to doom him to a lonely grave in the Presbyterian graveyard over-harbour. His people were all buried in the Methodist cemetery; so Alec Davis went back to his own in death and his widow consoled herself by erecting a monument which cost more than any of the Methodists could afford. The Meredith children hated it, without just knowing why, but they loved the old, flat, bench-like stones with the tall grasses growing rankly about them. They made jolly seats for one thing. They were all sitting on one now. Jerry, tired of leap frog, was playing on a jews-harp. Carl was lovingly poring over a strange beetle he had found; Una was trying to make a doll's dress, and Faith, leaning back on her slender brown wrists, was swinging her bare feet in lively time to the jews-harp.

Jerry had his father's black hair and large black eyes, but in him the latter were flashing instead of dreamy. Faith, who came next to him, wore her beauty like a rose, careless and glowing. She had golden-brown eyes, golden-brown curls and crimson cheeks. She laughed too much to please her father's congregation and had shocked old Mrs. Taylor, the disconsolate spouse of several departed husbands, by saucily declaring,—in the church porch at that,—"The world *isn't* a vale of tears, Mrs. Taylor. It's a world of laughter."

Little dreamy Una was not given to laughter. Her braids of straight, dead-black hair betrayed no lawless kinks, and her almond-shaped, dark-blue eyes had something wistful and sorrowful in them. Her mouth had a trick of falling open over her tiny white teeth, and a shy, meditative smile occasionally crept over her small face. She was much more sensitive to public opinion than Faith, and had an uneasy consciousness that there was something askew in their way of living. She longed to put it right, but did not know how. Now and then she dusted the furniture—but it was so seldom she could find the duster because it was never in the same place twice. And when the clothes brush was to the fore she tried to brush her father's best suit on Saturdays, and once sewed on a missing button with coarse white thread. When Mr. Meredith went to church next day every female eye saw that button and the peace of the Ladies' Aid was upset for weeks.

Carl had the clear, bright, dark-blue eyes, fearless and direct, of his dead mother, and her brown hair with its glints of gold. He knew the secrets of bugs and had a sort of freemasonry with bees and beetles. Una never liked to sit near him because she never knew what uncanny creature might be secreted about him. Jerry refused to sleep with him because Carl had once taken a young garter snake to bed with him;

so Carl slept in his old cot, which was so short that he could never stretch out, and had strange bed-fellows. Perhaps it was just as well that Aunt Martha was half blind when she made that bed. Altogether they were a jolly, lovable little crew, and Cecilia Meredith's heart must have ached bitterly when she faced the knowledge that she must leave them.

"Where would you like to be buried if you were a Methodist?" asked Faith cheerfully.

This opened up an interesting field of speculation.

"There isn't much choice. The place is full," said Jerry. "*I'd* like that corner near the road, I guess. I could hear the teams going past and the people talking."

"I'd like that little hollow under the weeping birch," said Una. "That birch is such a place for birds and they sing like mad in the mornings."

"I'd take the Porter lot where there's so many children buried. *I* like lots of company," said Faith. "Carl, where'd you?"

"I'd rather not be buried at all," said Carl, "but if I had to be I'd like the ant-bed. Ants are *awf'ly* int'resting."

"How very good all the people who are buried here must have been," said Una, who had been reading the laudatory old epitaphs. "There doesn't seem to be a single bad person in the whole graveyard. Methodists must be better than Presbyterians after all."

"Maybe the Methodists bury their bad people just just like they do cats," suggested Carl. "Maybe they don't bother bringing them to the graveyard at all."

"Nonsense," said Faith. "The people that are buried here weren't any better than other folks, Una. But when any one is dead you mustn't say anything of him but good or he'll come back and ha'nt you. Aunt Martha told me that. I asked father if it was true and he just looked through me and muttered, 'True? True? What is truth? What *is* truth, O jesting Pilate?' I concluded from that it must be true."

"I wonder if Mr. Alec Davis would come back and ha'nt me if I threw a stone at the urn on top of his tombstone," said Jerry.

"Mrs. Davis would," giggled Faith. "She just watches us in church like a cat watching mice. Last Sunday I made a face at her nephew and he made one back at me and you should have seen her glare. I'll bet she boxed *his* ears when they got out. Mrs. Marshall Elliott told me we mustn't offend her on any account or I'd have made a face at her, too!"

"They say Jem Blythe stuck out his tongue at her once and she never would have his father again, even when her husband was dying," said Jerry. "I wonder what the Blythe gang will be like."

"I liked their looks," said Faith. The manse children had been at the station that afternoon when the Blythe small fry had arrived. "I liked Jem's looks *especially.*"

"They say in school that Walter's a sissy," said Jerry.

"I don't believe it," said Una, who had thought Walter very handsome.

"Well, he writes poetry, anyhow. He won the prize the teacher offered last year for writing a poem, Bertie Shakespeare Drew told me. Bertie's mother thought *he* should have got the prize because of his name, but Bertie said he couldn't write poetry to save his soul, name or no name."

"I suppose we'll get acquainted with them as soon as they begin going to school," mused Faith. "I hope the girls are nice. I don't like most of the girls round here. Even the nice ones are poky. But the Blythe twins look jolly. I thought twins always looked alike, but they don't. I think the red-haired one is the nicest."

"I liked their mother's looks," said Una with a little sigh. Una envied all children with mothers. She had been only six when her mother died, but she had some very precious memories, treasured in her soul like jewels, of twilight cuddlings and morning frolics, of loving eyes, a tender voice, and the sweetest, gayest laugh.

"They say she isn't like other people," said Jerry.

"Mrs. Elliott says that is because she never really grew up," said Faith.

"She's taller than Mrs. Elliott."

"Yes, yes, but it is inside—Mrs. Elliott says Mrs. Blythe just stayed a little girl inside."

"What do I smell?" interrupted Carl, sniffing.

They all smelled it now. A most delectable odour

came floating up on the still evening air from the direction of the little woodsy dell below the manse hill.

"That makes me hungry," said Jerry.

"We had only bread and molasses for supper and cold ditto for dinner," said Una plaintively.

Aunt Martha's habit was to boil a large slab of mutton early in the week and serve it up every day, cold and greasy, as long as it lasted. To this Faith, in a moment of inspiration, had given the name of "ditto" and by this it was invariably known at the manse.

"Let's go and see where that smell is coming from," said Jerry.

They all sprang up, frolicked over the lawn with the abandon of young puppies, climbed a fence, and tore down the mossy slope, guided by the savory lure that ever grew stronger. A few minutes later they arrived breathlessly in the sanctum sanctorum of Rainbow Valley where the Blythe children were just about to give thanks and eat.

They halted shyly. Una wished they had not been so precipitate: but Di Blythe was equal to that and any occasion. She stepped forward, with a comrade's smile.

"I guess I know who you are," she said. "You belong to the manse, don't you?"

Faith nodded, her face creased with dimples.

"We smelled your trout cooking and wondered what it was."

"You must sit down and help us eat them," said Di.

"Maybe you haven't more than you want yourselves," said Jerry, looking hungrily at the tin platter.

"We've heaps—three apiece," said Jem. "Sit down."

No more ceremony was necessary. Down they all sat on mossy stones. Merry was that feast and long. Nan and Di would probably have died of horror had they known what Faith and Una knew perfectly well—that Carl had two young mice in his jacket pocket. But they never knew it, so it never hurt them. Where can folks get better acquainted than over a meal table? When the last trout had vanished, the manse children and the Ingleside children were sworn friends and allies. They had always known each other and always would. The race of Joseph recognized its own.

They poured out the history of their little pasts. The manse children heard of Avonlea and Green Gables, of Rainbow Valley traditions, and of the little house by the harbour shore where Jem had been born. The Ingleside children heard of Maywater, where the Merediths had lived before coming to the Glen, of Una's beloved, one-eyed doll and Faith's pet rooster.

Faith was inclined to resent the fact that people laughed at her for petting a rooster. She liked the Blythes because they accepted it without question.

"A handsome rooster like Adam is just as nice a pet as a dog or cat, *I* think," she said. "If he was a canary nobody would wonder. And I brought him up from a little, wee, yellow chicken. Mrs. Johnson at Maywater gave him to me. A weasel had killed all his brothers and sisters. I called him after her husband. I never liked dolls or cats. Cats are too sneaky and dolls are *dead*."

"Who lives in that house away up there?" asked Jerry.

"The Miss Wests—Rosemary and Ellen," answered Nan. "Di and I are going to take music lessons from Miss Rosemary this summer."

Una gazed at the lucky twins with eyes whose longing was too gentle for envy. Oh, if she could only have music lessons! It was one of the dreams of her little hidden life. But nobody ever thought of such a thing.

"Miss Rosemary is so sweet and she always dresses so pretty," said Di. "Her hair is just the colour of new molasses taffy," she added wistfully—for Di, like her mother before her, was not resigned to her own ruddy tresses.

"I like Miss Ellen, too," said Nan. "She always used to give me candies when she came to church. But Di is afraid of her."

"Her brows are so black and she has such a great deep voice," said Di. "Oh, how scared of her Kenneth Ford used to be when he was little! Mother says the first Sunday Mrs. Ford brought him to church Miss Ellen happened to be there, sitting right behind them. And the minute Kenneth saw her he just screamed and screamed until Mrs. Ford had to carry him out."

"Who is Mrs. Ford?" asked Una wonderingly.

"Oh, the Fords don't live here. They only come here in the summer. And they're not coming this summer. They live in that little house 'way, 'way down on the harbour shore where father and mother used to live. I wish you could see Persis Ford. She is just like a picture."

"I've heard of Mrs. Ford," broke in Faith. "Bertie Shakespeare Drew told me about her. She was married fourteen years to a dead man and then he came to life."

"Nonsense," said Nan. "That isn't the way of it at all. Bertie Shakespeare can never get anything straight. I know the whole story and I'll tell it to you some time, but not now, for it's too long and it's time for us to go home. Mother doesn't like us to be out late these damp evenings."

Nobody cared whether the manse children were out in the damp or not. Aunt Martha was already in bed and the minister was still too deeply lost in speculations concerning the immortality of the soul to remember the mortality of the body. But they went home, too, with visions of good times coming in their heads.

"I think Rainbow Valley is even nicer than the graveyard," said Una. "And I just love those dear Blythes. It's *so* nice when you can love people because so often you *can't*. Father said in his sermon last

Sunday that we should love everybody. But how can we? How could we love Mrs. Alec Davis?"

"Oh, father only said that in the pulpit," said Faith airily. "He has more sense than to really think it outside."

The Blythe children went up to Ingleside, except Jem, who slipped away for a few moments on a solitary expedition to a remote corner of Rainbow Valley. Mayflowers grew there and Jem never forgot to take his mother a bouquet as long as they lasted.

CHAPTER V

The Advent of Mary Vance

"THIS is just the sort of day you feel as if things might happen," said Faith, responsive to the lure of crystal air and blue hills. She hugged herself with delight and danced a hornpipe on old Hezekiah Pollock's bench tombstone, much to the horror of two ancient maidens who happened to be driving past just as Faith hopped on one foot around the stone, waving the other and her arms in the air.

"And that," groaned one ancient maiden, "is our minister's daughter."

"What else could you expect of a widower's family?" groaned the other ancient maiden. And then they both shook their heads.

It was early on Saturday morning and the Merediths were out in the dew-drenched world with a delightful consciousness of the holiday. They had never had anything to do on a holiday. Even Nan and Di Blythe had certain household tasks for Saturday mornings, but the daughters of the manse were free to roam from blushing morn to dewy eve if so it pleased them. It *did* please Faith, but Una felt a secret, bitter humiliation because they never learned to do anything. The other girls in her class at school could cook and sew and knit; she only was a little ignoramus.

Jerry suggested that they go exploring; so they went lingeringly through the fir grove, picking up Carl on the way, who was on his knees in the dripping grass studying his darling ants. Beyond the grove they came out in Mr. Taylor's pasture field, sprinkled over with the white ghosts of dandelions; in a remote corner was an old tumbledown barn, where Mr. Taylor sometimes stored his surplus hay crop but which was never used for any other purpose. Thither the Meredith children trooped, and prowled about the ground floor for several minutes.

"What was that?" whispered Una suddenly.

They all listened. There was a faint but distinct rustle in the hayloft above. The Merediths looked at each other.

"There's something up there," breathed Faith.

"I'm going up to see what it is," said Jerry resolutely.

"Oh, don't," begged Una, catching his arm.

"I'm going."

"We'll all go, too, then," said Faith.

The whole four climbed the shaky ladder, Jerry and Faith quite dauntless, Una pale from fright, and Carl rather absent-mindedly speculating on the possibility of finding a bat up in the loft. He longed to see a bat in daylight.

When they stepped off the ladder they saw what had made the rustle and the sight struck them dumb for a few moments.

In a little nest in the hay a girl was curled up, looking as if she had just awakened from sleep. When she saw them she stood up, rather shakily, as it seemed, and in the bright sunlight that streamed through the cobwebbed window behind her, they saw that her thin, sunburned face was very pale under its tan. She had two braids of lank, thick, tow-coloured hair and very odd eyes—"white-eyes," the manse children thought, as she stared at them half defiantly, half piteously. They were really of so pale a blue that they did seem almost white, especially when contrasted with the narrow black ring that circled the iris. She was barefooted and bareheaded, and was clad in a faded, ragged, old plaid dress, much too short and tight for her. As for years, she might have been almost any age, judging from her wizened little face, but her height seemed to be somewhere in the neighbourhood of twelve.

"Who are you?" asked Jerry.

The girl looked about her as if seeking a way of escape. Then she seemed to give in with a little shiver of despair.

"I'm Mary Vance," she said.

"Where'd you come from?" pursued Jerry.

Mary, instead of replying, suddenly sat, or fell, down on the hay and began to cry. Instantly Faith had flung herself down beside her and put her arm about the thin, shaking shoulders.

"You stop bothering her," she commanded Jerry.

Then she hugged the waif. "Don't cry, dear. Just tell us what's the matter. *We're* friends."

"I'm so—so—hungry," wailed Mary. "I—I haint had a thing to eat since Thursday morning, 'cept a little water from the brook out there."

The manse children gazed at each other in horror. Faith sprang up.

"You come right up to the manse and get something to eat before you say another word."

Mary shrank.

"Oh,—I can't. What will your pa and ma say? Besides, they'd send me back."

"We've no mother, and father won't bother about you. Neither will Aunt Martha. Come, I say." Faith stamped her foot impatiently. Was this queer girl going to insist on starving to death almost at their very door?

Mary yielded. She was so weak that she could hardly climb down the ladder, but somehow they got her down and over the field and into the manse kitchen. Aunt Martha, muddling through her Saturday cooking, took no notice of her. Faith and Una flew to the pantry and ransacked it for such eatables as it contained—some "ditto," bread, butter, milk and a doubtful pie. Mary Vance attacked the food ravenously and uncritically, while the manse children stood around and watched her. Jerry noticed that she had a pretty mouth and very nice, even, white teeth. Faith decided, with secret horror, that Mary had not one stitch on her except that ragged, faded dress. Una was full of pure pity, Carl of amused wonder, and all of them of curiosity.

"Now come out to the graveyard and tell us about yourself," ordered Faith, when Mary's appetite showed signs of failing her. Mary was now nothing loth. Food had restored her natural vivacity and unloosed her by no means reluctant tongue.

"You won't tell your pa or anybody if I tell you?" she stipulated, when she was enthroned on Mr. Pollock's tombstone. Opposite her the manse children lined up on another. Here was spice and mystery and adventure. Something *had* happened.

"No, we won't."

"Cross your hearts?"

"Cross our hearts."

"Well, I've run away. I was living with Mrs. Wiley over-harbour. Do you know Mrs. Wiley?"

"No."

"Well, you don't want to know her. She's an awful woman. My, how I hate her! She worked me to death and wouldn't give me half enough to eat, and she used to larrup me 'most every day. Look a-here."

Mary rolled up her ragged sleeves and held up her scrawny arms and thin hands, chapped almost to rawness. They were black with bruises. The manse children shivered. Faith flushed crimson with indignation. Una's blue eyes filled with tears.

"She licked me Wednesday night with a stick," said

Mary, indifferently. "It was 'cause I let the cow kick over a pail of milk. How'd I know the darn old cow was going to kick?"

A not unpleasant thrill ran over her listeners. They would never dream of using such dubious words, but it was rather titivating to hear some one else use them—and a girl, at that. Certainly this Mary Vance was an interesting creature.

"I don't blame you for running away," said Faith.

"Oh, I didn't run away 'cause she licked me. A licking was all in the day's work with me. I was darn well used to it. Nope, I'd meant to run away for a week 'cause I'd found out that Mrs. Wiley was going to rent her farm and go to Lowbridge to live and give me to a cousin of hers up Charlottetown way. I wasn't going to stand for *that*. She was a worse sort than Mrs. Wiley even. Mrs. Wiley lent me to her for a month last summer and I'd rather live with the devil himself."

Sensation number two. But Una looked doubtful.

"So I made up my mind I'd beat it. I had seventy cents saved up that Mrs. John Crawford give me in the spring for planting potatoes for her. Mrs. Wiley didn't know about it. She was away visiting her cousin when I planted them. I thought I'd sneak up here to the Glen and buy a ticket to Charlottetown and try to get work there. I'm a hustler, let me tell you. There ain't a lazy bone in *my* body. So I lit out Thursday morning 'fore Mrs. Wiley was up and walked to the Glen—six miles. And when I got to the station I found I'd lost my money. Dunno how—dunno where. Anyhow, it was gone. I didn't know what to do. If I went back to old Lady Wiley she'd take the hide off me. So I went and hid in that old barn."

"And what will you do now?" asked Jerry.

"Dunno. I s'pose I'll have to go back and take my medicine. Now that I've got some grub in my stomach I guess I can stand it."

But there was fear behind the bravado in Mary's eyes. Una suddenly slipped from the one tombstone to the other and put her arm about Mary.

"Don't go back. Just stay here with us."

"Oh, Mrs. Wiley'll hunt me up," said Mary. "It's likely she's on my trail before this. I might stay here till she finds me, I s'pose, if your folks don't mind. I was a darn fool ever to think of skipping out. She'd run a weasel to earth. But I was so misrebul."

Mary's voice quivered, but she was ashamed of showing her weakness.

"I hain't had the life of a dog for these four years," she explained defiantly.

"You've been four years with Mrs. Wiley?"

"Yip. She took me out of the asylum over in Hopetown when I was eight."

"That's the same place Mrs. Blythe came from," exclaimed Faith.

"I was two years in the asylum. I was put there

when I was six. My ma had hung herself and my pa had cut his throat."

"Holy cats! Why?" said Jerry.

"Booze," said Mary laconically.

"And you've no relations?"

"Not a darn one that I know of. Must have had some once, though. I was called after half a dozen of them. My full name is Mary Martha Lucilla Moore Ball Vance. Can you beat that? My grandfather was a rich man. I'll bet he was richer than *your* grandfather. But pa drunk it all up and ma, she did her part. *They* used to beat me, too. Laws, I've been licked so much I kind of like it."

Mary tossed her head. She divined that the manse children were pitying her for her many stripes and she did not want pity. She wanted to be envied. She looked gaily about her. Her strange eyes, now that the dullness of famine was removed from them, were brilliant. She would show these youngsters what a personage she was.

"I've been sick an awful lot," she said proudly. "There's not many kids could have come through what I have. I've had scarlet fever and measles and ersipelas and mumps and whooping cough and pew-monia."

"Were you ever fatally sick?" asked Una.

"I don't know," said Mary doubtfully.

"Of course she wasn't," scoffed Jerry. "If you're fatally sick you die."

"Oh, well, I never died exactly," said Mary, "but I come blamed near it once. They thought I was dead and they were getting ready to lay me out when I up and come to."

"What is it like to be half dead?" asked Jerry curiously.

"Like nothing. I didn't know it for days afterwards. It was when I had the pewmonia. Mrs. Wiley wouldn't have the doctor—said she wasn't going to no such expense for a home girl. Old Aunt Christina McAllister nursed me with poultices. She brung me round. But sometimes I wish I'd just died the other half and done with it. I'd been better off."

"If you went to heaven I s'pose you would," said Faith rather dubiously.

"Well, what other place is there to go to?" demanded Mary in a puzzled tone.

"There's hell, you know," said Una, dropping her voice and hugging Mary to lessen the awfulness of the suggestion.

"Hell? What's that?"

"Why, it's where the devil lives," said Jerry. "You've heard of him—you spoke about him."

"Oh, yes, but I didn't know he lived anywhere. I thought he just roamed round. Mr. Wiley used to mention hell when he was alive. He was always telling folks to go there. I thought it was some place over in New Brunswick where he come from."

"Hell is an awful place," said Faith, with the dramatic enjoyment that is born of telling dreadful things. "Bad people go there when they die and burn in fire for ever and ever and ever."

"Who told you that?" demanded Mary incredulously.

"It's in the Bible. And Mr. Isaac Crothers at Maywater told us, too, in Sunday School. He was an elder and a pillar in the church and knew all about it. But you needn't worry. If you're good you'll go to heaven and if you're bad I guess you'd rather go to hell."

"I wouldn't," said Mary positively. "No matter how bad I was I wouldn't want to be burned and burned. *I* know what it's like. I picked up a red hot poker once by accident. What must you do to be good?"

"You must go to church and Sunday School and read your Bible and pray every night and give to missions," said Una.

"It sounds like a large order," said Mary. "Anything else?"

"You must ask God to forgive the sins you've committed."

"But I've never com—committed any," said Mary. "What's a sin any way?"

"Oh, Mary, you must have. Everybody does. Did you never tell a lie?"

"Heaps of 'em," said Mary.

"That's a dreadful sin," said Una solemnly.

"Do you mean to tell me," demanded Mary, "that

I'd be sent to hell for telling a lie now and then? Why, I *had* to. Mr. Wiley would have broken every bone in my body one time if I hadn't told him a lie. Lies have saved me many a whack, I can tell you."

Una sighed. Here were too many difficulties for her to solve. She shuddered as she thought of being cruelly whipped. Very likely she would have lied too. She squeezed Mary's little calloused hand.

"Is that the only dress you've got?" asked Faith, whose joyous nature refused to dwell on disagreeable subjects.

"I just put on this dress because it was no good," cried Mary flushing. "Mrs. Wiley'd bought my clothes and I wasn't going to be beholden to her for anything. And I'm honest. If I was going to run away I wasn't going to take what belonged to *her* that was worth anything. When I grow up I'm going to have a blue sating dress. Your own clothes don't look so stylish. I thought minister's children were always dressed up."

It was plain that Mary had a temper and was sensitive on some points. But there was a queer, wild charm about her which captivated them all. She was taken to Rainbow Valley that afternoon and introduced to the Blythes as "a friend of ours from over harbour who is visiting us." The Blythes accepted her unquestioningly, perhaps because she was outwardly fairly respectable now. After dinner—through which Aunt Martha had mumbled and Mr. Meredith had been in a state of semi-unconsciousness while brooding his Sunday sermon—Faith had prevailed on Mary to put on one of her dresses, as well as certain other articles of clothing. With her hair neatly braided Mary passed muster tolerably well. She was an acceptable playmate, for she knew several new and exciting games, and her conversation lacked not spice. In fact, some of her expressions made Nan and Di look at her rather askance. They were not quite sure what their mother would have thought of her, but they knew quite well what Susan would. However, she was a visitor at the manse, so she must be all right.

When bedtime came there was the problem of where Mary should sleep.

"We can't put her in the spare room, you know," said Faith perplexedly to Una.

"I haven't got anything in my head," cried Mary in an injured tone.

"Oh, I didn't mean *that,*" protested Faith. "The spare room is all torn up. The mice have gnawed a big hole in the feather tick and made a nest in it. We never found it out till Aunt Martha put the Rev. Mr. Fisher from Charlottetown there to sleep last week. *He* soon found it out. Then father had to give him his bed and sleep on the study lounge. Aunt Martha hasn't had time to fix the spare room bed up yet, so she says; so *nobody* can sleep there, no matter how clean their heads are. And our room is so small, and the bed so small you can't sleep with us."

"I can go back to the hay in the old barn for the

night if you'll lend me a quilt," said Mary philosophically. "It was kind of chilly last night, but 'cept for that I've had worse beds."

"Oh, no, no, you mustn't do that," said Una. "I've thought of a plan, Faith. You know that little trestle bed in the garret room, with the old mattress on it, that the last minister left there? Let's take up the spare room bedclothes and make Mary a bed there. You won't mind sleeping in the garret, will you, Mary? It's just above our room."

"Any place'll do me. Laws, I never had a decent place to sleep in in my life. I slept in the loft over the kitchen at Mrs. Wiley's. The roof leaked rain in summer and the snow druv in in winter. My bed was a straw tick on the floor. You won't find me a mite huffy about where *I* sleep."

The manse garret was a long, low, shadowy place, with one gable end partitioned off. Here a bed was made up for Mary of the dainty hemstitched sheets and embroidered spread which Cecilia Meredith had once so proudly made for her spare room, and which still survived Aunt Martha's uncertain washings. The goodnights were said and silence fell over the manse. Una was just falling asleep when she heard a sound in the room just above that made her sit up suddenly.

"Listen, Faith—Mary's crying," she whispered. Faith replied not, being already asleep. Una slipped out of bed, and made her way in her little white gown down the hall and up the garret stairs. The creaking garret floor gave ample notice of her coming, and when she reached the corner room all was moonlit silence and the trestle bed showed only a hump in the middle.

"Mary," whispered Una.

There was no response.

Una crept close to the bed and pulled at the spread. "Mary, I know you are crying. I heard you. Are you lonesome?"

Mary suddenly appeared to view but said nothing.

"Let me in beside you. I'm cold," said Una shivering in the chilly air, for the little garret window was open and the keen breath of the north shore at night blew in.

Mary moved over and Una snuggled down beside her.

"*Now* you won't be lonesome. We shouldn't have left you here alone the first night."

"I wasn't lonesome," sniffed Mary.

"What were you crying for then?"

"Oh, I just got to thinking of things when I was here alone. I thought of having to go back to Mrs. Wiley—and of being licked for running away—and—and—and of going to hell for telling lies. It all worried me something scandalous."

"Oh, Mary," said poor Una in distress. "I don't believe God will send you to hell for telling lies when you didn't know it was wrong. He *couldn't*. Why, He's kind and good. Of course, you mustn't tell any more now that you know it's wrong."

"If I can't tell lies what's to become of me?" said Mary with a sob. "*You* don't understand. You don't know anything about it. You got a home and a kind father—though it does seem to me that he isn't more'n about half there. But anyway he doesn't lick you, and you get enough to eat such as it is—though that old aunt of yours doesn't know *anything* about cooking. Why, this is the first day I ever remember of feeling 'sif I'd enough to eat. I've been knocked about all my life, 'cept for the two years I was at the asylum. They didn't lick me there and it wasn't too bad, though the matron was cross. She always looked ready to bite the head off a nail. But Mrs. Wiley is a holy terror, that's what *she* is, and I'm just scared stiff when I think of going back to her."

"Perhaps you won't have to. Perhaps we'll be able to think of a way out. Let's both ask God to keep you from having to go back to Mrs. Wiley. You say your prayers, don't you Mary?"

"Oh, yes, I always go over an old rhyme 'fore I get into bed," said Mary indifferently. "I never thought of asking for anything in particular though. Nobody in this world ever bothered themselves about me so I didn't s'pose God would. He *might* take more trouble for you, seeing you're a minister's daughter."

"He'd take every bit as much trouble for you, Mary, I'm sure," said Una. "It doesn't matter whose child you are. You just ask Him—and I will, too."

"All right," agreed Mary. "It won't do any harm

if it doesn't do much good. If you knew Mrs. Wiley as well as I do you wouldn't think God would want to meddle with her. Anyhow, I won't cry any more about it. This is a big sight better'n last night down in that old barn, with the mice running about. Look at the Four Winds light. Ain't it pretty?"

"This is the only window we can see it from," said Una. "I love to watch it."

"Do you? So do I. I could see it from the Wiley loft and it was the only comfort I had. When I was all sore from being licked I'd watch it and forget about the places that hurt. I'd think of the ships sailing away and away from it and wish I was on one of them sailing far away too—away from everything. In winter nights when it didn't shine, I just felt real lonesome. Say, Una, what makes all you folks so kind to me when I'm just a stranger?"

"Because it's right to be. The Bible tells us to be kind to everybody."

"Does it? Well, I guess most folks don't mind it much then. I never remember of any one being kind to me before—true's you live I don't. Say, Una, ain't them shadows on the wall pretty? They look just like a flock of little dancing birds. And say, Una, I like all you folks and them Blythe boys and Di, but I don't like that Nan. She's a proud one."

"Oh, no, Mary, she isn't a bit proud," said Una eagerly. "Not a single bit."

"Don't tell me. Any one that holds her head like that *is* proud. I don't like her."

"*We* all like her very much."

"Oh, I s'pose you like her better'n me?" said Mary jealously. "Do you?"

"Why, Mary—we've known her for weeks and we've only known you a few hours," stammered Una.

"So you do like her better then?" said Mary in a rage. "All right! Like her all you want to. *I* don't care. *I* can get along without you."

She flung herself over against the wall of the garret with a slam.

"Oh, Mary," said Una, pushing a tender arm over Mary's uncompromising back, "don't talk like that. I *do* like you ever so much. And you make me feel so bad."

No answer. Presently Una gave a sob. Instantly Mary squirmed around again and engulfed Una in a bear's hug.

"Hush up," she ordered. "Don't go crying over what I said. I was as mean as the devil to talk that way. I orter to be skinned alive—and you all so good to me. I should think you *would* like any one better'n me. I deserve every licking I ever got. Hush, now. If you cry any more I'll go and walk right down to the harbour in this night dress and drown myself."

This terrible threat made Una choke back her sobs. Her tears were wiped away by Mary with the lace frill of the spare room pillow and forgiver and forgiven cuddled down together again, harmony restored, to watch the shadows of the vine leaves on the moonlit wall until they fell asleep.

And in the study below the Rev. John Meredith walked the floor with rapt face and shining eyes, thinking out his message of the morrow, and knew not that under his own roof there was a little forlorn soul, stumbling in darkness and ignorance, beset by terror and compassed about with difficulties too great for it to grapple in its unequal struggle with a big indifferent world.

CHAPTER VI

MARY STAYS AT THE MANSE

THE manse children took Mary Vance to church with them the next day. At first Mary objected to the idea.

"Didn't you go to church over-harbour?" asked Una.

"You bet. Mrs. Wiley never troubled church much, but I went every Sunday I could get off. I was mighty thankful to go to some place where I could sit down for a spell. But I can't go to church in this old ragged dress."

This difficulty was removed by Faith offering the loan of her second best dress.

"It's faded a little and two of the buttons are off, but I guess it'll do."

"I'll sew the buttons on in a jiffy," said Mary.

"Not on Sunday," said Una, shocked.

"Sure. The better the day the better the deed. You just gimme a needle and thread and look the other way if you're squeamish."

Faith's school boots, and an old black velvet cap that had once been Cecilia Meredith's, completed Mary's costume, and to church she went. Her behaviour was quite conventional, and though some wondered who the shabby little girl with the manse children was she did not attract much attention. She listened to the sermon with outward decorum and joined lustily in the singing. She had, it appeared, a clear, strong voice and a good ear.

"His blood can make the *violets* clean," carolled Mary blithely. Mrs. Jimmy Milgrave, whose pew was just in front of the manse pew, turned suddenly and looked the child over from top to toe. Mary, in a mere superfluity of naughtiness, stuck her tongue out at Mrs. Milgrave, much to Una's horror.

"I couldn't help it," she declared after church. "What'd she want to stare at me like that for? Such manners! I'm *glad* I stuck my tongue out at her. I wish I'd stuck it further out. Say, I saw Rob MacAllister from over-harbour there. Wonder if he'll tell Mrs. Wiley on me."

No Mrs. Wiley appeared, however, and in a few days the children forgot to look for her. Mary was apparently a fixture at the manse. But she refused to go to school with the others.

"Nope. I've finished my education," she said, when Faith urged her to go. "I went to school four winters since I come to Mrs. Wiley's and I've had all I want of *that*. I'm sick and tired of being everlastingly jawed at 'cause I didn't get my home lessons done. *I'd* no time to do home lessons."

"Our teacher won't jaw you. He is awfully nice," said Faith.

"Well, I ain't going. I can read and write and

cipher up to fractions. That's all I want. You fellows go and I'll stay home. You needn't be scared I'll steal anything. I swear I'm honest."

Mary employed herself while the others were in school in cleaning up the manse. In a few days it was a different place. Floors were swept, furniture dusted, everything straightened out. She mended the spare-room bed-tick, she sewed on missing buttons, she patched clothes neatly, she even invaded the study with broom and dust-pan and ordered Mr. Meredith out while she put it to rights. But there was one department with which Aunt Martha refused to let her interfere. Aunt Martha might be deaf and half blind and very childish, but she was resolved to keep the commissariat in her own hands, in spite of all Mary's wiles and stratagems.

"I can tell you if old Martha'd let *me* cook you'd have some decent meals," she told the manse children indignantly. "There'd be no more 'ditto'—and no more lumpy porridge and blue milk either. What *does* she do with all the cream?"

"She gives it to the cat. He's hers, you know," said Faith.

"I'd like to *cat* her," exclaimed Mary bitterly. "I've no use for cats anyhow. They belong to the old Nick. You can tell that by their eyes. Well, if old Martha won't, she won't, I s'pose. But it gits on my nerves to see good vittles spoiled."

When school came out they always went to Rainbow

Valley. Mary refused to play in the graveyard. She declared she was afraid of ghosts.

"There's no such thing as ghosts," declared Jem Blythe.

"Oh, ain't there?"

"Did you ever see any?"

"Hundreds of 'em," said Mary promptly.

"What are they like?" said Carl.

"Awful-looking. Dressed all in white with skellington hands and heads," said Mary.

"What did you do?" asked Una.

"Run like the devil," said Mary. Then she caught Walter's eyes and blushed. Mary was a good deal in awe of Walter. She declared to the manse girls that his eyes made her nervous.

"I think of all the lies I've ever told when I look into them," she said, "and wish I hadn't."

Jem was Mary's favourite. When he took her to the attic at Ingleside and showed her the museum of curios that Captain Jim Boyd had bequeathed to him she was immensely pleased and flattered. She also won Carl's heart entirely by her interest in his beetles and ants. It could not be denied that Mary got on rather better with the boys than with the girls. She quarrelled bitterly with Nan Blythe the second day.

"Your mother is a witch," she told Nan scornfully. "Red-haired women are always witches." Then she and Faith fell out about the rooster. Mary said its tail was too short. Faith angrily retorted that she

guessed God knew what length to make a rooster's tail. They did not "speak" for a day over this. Mary treated Una's hairless, one-eyed doll with consideration; but when Una showed her other prized treasure—a picture of an angel carrying a baby, presumably to heaven, Mary declared that it looked too much like a ghost for her. Una crept away to her room and cried over this, but Mary hunted her out, hugged her repentantly and implored forgiveness. No one could keep up a quarrel long with Mary—not even Nan, who was rather prone to hold grudges and never quite forgave the insult to her mother. Mary was jolly. She could and did tell the most thrilling ghost stories. Rainbow Valley seances were undeniably more exciting after Mary came. She learned to play on the jews-harp and soon eclipsed Jerry.

"Never struck anything yet I couldn't do if I put my mind to it," she declared. Mary seldom lost a chance of tooting her own horn. She taught them how to make "blow-bags" out of the thick leaves of the "live-forever" that flourished in the old Bailey garden, she initiated them into the toothsome qualities of the "sours" that grew in the niches of the graveyard dyke, and she could make the most wonderful shadow pictures on the walls with her long, flexible fingers. And when they all went picking gum in Rainbow Valley Mary always got "the biggest chew" and bragged about it. There were times when they hated her and times when they loved her. But at all times they found her interesting. So they submitted quite meekly to her bossing, and by the end of a fortnight had come to feel that she must always have been with them.

"It's the queerest thing that Mrs. Wiley hain't been after me," said Mary. "I can't understand it."

"Maybe she isn't going to bother about you at all," said Una. "Then you can just go on staying here."

"This house ain't hardly big enough for me and old Martha," said Mary darkly. "It's a very fine thing to have enough to eat—I've often wondered what it would be like—but I'm p'ticler about my cooking. And Mrs. Wiley'll be here yet. *She's* got a rod in pickle for me all right. I don't think about it so much in day-time but say, girls, up there in that garret at night I git to thinking and thinking of it, till I just almost wish she'd come and have it over with. I dunno's one real good whipping would be much worse'n all the dozen I've lived through in my mind ever since I run away. Were any of you ever licked?"

"No, of course not," said Faith indignantly. "Father would never do such a thing."

"You don't know you're alive," said Mary with a sigh half of envy, half of superiority. "You don't know what I've come through. And I s'pose the Blythes were never licked either?"

"No-o-o, I guess not. But I *think* they were sometimes spanked when they were small."

"A spanking doesn't amount to anything," said

Mary contemptuously. "If my folks had just spanked me I'd have thought they were petting me. Well, it ain't a fair world. I wouldn't mind taking my share of wallopings but I've had a darn sight too many."

"It isn't right to say that word, Mary," said Una reproachfully. "You promised me you wouldn't say it."

"G'way," responded Mary. "If you knew some of the words I *could* say if I liked you wouldn't make such a fuss over darn. And you know very well I hain't ever told any lies since I come here."

"What about all those ghosts you said you saw?" asked Faith.

Mary blushed.

"That was diff'runt," she said defiantly. "I knew you wouldn't believe them yarns and I didn't intend you to. And I really did see something queer one night when I was passing the over-harbour graveyard, true's you live. I dunno whether 'twas a ghost or Sandy Crawford's old white nag, but it looked blamed queer and I tell you I scooted at the rate of no man's business."

CHAPTER VII

A Fishy Episode

RILLA BLYTHE walked proudly, and perhaps a little primly, through the main "street" of the Glen and up the manse hill, carefully carrying a small basketful of early strawberries, which Susan had coaxed into lusciousness in one of the sunny nooks of Ingleside. Susan had charged Rilla to give the basket to nobody except Aunt Martha or Mr. Meredith, and Rilla, very proud of being entrusted with such an errand, was resolved to carry out her instructions to the letter.

Susan had dressed her daintily in a white, starched, and embroidered dress, with sash of blue and beaded slippers. Her long ruddy curls were sleek and round, and Susan had let her put on her best hat, out of compliment to the manse. It was a somewhat elaborate affair, wherein Susan's taste had had more to say than Anne's, and Rilla's small soul gloried in its splendours of silk and lace and flowers. She was very conscious of her hat, and I am afraid she strutted up the manse hill. The strut, or the hat, or both, got on the nerves of Mary Vance, who was swinging on the lawn gate. Mary's temper was somewhat ruffled just then, into the bargain. Aunt Martha had refused to let her peel the potatoes and had ordered her out of the kitchen.

"Yah! You'll bring the potatoes to the table with strips of skin hanging to them and half boiled as usual! My, but it'll be nice to go to your funeral," shrieked Mary. She went out of the kitchen, giving the door such a bang that even Aunt Martha heard it, and Mr. Meredith in his study felt the vibration and thought absently that there must have been a slight earthquake shock. Then he went on with his sermon.

Mary slipped from the gate and confronted the spick and span damsel of Ingleside.

"What you got there?" she demanded, trying to take the basket.

Rilla resisted. "It'th for Mithter Meredith," she lisped.

"Give it to me. *I'll* give it to him," said Mary.

"No. Thuthan thaid I wathn't to give it to anybody but Mithter Mer'dith or Aunt Martha," insisted Rilla.

Mary eyed her sourly.

"You think you're something, don't you, all dressed up like a doll? Look at me. My dress is all rags and *I* don't care! I'd rather be ragged than a doll baby. Go home and tell them to put you in a glass case. Look at me—look at me—look at me!"

Mary executed a wild dance around the dismayed and bewildered Rilla, flirting her ragged skirt and vociferating "Look at me—look at me" until poor Rilla was dizzy. But as the latter tried to edge away towards the gate Mary pounced on her again.

"You give me that basket," she ordered with a

grimace. Mary was past mistress in the art of "making faces." She could give her countenance a most grotesque and unearthly appearance out of which her strange, brilliant, white eyes gleamed with weird effect.

"I won't," gasped Rilla, frightened but staunch. "You let me go, Mary Vanth."

Mary let go for a minute and looked around her. Just inside the gate was a small "flake," on which half a dozen large codfish were drying. One of Mr. Meredith's parishioners had presented him with them one day, perhaps in lieu of the subscription he was supposed to pay to the stipend and never did. Mr. Meredith had thanked him and then forgotten all about the fish, which would have promptly spoiled had not the indefatigable Mary prepared them for drying and rigged up the "flake" herself on which to dry them.

Mary had a diabolical inspiration. She flew to the "flake" and seized the largest fish there—a huge, flat thing, nearly as big as herself. With a whoop she swooped down on the terrified Rilla, brandishing her weird missile. Rilla's courage gave way. To be lambasted with a dried codfish was such an unheard-of thing that Rilla could not face it. With a shriek she dropped her basket and fled. The beautiful berries, which Susan had so tenderly selected for the minister, rolled in a rosy torrent over the dusty road and were trodden on by the flying feet of pursuer and pursued. The basket and contents were no longer in Mary's mind. She thought only of the delight of giving Rilla Blythe the scare of her life. She would teach *her* to come giving herself airs because of her fine clothes.

Rilla flew down the hill and along the street. Terror lent wings to her feet, and she just managed to keep ahead of Mary, who was somewhat hampered by her own laughter, but who had breath enough to give occasional blood-curdling whoops as she ran, flourishing her codfish in the air. Through the Glen street they swept, while everybody ran to the windows and gates to see them. Mary felt she was making a tremendous sensation and enjoyed it. Rilla, blind with terror and spent of breath, felt that she could run no longer. In another instant that terrible girl would be on her with the codfish. At this point the poor mite stumbled and fell into the mud-puddle at the end of the street just as Miss Cornelia came out of Carter Flagg's store.

Miss Cornelia took the whole situation in at a glance. So did Mary. The latter stopped short in her mad career and before Miss Cornelia could speak she had whirled around and was running up as fast as she had run down. Miss Cornelia's lips tightened ominously, but she knew it was no use to think of chasing her. So she picked up poor, sobbing, dishevelled Rilla instead and took her home. Rilla was heart broken. Her dress and slippers and hat were ruined and her six year old pride had received terrible bruises.

Susan, white with indignation, heard Miss Cornelia's story of Mary Vance's exploit.

"Oh, the hussy—oh, the little hussy!" she said, as she carried Rilla away for purification and comfort.

"This thing has gone far enough, Anne dearie," said Miss Cornelia resolutely. "Something must be done. *Who* is this creature who is staying at the manse and where does she come from?"

"I understood she was a little girl from over-harbour who was visiting at the manse," answered Anne, who saw the comical side of the codfish chase and secretly thought Rilla was rather vain and needed a lesson or two.

"I know all the over-harbour families who come to our church and that imp doesn't belong to any of them," retorted Miss Cornelia. "She is almost in rags and when she goes to church she wears Faith Meredith's old clothes. There's some mystery here, and I'm going to investigate it, since it seems nobody else will. I believe she was at the bottom of their goings-on in Warren Mead's spruce bush the other day. Did you hear of their frightening his mother into a fit?"

"No. I knew Gilbert had been called to see her, but I did not hear what the trouble was."

"Well, you know she has a weak heart. And one day last week, when she was all alone on the veranda, she heard the most awful shrieks of "murder" and "help" coming from the bush—positively frightful sounds, Anne dearie. Her heart gave out at once. Warren heard them himself at the barn, and went straight to the bush to investigate, and there he found all the manse children sitting on a fallen tree and screaming "murder" at the top of their lungs. They told him they were only in fun and didn't think any one would hear them. They were just playing Indian ambush. Warren went back to the house and found his poor mother unconscious on the veranda."

Susan, who had returned, sniffed contemptuously.

"I think she was very far from being unconscious, Mrs. Marshall Elliott, and that you may tie to. I have been hearing of Amelia Warren's weak heart for forty years. She had it when she was twenty. She enjoys making a fuss and having the doctor, and any excuse will do."

"I don't think Gilbert thought her attack very serious," said Anne.

"Oh, that may very well be," said Miss Cornelia. "But the matter has made an awful lot of talk and the Meads being Methodists makes it that much worse. What is going to become of those children? Sometimes I can't sleep at nights for thinking about them, Anne dearie. I really do question if they get enough to eat, even, for their father is so lost in dreams that he doesn't often remember he has a stomach, and that lazy old woman doesn't bother cooking what she ought. They are just running wild and now that school is closing they'll be worse than ever."

"They do have jolly times," said Anne; laughing

over the recollections of some Rainbow Valley happenings that had come to her ears. "And they are all brave and frank and loyal and truthful."

"That's a true word, Anne dearie, and when you come to think of all the trouble in the church those two tattling, deceitful youngsters of the last minister's made I'm inclined to overlook a good deal in the Merediths."

"When all is said and done, Mrs. Dr. dear, they are very nice children," said Susan. "They have got plenty of original sin in them and that I will admit, but maybe it is just as well, for if they had not they might spoil from over-sweetness. Only I do think it is not proper for them to play in a graveyard and that I will maintain."

"But they really play quite quietly there," excused Anne. "They don't run and yell as they do elsewhere. Such howls as drift up here from Rainbow Valley sometimes! Though I fancy my own small fry bear a valiant part in them. They had a sham battle there last night and had to "roar" themselves, because they had no artillery to do it, so Jem says. Jem is passing through the stage where all boys hanker to be soldiers."

"Well, thank goodness, he'll never be a soldier," said Miss Cornelia. "I never approved of our boys going to that South African fracas. But it's over, and not likely anything of the kind will ever happen again. I think the world is getting more sensible. As for the

Merediths, I've said many a time and I say it again, if Mr. Meredith had a wife all would be well."

"He called twice at the Kirks' last week, so I am told," said Susan.

"Well," said Miss Cornelia thoughtfully, "as a rule, I don't approve of a minister marrying in his congregation. It generally spoils him. But in this case it would do no harm, for every one likes Elizabeth Kirk and nobody else is hankering for the job of stepmothering those youngsters. Even the Hill girls balk at that. They haven't been found laying traps for Mr. Meredith. Elizabeth would make him a good wife if he only thought so. But the trouble is, she really is homely and, Anne dearie, Mr. Meredith, abstracted as he is, has an eye for a good-looking woman, manlike. He isn't *so* other-worldly when it comes to that, believe *me*."

"Elizabeth Kirk is a very nice person, but they do say that people have nearly frozen to death in her mother's spare-room bed before now, Mrs. Dr. dear," said Susan darkly. "If *I* felt I had any right to express an opinion concerning such a solemn matter as a minister's marriage I would say that I think Elizabeth's cousin Sarah, over-harbour, would make Mr. Meredith a better wife."

"Why, Sarah Kirk is a Methodist," said Miss Cornelia, much as if Susan had suggested a Hottentot as a manse bride.

"She would likely turn Presbyterian if she married Mr. Meredith," retorted Susan.

Miss Cornelia shook her head. Evidently with her it was, once a Methodist, always a Methodist.

"Sarah Kirk is entirely out of the question," she said positively. "And so is Emmeline Drew—though the Drews are all trying to make the match. They are literally throwing poor Emmeline at his head, and he hasn't the least idea of it."

"Emmeline Drew has no gumption, I must allow," said Susan. "She is the kind of woman, Mrs. Dr. dear, who would put a hot water bottle in your bed on a dog-night and then have her feelings hurt because you were not grateful. And her mother was a *very* poor housekeeper. Did you ever hear the story of her dishcloth? She lost her dishcloth one day. But the next day she found it. Oh, yes, Mrs. Dr. dear, she found it, in the goose at the dinner table, mixed up with the stuffing. Do you think a woman like that would do for a minister's mother-in-law? *I* do not. But no doubt I would be better employed in mending little Jem's trousers than in talking gossip about my neighbours. He tore them something scandalous last night in Rainbow Valley."

"Where is Walter?" asked Anne.

"He is up to no good, I fear, Mrs. Dr. dear. He is in the attic writing something in an exercise book. And he has not done as well in arithmetic this term as he should, so the teacher tells me. Too well I know the reason why. He has been writing silly rhymes when he should have been doing his sums. I am afraid that boy is going to be a poet, Mrs. Dr. dear."

"He *is* a poet now, Susan."

"Well, you take it real calm, Mrs. Dr. dear. I suppose it is the best way, when a person has the strength. I had an uncle who began by being a poet and ended up by being a tramp. Our family were dreadfully ashamed of him."

"You don't seem to think very highly of poets, Susan," said Anne, laughing.

"Who does, Mrs. Dr. dear?" asked Susan in genuine astonishment.

"What about Milton and Shakespeare? And the poets of the Bible?"

"They tell me Milton could not get along with his wife, and Shakespeare was no more than respectable by times. As for the Bible, of course things were different in those sacred days—although I never had a high opinion of King David, say what you will. I never knew any good to come of writing poetry, and I hope and pray that blessed boy will outgrow the tendency. If he does not—we must see what emulsion of cod-liver oil will do."

CHAPTER VIII

Miss Cornelia Intervenes

MISS CORNELIA descended upon the manse the next day and cross-questioned Mary, who, being a young person of considerable discernment and astuteness, told her story simply and truthfully, with an entire absence of complaint or bravado. Miss Cornelia was more favourably impressed than she had expected to be, but deemed it her duty to be severe.

"Do you think," she said sternly, "that you showed your gratitude to this family, who have been far too kind to you, by insulting and chasing one of their little friends as you did yesterday?"

"Say, it was rotten mean of me," admitted Mary easily. "I dunno what possessed me. That old codfish seemed to come in so blamed handy. But I was awful sorry—I cried last night after I went to bed about it, honest I did. You ask Una if I didn't. I wouldn't tell her what for 'cause I was ashamed of it, and then she cried, too, because she was afraid some one had hurt my feelings. Laws, *I* ain't got any feelings to hurt worth speaking of. What worries me is why Mrs. Wiley hain't been hunting for me. It ain't like her."

Miss Cornelia herself thought it rather peculiar, but

she merely admonished Mary sharply not to take any further liberties with the minister's codfish, and went to report progress at Ingleside.

"If the child's story is true the matter ought to be looked into," she said. "I know something about that Wiley woman, believe *me*. Marshall used to be well acquainted with her when he lived over-harbour. I heard him say something last summer about her and a home child she had—likely this very Mary-creature. He said some one told him she was working the child to death and not half feeding and clothing it. You know, Anne dearie, it has always been my habit neither to make nor meddle with those over-harbour folks. But I shall send Marshall over to-morrow to find out the rights of this if he can. And *then* I'll speak to the minister. Mind you, Anne dearie, the Merediths found this girl literally starving in James Taylor's old hay barn. She had been there all night, cold and hungry and alone. And us sleeping warm in our beds after good suppers."

"The poor little thing," said Anne, picturing one of her own dear babies, cold and hungry and alone in such circumstances. "If she has been ill-used, Miss Cornelia, she mustn't be taken back to such a place. *I* was an orphan once in a very similar situation."

"We'll have to consult the Hopetown asylum folks," said Miss Cornelia. "Anyway, she can't be left at the manse. Dear knows what those poor children might learn from her. I understand that she has been known to swear. But just think of her being there two whole weeks and Mr. Meredith never waking up to it! What business has a man like that to have a family? Why, Anne dearie, he ought to be a monk."

Two evenings later Miss Cornelia was back at Ingleside.

"It's the most amazing thing!" she said. "Mrs. Wiley was found dead in her bed the very morning after this Mary-creature ran away. She has had a bad heart for years and the doctor had warned her it might happen at any time. She had sent away her hired man and there was nobody in the house. Some neighbours found her the next day. They missed the child, it seems, but supposed Mrs. Wiley had sent her to her cousin near Charlottetown as she had said she was going to do. The cousin didn't come to the funeral and so nobody ever knew that Mary wasn't with her. The people Marshall talked to told him some things about the way Mrs. Wiley used this Mary that made his blood boil, so he declares. You know, it puts Marshall in a regular fury to hear of a child being ill-used. They said she whipped her mercilessly for every little fault or mistake. Some folks talked of writing to the asylum authorities but everybody's business is nobody's business and it was never done."

"I am very sorry that Wiley person is dead," said Susan fiercely. "I should like to go over-harbour and give her a piece of my mind. Starving and beating a child, Mrs. Dr. dear! As you know, I hold with lawful spanking, but I go no further. And what is to become of this poor child now, Mrs. Marshall Elliott?"

"I suppose she must be sent back to Hopetown," said Miss Cornelia. "I think every one hereabouts who wants a home child has one. I'll see Mr. Meredith to-morrow and tell him my opinion of the whole affair."

"And no doubt she will, Mrs. Dr. dear," said Susan, after Miss Cornelia had gone. "She would stick at nothing, not even at shingling the church spire if she took it into her head. But I cannot understand how even Cornelia Bryant can talk to a minister as she does. You would think he was just any common person."

When Miss Cornelia had gone, Nan Blythe uncurled herself from the hammock where she had been studying her lessons and slipped away to Rainbow Valley. The others were already there. Jem and Jerry were playing quoits with old horseshoes borrowed from the Glen blacksmith. Carl was stalking ants on a sunny hillock. Walter, lying on his stomach among the fern, was reading aloud to Mary and Di and Faith and Una from a wonderful book of myths wherein were fascinating accounts of Prester John and the Wandering Jew, divining rods and tailed men, of Schamir, the worm that split rocks and opened the way to golden treasure, of Fortunate Isles and swan-maidens. It was a great shock to Walter to learn that William Tell and Gelert were myths also; and the story of Bishop

Hatto was to keep him awake all that night; but best of all he loved the stories of the Pied Piper and the San Greal. He read them thrillingly, while the bells on the Tree Lovers tinkled in the summer wind and the coolness of the evening shadows crept across the valley.

"Say, ain't them in'resting lies?" said Mary admiringly when Walter had closed the book.

"They aren't lies," said Di indignantly.

"You don't mean they're true?" asked Mary incredulously.

"No—not exactly. They're like those ghost-stories of yours. They weren't true—but you didn't expect us to believe them, so they weren't lies."

"That yarn about the divining rod is no lie, anyhow," said Mary. "Old Jake Crawford over-harbour can work it. They send for him from everywhere when they want to dig a well. And I believe I know the Wandering Jew."

"Oh, Mary," said Una, awe-struck.

"I do—true's you're alive. There was an old man at Mrs. Wiley's one day last fall. He looked old enough to be *anything*. She was asking him about cedar posts, if he thought they'd last well. And he said, 'Last well? They'll last a thousand years. I know, for I've tried them twice.' Now, if he was two thousand years old who was he but your Wandering Jew?"

"I don't believe the Wandering Jew would associate with a person like Mrs. Wiley," said Faith decidedly.

"I love the Pied Piper story," said Di, "and so does mother. I always feel so sorry for the poor little lame boy who couldn't keep up with the others and got shut out of the mountain. He must have been *so* disappointed. I think all the rest of his life he'd be wondering what wonderful thing he had missed and wishing he could have got in with the others."

"But how glad his mother must have been," said Una softly. "I think she had been sorry all her life that he was lame. Perhaps she even used to cry about it. But she would never be sorry again—never. She would be glad he was lame because that was why she hadn't lost him."

"Some day," said Walter dreamily, looking afar into the sky, "the Pied Piper will come over the hill up there and down Rainbow Valley, piping merrily and sweetly. And I will follow him—follow him down to the shore—down to the sea—away from you all. I don't think I'll want to go. Jem will want to go—it will be such an adventure—but I won't. Only I'll *have* to—the music will call and call and call me until I *must* follow."

"We'll all go," cried Di, catching fire at the flame of Walter's fancy, and half-believing she could see the mocking, retreating figure of the mystic piper in the far, dim end of the valley.

"No. You'll sit here and wait," said Walter, his great, splendid eyes full of strange glamour. "You'll wait for us to come back. And we may not come—for we cannot come as long as the Piper plays. He may pipe us round the world. And still you'll sit here and wait—and *wait.*"

"Oh, dry up," said Mary, shivering. "Don't look like that, Walter Blythe. You give me the creeps. Do you want to set me bawling? I could just see that horrid old Piper going away on, and you boys following him, and us girls sitting here waiting all alone. I dunno why it is—I never was one of the blubbering kind—but as soon as you start your spieling I always want to cry."

Walter smiled in triumph. He liked to exercise this power of his over his companions—to play on their feelings, waken their fears, thrill their souls. It satisfied some dramatic instinct in him. But under his triumph was a queer little chill of some mysterious dread. The Pied Piper had seemed very real to him—as if the fluttering veil that hid the future had for a moment been blown aside in the starlit dusk of Rainbow Valley and some dim glimpse of coming years granted to him.

Carl, coming up to their group with a report of the doings in ant-land, brought them all back to the realm of facts.

"Ants *are* darned in'resting," exclaimed Mary, glad to escape the shadowy Piper's thrall. "Carl and me watched that bed in the graveyard all Saturday afternoon. I never thought there was so much in bugs. Say, but they're quarrelsome little cusses—some of 'em like to start a fight 'thout any reason, far's we could see. And some of 'em are cowards. They got so scared they just doubled theirselves up into a ball and let the other fellows bang 'em round. They wouldn't put up a fight at all. Some of 'em are lazy and won't work. We watched 'em shirking. And there was one ant died of grief 'cause another ant got killed—wouldn't work—wouldn't eat—just died—it did, honest to Go—oodness."

A shocked silence prevailed. Every one knew that Mary had not started out to say "goodness." Faith and Di exchanged glances that would have done credit to Miss Cornelia herself. Walter and Carl looked uncomfortable, and Una's lip trembled.

Mary squirmed uncomfortably.

"That slipped out 'fore I thought—it did, honest to —I mean, true's you live, and I swallowed half of it. You folks over here are mighty squeamish seems to me. Wish you could have heard the Wileys when they had a fight."

"Ladies don't say such things," said Faith, very primly for her.

"It isn't right," whispered Una.

"I ain't a lady," said Mary. "What chance've I ever had of being a lady? But I won't say that again if I can help it. I promise you."

"Besides," said Una, "you can't expect God to answer your prayers if you take His name in vain, Mary."

"I don't expect Him to answer 'em anyhow," said Mary of little faith. "I've been asking Him for a week to clear up this Wiley affair and He hasn't done a thing. I'm going to give up."

At this juncture Nan arrived breathless.

"Oh, Mary, I've news for you. Mrs. Elliott has been over-harbour and what do you think she found out? Mrs. Wiley is dead—she was found dead in bed the morning after you ran away. So you'll never have to go back to her."

"Dead!" said Mary stupefied. Then she shivered.

"Do you s'pose my praying had anything to do with that?" she cried imploringly to Una. "If it had I'll never pray again as long as I live. Why, she may come back and ha'nt me."

"No, no, Mary," said Una comfortingly, "it hadn't. Why, Mrs. Wiley died long before you ever began to pray about it at all."

"That's so," said Mary recovering from her panic. "But I tell you it gave me a start. I wouldn't like to think I'd prayed anybody to death. I never thought of such a thing as her dying when I was praying. She didn't seem much like the dying kind. Did Mrs. Elliott say anything about me?"

"She said you would likely have to go back to the asylum."

"I thought as much," said Mary drearily. "And then they'll give me out again—likely to some one just like Mrs. Wiley. Well, I s'pose I can stand it. I'm tough."

"I'm going to pray that you won't have to go back," whispered Una, as she and Mary walked home to the manse.

"You can do as you like," said Mary decidedly, "but I vow *I* won't. I'm good and scared of this praying business. See what's come of it. If Mrs. Wiley *had* died after I started praying it would have been my doings."

"Oh, no, it wouldn't," said Una. "I wish I could explain things better—father could, I know, if you'd talk to him, Mary."

"Catch me! I don't know what to make of your father, that's the long and short of it. He goes by me and never sees me in broad daylight. I ain't proud—but I ain't a door mat, neither!"

"Oh, Mary, it's just father's way. Most of the time he never sees us, either. He is thinking deeply, that is all. And I *am* going to pray that God will keep you in Four Winds—because I like you, Mary."

"All right. Only don't let me hear of any more people dying on account of it," said Mary. "I'd like to stay in Four Winds fine. I like it and I like the harbour and the light house—and you and the Blythes. You're the only friends I ever had and I'd hate to leave you."

CHAPTER IX

UNA INTERVENES

MISS CORNELIA had an interview with Mr. Meredith which proved something of a shock to that abstracted gentleman. She pointed out to him, none too respectfully, his dereliction of duty in allowing a waif like Mary Vance to come into his family and associate with his children without knowing or learning anything about her.

"I don't say there is much harm done, of course," she concluded. "This Mary-creature isn't what you might call bad, when all is said and done. I've been questioning your children and the Blythes, and from what I can make out there's nothing much to be said against the child except that she's slangy and doesn't use very refined language. But think what *might* have happened if she'd been like some of those home children we know of. You know yourself what that poor little creature the Jim Flaggs' had, taught and told the Flagg children."

Mr. Meredith did know and was honestly shocked over his own carelessness in the matter.

"But what is to be done, Mrs. Elliott?" he asked helplessly. "We can't turn the poor child out. She *must* be cared for."

"Of course. We'd better write to the Hopetown

authorities at once. Meanwhile, I suppose she might as well stay here for a few more days till we hear from them. But keep your eyes and ears open, Mr. Meredith."

Susan would have died of horror on the spot if she had heard Miss Cornelia so admonishing a minister. But Miss Cornelia departed in a warm glow of satisfaction over duty done, and that night Mr. Meredith asked Mary to come into his study with him. Mary obeyed, looking literally ghastly with fright. But she got the surprise of her poor, battered little life. This man, of whom she had stood so terribly in awe, was the kindest, gentlest soul she had ever met. Before she knew what happened Mary found herself pouring all her troubles into his ear and receiving in return such sympathy and tender understanding as it had never occurred to her to imagine. Mary left the study with her face and eyes so softened that Una hardly knew her.

"Your father's all right, when he does wake up," she said with a sniff that just escaped being a sob. "It's a pity he doesn't wake up oftener. He said I wasn't to blame for Mrs. Wiley dying, but that I must try to think of her good points and not of her bad ones. I dunno what good points she had, unless it was keeping her house clean and making first class butter. I know I 'most wore my arms out scrubbing her old kitchen floor with the knots in it. But anything your father says goes with me after this."

Mary proved a rather dull companion in the following days, however. She confided to Una that the more she thought of going back to the asylum the more she hated it. Una racked her small brains for some way of averting it, but it was Nan Blythe who came to the rescue with a somewhat startling suggestion.

"Mrs. Elliott might take Mary herself. She has a great big house and Mr. Elliott is always wanting her to have help. It would be just a splendid place for Mary. Only she'd have to behave herself."

"Oh, Nan, do you think Mrs. Elliott would take her?"

"It wouldn't do any harm if you asked her," said Nan.

At first Una did not think she could. She was so shy that to ask a favour of anybody was agony to her. And she was very much in awe of the bustling, energetic Mrs. Elliott. She liked her very much and always enjoyed a visit to her house; but to go and ask her to adopt Mary Vance seemed such a height of presumption that Una's timid spirit quailed.

When the Hopetown authorities wrote to Mr. Meredith to send Mary to them without delay Mary cried herself to sleep in the manse attic that night and Una found a desperate courage. The next evening she slipped away from the manse to the harbour road. Far down in Rainbow Valley she heard joyous laughter but her way lay not there. She was terribly pale and terribly in earnest—so much so that she took no notice of the people she met—and old Mrs. Stanley Flagg was quite huffed and said Una Meredith would be as absent-minded as her father when she grew up.

Miss Cornelia lived half way between the Glen and Four Winds Point, in a house whose original glaring green hue had mellowed down to an agreeable greenish gray. Marshall Elliott had planted trees about it and set out a rose garden and a spruce hedge. It was quite a different place from what it had been in years agone. The manse children and the Ingleside children liked to go there. It was a beautiful walk down the old harbour road, and there was always a well-filled cooky jar at the end.

The misty sea was lapping softly far down on the sands. Three big boats were skimming down the harbour like great white sea-birds. A schooner was coming up the channel. The world of Four Winds was steeped in glowing colour, and subtle music, and strange glamour, and everybody should have been happy in it. But when Una turned in at Miss Cornelia's gate her very legs had almost refused to carry her.

Miss Cornelia was alone on the veranda. Una had hoped Mr. Elliott would be there. He was so big and hearty and twinkly that there would be encouragement in his presence. She sat on the little stool Miss Cornelia brought out and tried to eat the doughnut Miss Cornelia gave her. It stuck in her throat, but she swallowed desperately lest Miss Cornelia be offended.

She could not talk; she was still pale; and her big, dark-blue eyes looked so piteous that Miss Cornelia concluded the child was in some trouble.

"What's on your mind, dearie?" she asked. "There's something, that's plain to be seen."

Una swallowed the last twist of doughnut with a desperate gulp.

"Mrs. Elliott, won't *you* take Mary Vance?" she said beseechingly.

Miss Cornelia stared blankly.

"Me! Take Mary Vance! Do you mean keep her?"

"Yes—keep her—adopt her," said Una eagerly, gaining courage now that the ice was broken. "Oh, Mrs. Elliott, *please* do. She doesn't want to go back to the asylum—she cries every night about it. She's so afraid of being sent to another hard place. And she's *so* smart—there isn't anything she can't do. I know you wouldn't be sorry if you took her."

"I never thought of such a thing," said Miss Cornelia rather helplessly.

"*Won't* you think of it?" implored Una.

"But, dearie, I don't want help. I'm quite able to do all the work here. And I never thought I'd like to have a home girl if I did need help."

The light went out of Una's eyes. Her lips trembled. She sat down on her stool again, a pathetic little figure of disappointment, and began to cry.

"Don't—dearie—don't," exclaimed Miss Cornelia in

distress. She could never bear to hurt a child. "I don't say I *won't* take her—but the idea is so new it has just kerflummuxed me. I must think it over."

"Mary is *so* smart," said Una again.

"Humph! So I've heard. I've heard she swears, too. Is that true?"

"I've never heard her swear—*exactly,*" faltered Una uncomfortably. "But I'm afraid she *could.*"

"I believe you! Does she always tell the truth?"

"I think she does, except when she's afraid of a whipping."

"And yet you want me to take her?"

"*Some one* has to take her," sobbed Una. "*Some one* has to look after her, Mrs. Elliott."

"That's true. Perhaps it *is* my duty to do it," said Miss Cornelia with a sigh. "Well, I'll have to talk it over with Mr. Elliott. So don't say anything about it just yet. Take another doughnut, dearie."

Una took it and ate it with a better appetite.

"I'm very fond of doughnuts," she confessed. "Aunt Martha never makes any. But Miss Susan at Ingleside does, and sometimes she lets us have a plateful in Rainbow Valley. Do you know what I do when I'm hungry for doughnuts and can't get any, Mrs. Elliott?"

"No, dearie. What?"

"I get out mother's old cook book and read the doughnut recipe—and the other recipes. They sound *so* nice. I always do that when I'm hungry—especially after we've had ditto for dinner. *Then* I read the fried chicken and the roast goose recipes. Mother could make all those nice things."

"Those manse children will starve to death yet if Mr. Meredith doesn't get married," Miss Cornelia told her husband indignantly after Una had gone. "And he won't—and what's to be done? And *shall* we take this Mary-creature, Marshall?"

"Yes, take her," said Marshall laconically.

"Just like a man," said his wife, despairingly. " 'Take her'—as if that was all. There are a hundred things to be considered, believe *me*."

"Take her—and we'll consider them afterwards, Cornelia," said her husband.

In the end Miss Cornelia did take her and went up to announce her decision to the Ingleside people first.

"Splendid!" said Anne delightedly. "I've been hoping you would do that very thing, Miss Cornelia. I want that poor child to get a good home. *I* was a homeless little orphan just like her once."

"I don't think this Mary-creature is or ever will be much like you," retorted Miss Cornelia gloomily. "She's a cat of another colour. But she's also a human being with an immortal soul to save. I've got a shorter catechism and a small tooth comb and I'm going to do my duty by her, now that I've set my hand to the plough, believe me."

Mary received the news with chastened satisfaction.

"It's better luck than I expected," she said.

"You'll have to mind your p's and q's with Mrs. Elliott," said Nan.

"Well, I can do that," flashed Mary. "I know how to behave when I want to just as well as you, Nan Blythe."

"You mustn't use bad words, you know, Mary," said Una anxiously.

"I s'pose she'd die of horror if I did," grinned Mary, her white eyes shining with unholy glee over the idea. "But you needn't worry, Una. Butter won't melt in my mouth after this. I'll be all prunes and prisms."

"Nor tell lies," added Faith.

"Not even to get off from a whipping?" pleaded Mary.

"Mrs. Elliott will *never* whip you—*never*," exclaimed Di.

"Won't she?" said Mary skeptically. "If I ever find myself in a place where I ain't licked I'll think it's heaven all right. No fear of me telling lies then. I ain't fond of telling 'em—I'd ruther not, if it comes to that."

The day before Mary's departure from the manse they had a picnic in her honour in Rainbow Valley, and that evening all the manse children gave her something from their scanty store of treasured things for a keepsake. Carl gave her his Noah's ark and Jerry his second best jews-harp. Faith gave her a little hair brush with a mirror in the back of it, which Mary had always considered very wonderful. Una hesitated between an old beaded purse and a gay picture of Daniel in the lion's den, and finally offered Mary her choice. Mary really hankered after the beaded purse, but she knew Una loved it, so she said,

"Give me Daniel. I'd ruther have it 'cause I'm partial to lions. Only I wish they'd et Daniel up. It would have been more exciting."

At bedtime Mary coaxed Una to sleep with her.

"It's for the last time," she said, "and it's raining to-night, and I hate sleeping up there alone when it's raining on account of that graveyard. I don't mind it on fine nights, but a night like this I can't see anything but the rain pouring down on them old white stones, and the wind round the window sounds as if them dead people were trying to get in and crying 'cause they couldn't."

"I like rainy nights," said Una, when they were cuddled down together in the little attic room, "and so do the Blythe girls."

"I don't mind 'em when I'm not handy to graveyards," said Mary. "If I was alone here I'd cry my eyes out I'd be so lonesome. I feel awful bad to be leaving you all."

"Mrs. Elliott will let you come up and play in Rainbow Valley quite often I'm sure," said Una. "And you *will* be a good girl, won't you, Mary?"

"Oh, I'll try," sighed Mary. "But it won't be as easy for me to be good—inside, I mean, as well as outside—as it is for you. You hadn't such scalawags of relations as I had."

"But your people must have had some good qualities as well as bad ones," argued Una. "You must live up to them and never mind their bad ones."

"I don't believe they had any good qualities," said Mary gloomily. "*I* never heard of any. My grandfather had money, but they say he was a rascal. No, I'll just have to start out on my own hook and do the best I can."

"And God will help you, you know, Mary, if you ask Him."

"I don't know about that."

"Oh, Mary. You know we asked God to get a home for you and He did."

"I don't see what He had to do with it," retorted Mary. "It was you put it into Mrs. Elliott's head."

"But God put it into her *heart* to take you. All my putting it into her *head* wouldn't have done any good if He hadn't."

"Well, there may be something in that," admitted Mary. "Mind you, I haven't got anything against God, Una. I'm willing to give Him a chance. But, honest, I think He's an awful lot like your father—just absent-minded and never taking any notice of a body most of the time, but sometimes waking up all of a suddent and being awful good and kind and sensible."

"Oh, Mary, no!" exclaimed horrified Una. "God

isn't a bit like father—I mean He's a thousand times better and kinder."

"If He's as good as your father He'll do for me," said Mary. "When your father was talking to me I felt as if I never could be bad any more."

"I wish you'd talk to father about Him," sighed Una. "He can explain it all so much better than I can."

"Why, so I will, next time he wakes up," promised Mary. "That night he talked to me in the study he showed me real clear that my praying didn't kill Mrs. Wiley. My mind's been easy since, but I'm real cautious about praying. I guess the old rhyme is the safest. Say, Una, it seems to me if one has to pray to anybody it'd be better to pray to the devil than to God. God's good, anyhow, so you say, so He won't do you any harm, but from all I can make out the devil needs to be peacified. *I* think the sensible way would be to say to *him*, 'Good devil, please don't tempt me. Just leave me alone, please.' Now, don't you?"

"Oh, no, no, Mary. I'm sure it couldn't be right to pray to the devil. And it wouldn't do any good because he's bad. It might aggravate him and he'd be worse than ever."

"Well, as to this God-matter," said Mary stubbornly, "since you and I can't settle it, there ain't no use in talking more about it until we've a chanct to find out the rights of it. I'l do the best I can alone till then."

"If mother was alive she could tell us everything," said Una with a sigh.

"I wisht she was alive," said Mary. "I don't know what's going to become of you youngsters when I'm gone. Anyhow, *do* try and keep the house a little tidy. The way people talks about it is scandalous. And first thing you know your father will be getting married again and then your noses will be out of joint."

Una was startled. The idea of her father marrying again had never presented itself to her before. She did not like it and she lay silent under the chill of it.

"Stepmothers are *awful* creatures," Mary went on. "I could make your blood run cold if I was to tell you all I know about 'em. The Wilson kids across the road from Wileys' had a stepmother. She was just as bad to 'em as Mrs. Wiley was to me. It'll be awful if you get a stepmother."

"I'm sure we won't," said Una tremulously. "Father won't marry anybody else."

"He'll be hounded into it, I expect," said Mary darkly. "All the old maids in the settlement are after him. There's no being up to them. And the worst of stepmothers is, they always set your father against you. He'd never care anything about you again. He'd always take her part and her children's part. You see, she'd make him believe you were all bad."

"I wish you hadn't told me this, Mary," cried Una. "It makes me feel so unhappy."

"I only wanted to warn you," said Mary, rather

repentantly. "Of course, your father's so absent-minded he mightn't happen to think of getting married again. But it's better to be prepared."

Long after Mary slept serenely little Una lay awake, her eyes smarting with tears. Oh, how dreadful it would be if her father should marry somebody who would make him hate her and Jerry and Faith and Carl! She couldn't bear it—she couldn't!

Mary had not instilled any poison of the kind Miss Cornelia had feared into the manse children's minds. Yet she had certainly contrived to do a little mischief with the best of intentions. But she slept dreamlessly, while Una lay awake and the rain fell and the wind wailed around the old gray manse. And the Rev. John Meredith forgot to go to bed at all because he was absorbed in reading a life of St. Augustine. It was gray dawn when he finished it and went upstairs, wrestling with the problems of two thousand years ago. The door of the girls' room was open and he saw Faith lying asleep, rosy and beautiful. He wondered where Una was. Perhaps she had gone over to "stay all night" with the Blythe girls. She did this occasionally, deeming it a great treat. John Meredith sighed. He felt that Una's whereabouts ought not to be a mystery to him. Cecilia would have looked after her better than that.

If only Cecilia were still with him! How pretty and gay she had been! How the old manse up at Maywater had echoed to her songs! And she had gone away so suddenly, taking her laughter and music and leaving silence—so suddenly that he had never quite got over his feeling of amazement. How could *she,* the beautiful and vivid, have died?

The idea of a second marriage had never presented itself seriously to John Meredith. He had loved his wife so deeply that he believed he could never care for any woman again. He had a vague idea that before very long Faith would be old enough to take her mother's place. Until then, he must do the best he could alone. He sighed and went to his room, where the bed was still unmade. Aunt Martha had forgotten it, and Mary had not dared to make it because Aunt Martha had forbidden her to meddle with anything in the minister's room. But Mr. Meredith did not notice that it was unmade. His last thoughts were of St. Augustine.

CHAPTER X

The Manse Girls Clean House

"UGH," said Faith, sitting up in bed with a shiver. "It's raining. I do hate a rainy Sunday. Sunday is dull enough even when it's fine."

"We oughtn't to find Sunday dull," said Una sleepily, trying to pull her drowsy wits together with an uneasy conviction that they had overslept.

"But we *do,* you know," said Faith candidly. "Mary Vance says most Sundays are so dull she could hang herself."

"We ought to like Sunday better than Mary Vance," said Una remorsefully. "We're the minister's children."

"I wish we were a blacksmith's children," protested Faith angrily, hunting for her stockings. "*Then* people wouldn't expect us to be better than other children. *Just* look at the holes in my heels. Mary darned them all up before she went away, but they're as bad as ever now. Una, get up. I can't get the breakfast alone. Oh, dear. I wish father and Jerry were home. You wouldn't think we'd miss father much—we don't see much of him when he *is* home. And yet *everything* seems gone. I must run in and see how Aunt Martha is."

"Is she any better?" asked Una, when Faith returned.

"No, she isn't. She's groaning with the misery still. Maybe we ought to tell Dr. Blythe. But she says not—she never had a doctor in her life and she isn't going to begin now. She says doctors just live by poisoning people. Do you suppose they do?"

"No, of course not," said Una indignantly. "I'm sure Dr. Blythe wouldn't poison anybody."

"Well, we'll have to rub Aunt Martha's back again after breakfast. We'd better not make the flannels as hot as we did yesterday."

Faith giggled over the remembrance. They had nearly scalded the skin off poor Aunt Martha's back. Una sighed. Mary Vance would have known just what the precise temperature of flannels for a misery back should be. Mary knew everything. They knew nothing. And how could they learn, save by bitter experience for which, in this instance, unfortunate Aunt Martha had paid?

The preceding Monday Mr. Meredith had left for Nova Scotia to spend his short vacation, taking Jerry with him. On Wednesday Aunt Martha was suddenly seized with a recurring and mysterious ailment which she always called "the misery," and which was tolerably certain to attack her at the most inconvenient times. She could not rise from her bed, any movement causing agony. A doctor she flatly refused to have. Faith and Una cooked the meals and waited on her.

The less said about the meals the better—yet they were not much worse than Aunt Martha's had been. There were many women in the village who would have been glad to come and help, but Aunt Martha refused to let her plight be known.

"You must worry on till I kin git around," she groaned. "Thank goodness, John isn't here. There's a plenty o' cold biled meat and bread and you kin try your hand at making porridge."

The girls had tried their hand, but so far without much success. The first day it had been too thin. The next day so thick that you could cut it in slices. And both days it had been burned.

"I hate porridge," said Faith viciously. "When I have a house of my own I'm *never* going to have a single bit of porridge in it."

"What'll your children do then?" asked Una. "Children have to have porridge or they won't grow. Everybody says so."

"They'll have to get along without it or stay runts," retorted Faith stubbornly. "Here, Una, you stir it while I set the table. If I leave it for a minute the horrid stuff will burn. It's half past nine. We'll be late for Sunday School."

"I haven't seen any one going past yet," said Una. "There won't likely be many out. Just see how it's pouring. And when there's no preaching the folks won't come from a distance to bring the children."

"Go and call Carl," said Faith.

Carl, it appeared, had a sore throat, induced by getting wet in the Rainbow Valley marsh the previous evening while pursuing dragon-flies. He had come home with dripping stockings and boots and had sat out the evening in them. He could not eat any breakfast and Faith made him go back to bed again. She and Una left the table as it was and went to Sunday School. There was no one in the school room when they got there and no one came. They waited until eleven and then went home.

"There doesn't seem to be anybody at the Methodist Sunday School either," said Una.

"I'm *glad,*" said Faith. "I'd hate to think the Methodists were better at going to Sunday School on rainy Sundays than the Presbyterians. But there's no preaching in their Church to-day, either, so likely their Sunday School is in the afternoon."

Una washed the dishes, doing them quite nicely, for so much had she learned from Mary Vance. Faith swept the floor after a fashion and peeled the potatoes for dinner, cutting her finger in the process.

"I wish we had something for dinner besides ditto," sighed Una. "I'm so tired of it. The Blythe children don't know what ditto is. And we *never* have any pudding. Nan says Susan would faint if they had no pudding on Sundays. Why aren't we like other people, Faith?"

"I don't want to be like other people," laughed Faith, tying up her bleeding finger. "I like being myself.

It's more interesting. Jessie Drew is as good a housekeeper as her mother, but would you want to be as stupid as she is?"

"But our house isn't right. Mary Vance says so. She says people talk about it being so untidy."

Faith had an inspiration.

"We'll clean it all up," she cried. "We'll go right to work to-morrow. It's a real good chance when Aunt Martha is laid up and can't interfere with us. We'll have it all lovely and clean when father comes home, just like it was when Mary went away. *Any one* can sweep and dust and wash windows. People won't be able to talk about us any more. Jem Blythe says it's only old cats that talk, but their talk hurts just as much as anybody's."

"I hope it will be fine to-morrow," said Una, fired with enthusiasm. "Oh, Faith, it will be splendid to be all cleaned up and like other people."

"I hope Aunt Martha's misery will last over to-morrow," said Faith. "If it doesn't we won't get a single thing done."

Faith's amiable wish was fulfilled. The next day found Aunt Martha still unable to rise. Carl, too, was still sick and easily prevailed on to stay in bed. Neither Faith nor Una had any idea how sick the boy really was; a watchful mother would have had a doctor without delay; but there was no mother, and poor little Carl, with his sore throat and aching head and crimson cheeks, rolled himself up in his twisted bedclothes and suffered alone, somewhat comforted by the companionship of a small green lizard in the pocket of his ragged nighty.

The world was full of summer sunshine after the rain. It was a peerless day for housecleaning and Faith and Una went gaily to work.

"We'll clean the dining room and the parlor," said Faith. "It wouldn't do to meddle with the study, and it doesn't matter much about the upstairs. The first thing is to take everything out."

Accordingly, everything was taken out. The furniture was piled on the veranda and lawn and the Methodist graveyard fence was gaily draped with rugs. An orgy of sweeping followed, with an attempt at dusting on Una's part, while Faith washed the windows of the dining room, breaking one pane and cracking two in the process. Una surveyed the streaked result dubiously.

"They don't look right, somehow," she said. "Mrs. Elliott's and Susan's windows just shine and sparkle."

"Never mind. They let the sunshine through just as well," said Faith cheerfully. "They *must* be clean after all the soap and water I've used, and that's the main thing. Now, it's past eleven, so I'll wipe up this mess on the floor and we'll go outside. You dust the furniture and I'll shake the rugs. I'm going to do it in the graveyard. I don't want to send dust flying all over the lawn."

Faith enjoyed the rug shaking. To stand on Hezekiah Pollock's tombstone, flapping and shaking rugs, was real fun. To be sure, Elder Abraham Clow and his wife, driving past in their capacious double-seated buggy, seemed to gaze at her in grim disapproval.

"Isn't that a terrible sight?" said Elder Abraham solemnly.

"I would never have believed it if I hadn't seen it with my own eyes," said Mrs. Elder Abraham, more solemnly still.

Faith waved a door mat cheerily at the Clow party. It did not worry her that the elder and his wife did not return her greeting. Everybody knew that Elder Abraham had never been known to smile since he had been appointed Superintendent of the Sunday School fourteen years previously. But it hurt her that Minnie and Adella Clow did not wave back. Faith liked Minnie and Adella. Next to the Blythes, they were her best friends in school and she always helped Adella with her sums. This was gratitude for you. Her friends cut her because she was shaking rugs in an old graveyard where, as Mary Vance said, not a living soul had been buried for years. Faith flounced around to the veranda, where she found Una grieved in spirit because the Clow girls had not waved to her, either.

"I suppose they're mad over something," said Faith. "Perhaps they're jealous because we play so much in Rainbow Valley with the Blythes. Well, just wait till school opens and Adella wants me to show her how to do her sums! We'll get square then. Come on, let's put the things back in. I'm tired to death and I don't believe the rooms will look much better than before we started—though I shook out pecks of dust in the graveyard. I *hate* house-cleaning."

It was two o'clock before the tired girls finished the two rooms. They got a dreary bite in the kitchen and intended to wash the dishes at once. But Faith happened to pick up a new story book Di Blythe had lent her and was lost to the world until sunset. Una took a cup of rank tea up to Carl but found him asleep; so she curled herself up on Jerry's bed and went to sleep too. Meanwhile, a weird story flew through Glen St. Mary and folks asked each other seriously *what* was to be done with those manse youngsters.

"This is past laughing at, believe *me,*" said Miss Cornelia to her husband, with a heavy sigh. "I couldn't believe it at first. Miranda Drew brought the story home from the Methodist Sunday School this afternoon and I simply scoffed at it. But Mrs. Elder Abraham says she and the Elder saw it with their own eyes."

"Saw what?" asked Marshall.

"Faith and Una Meredith stayed home from Sunday School this morning and *cleaned house,*" said Miss Cornelia, in accents of despair. "When Elder Abraham went home from the church—he had stayed behind to straighten out the library books—he saw them shaking rugs in the Methodist graveyard. I can never look a Methodist in the face again. Just think what a scandal it will make!"

A scandal it assuredly did make, growing more scandalous as it spread, until the over-harbour people heard that the manse children had not only cleaned house and put out a washing on Sunday, but had wound up with an afternoon picnic in the graveyard while the Methodist Sunday School was going on. The only household which remained in blissful ignorance of the terrible thing was the manse itself; on what Faith and Una fondly believed to be Tuesday it rained again; for the next three days it rained; nobody came near the manse; the manse folk went nowhere; they might have waded through the misty Rainbow Valley up to Ingleside, but all the Blythe family, save Susan and the doctor, were away on a visit to Avonlea.

"This is the last of our bread," said Faith, "and the ditto is done. If Aunt Martha doesn't get better soon *what* will we do?"

"We can buy some bread in the village and there's the codfish Mary dried," said Una. "But we don't know how to cook it."

"Oh, that's easy," laughed Faith. "You just boil it."

Boil it they did; but as it did not occur to them to soak it beforehand it was too salt to eat. That night they were very hungry; but by the following day their troubles were over. Sunshine returned to the world; Carl was well and Aunt Martha's misery left her as suddenly as it had come; the butcher called at the manse and chased famine away. To crown all, the Blythes returned home, and that evening they and the manse children and Mary Vance kept sunset tryst once more in Rainbow Valley, where the daisies were floating upon the grass like spirits of the dew and the bells on the Tree Lovers rang like fairy chimes in the scented twilight.

CHAPTER XI

A Dreadful Discovery

"WELL, you kids have gone and done it now," was Mary's greeting, as she joined them in the Valley. Miss Cornelia was up at Ingleside, holding agonized conclave with Anne and Susan, and Mary hoped that the session might be a long one, for it was all of two weeks since she had been allowed to revel with her chums in the dear valley of rainbows.

"Done what?" demanded everybody but Walter, who was day-dreaming as usual.

"It's you manse young ones, I mean," said Mary. "It was just awful of you. *I* wouldn't have done such a thing for the world, and *I* weren't brought up in a manse,—weren't brought up *anywhere*—just *come* up."

"What have *we* done?" asked Faith blankly.

"Done! You'd *better* ask! The talk is something terrible. I expect it's ruined your father in this congregation. He'll never be able to live it down, poor man! Everybody blames him for it, and that isn't fair. But nothing *is* fair in this world. You ought to be ashamed of yourselves."

"What *have* we done?" asked Una again, despairingly. Faith said nothing, but her eyes flashed golden-brown scorn at Mary.

"Oh, don't pretend innocence," said Mary, witheringly. "Everybody knows what you've done."

"*I* don't," interjected Jem Blythe indignantly. "Don't let me catch you making Una cry, Mary Vance. What are you talking about?"

"I s'pose you don't know, since you're just back from up west," said Mary, somewhat subdued. Jem could always manage her. "But everybody else knows, you'd better believe."

"Knows what?"

"That Faith and Una stayed home from Sunday School last Sunday and *cleaned house.*"

"We didn't," cried Faith and Una, in passionate denial.

Mary looked haughtily at them.

"I didn't suppose you'd deny it, after the way you've combed *me* down for lying," she said. "What's the good of saying you didn't? Everybody knows you *did*. Elder Clow and his wife saw you. Some people say it will break up the church, but *I* don't go that far. You *are* nice ones."

Nan Blythe stood up and put her arms around the dazed Faith and Una.

"They were nice enough to take you in and feed you and clothe you when you were starving in Mr. Taylor's barn, Mary Vance," she said. "You are *very* grateful, I must say."

"I *am* grateful," retorted Mary. "You'd know it if you'd heard me standing up for Mr. Meredith through thick and thin. I've blistered my tongue talking for him this week. I've said again and again that he isn't to blame if his young ones did clean house on Sunday. He was away—and they knew better."

"But we didn't," protested Una. "It was *Monday* we cleaned house. Wasn't it, Faith?"

"Of course it was," said Faith, with flashing eyes. "We went to Sunday School in spite of the rain—and no one came—not even Elder Abraham, for all his talk about fair-weather Christians."

"It was Saturday it rained," said Mary. "Sunday was fine as silk. I wasn't at Sunday School because I had toothache, but every one else was and they saw all your stuff out on the lawn. And Elder Abraham and Mrs. Elder Abraham saw you shaking rugs in the graveyard."

Una sat down among the daisies and began to cry.

"Look here," said Jem resolutely, "this thing must be cleared up. *Somebody* has made a mistake. Sunday *was* fine, Faith. How could you have thought Saturday was Sunday?"

"Prayer meeting was Thursday night," cried Faith, "and Adam flew into the soup-pot on Friday when Aunt Martha's cat chased him, and spoiled our dinner; and Saturday there was a snake in the cellar and Carl caught it with a forked stick and carried it out, and Sunday it rained. So there!"

"Prayer meeting was Wednesday night," said Mary. "Elder Baxter was to lead and he couldn't go Thursday night and it was changed to Wednesday. You were just a day out, Faith Meredith, and you *did* work on Sunday."

Suddenly Faith burst into a peal of laughter.

"I suppose we did. What a joke!"

"It isn't much of a joke for your father," said Mary sourly.

"It'll be all right when people find out it was just a mistake," said Faith carelessly. "We'll explain."

"You can explain till you're black in the face," said Mary, "but a lie like that'll travel faster'n further than you ever will. *I*'ve seen more of the world than you and *I* know. Besides, there are plenty of folks won't believe it was a mistake."

"They will if I tell them," said Faith.

"You can't tell everybody," said Mary. "No, I tell you you've disgraced your father."

Una's evening was spoiled by this dire reflection, but Faith refused to be made uncomfortable. Besides, she had a plan that would put everything right. So she put the past with its mistake behind her and gave herherself over to enjoyment of the present. Jem went away to fish and Walter came out of his reverie and proceeded to describe the woods of heaven. Mary pricked up her ears and listened respectfully. Despite her awe of Walter she revelled in his "book talk." It always gave her a delightful sensation. Walter had been reading his Coleridge that day, and he pictured a heaven where

"There were gardens bright with sinuous rills
Where blossomed many an incense bearing tree,
And there were forests ancient as the hills
Enfolding sunny spots of greenery."

"I didn't know there was any woods in heaven," said Mary, with a long breath. "I thought it was all streets—and streets—*and* streets."

"Of course there are woods," said Nan. "Mother can't live without trees and I can't, so what would be the use of going to heaven if there weren't any trees?"

"There are cities, too," said the young dreamer, "splendid cities—coloured just like that sunset, with sapphire towers and rainbow domes. They are built of gold and diamonds—whole streets of diamonds, flashing like the sun. In the squares there are crystal fountains kissed by the light, and everywhere the asphodel blooms—the flower of heaven."

"Fancy!" said Mary. "I saw the main street in Charlottetown once and I thought it was real grand, but I s'pose it's nothing to heaven. Well, it all sounds gorgeous the way you tell it, but won't it be kind of dull, too?"

"Oh, I guess we can have some fun when the angels' backs are turned," said Faith comfortably.

"Heaven is *all* fun," declared Di.

"The Bible doesn't say so," cried Mary, who had read so much of the Bible on Sunday afternoons under Miss Cornelia's eye that she now considered herself quite an authority on it.

"Mother says the Bible language is figurative," said Nan.

"Does that mean that it isn't true?" asked Mary hopefully.

"No—not exactly—but I think it means that heaven will be just like what you'd like it to be."

"I'd like it to be just like Rainbow Valley," said Mary, "with all you kids to gas and play with. *That's* good enough for me. Anyhow, we can't go to heaven till we're dead and maybe not then, so what's the use of worrying? Here's Jem with a string of trout and it's my turn to fry them."

"We ought to know more about heaven than Walter does when we're the minister's family," said Una, as they walked home that night.

"We *know* just as much, but Walter can *imagine,*" said Faith. "Mrs. Elliott says he gets it from his mother."

"I do wish we hadn't made that mistake about Sunday," sighed Una.

"Don't worry over that. I've thought of a great plan to explain so that everybody will know," said Faith. "Just wait till to-morrow night."

CHAPTER XII

AN EXPLANATION AND A DARE

THE Rev. Dr. Cooper preached in Glen St. Mary the next evening and the Presbyterian Church was crowded with people from near and far. The Reverend Doctor was reputed to be a very eloquent speaker; and, bearing in mind the old dictum that a minister should take his best clothes to the city and his best sermons to the country, he delivered a very scholarly and impressive discourse. But when the folks went home that night it was not of Dr. Cooper's sermon they talked. They had completely forgotten all about it.

Dr. Cooper had concluded with a fervent appeal, had wiped the perspiration from his massive brow, had said "Let us pray" as he was famed for saying it, and had duly prayed. There was a slight pause. In Glen St. Mary Church the old fashion of taking the collection after the sermon instead of before still held—mainly because the Methodists had adopted the new fashion first, and Miss Cornelia and Elder Clow would not hear of following where Methodists had led. Charles Baxter and Thomas Douglas, whose duty it was to pass the plates, were on the point of rising to their feet. The organist had got out the music of her anthem and the choir had cleared its throat. Suddenly

Faith Meredith rose in the manse pew, walked up to the pulpit platform, and faced the amazed audience.

Miss Cornelia half rose in her seat and then sat down again. Her pew was far back and it occurred to her that whatever Faith meant to do or say would be half done or said before she could reach her. There was no use making the exhibition worse than it had to be. With an anguished glance at Mrs. Dr. Blythe, and another at Deacon Warren of the Methodist Church, Miss Cornelia resigned herself to another scandal.

"If the child was only dressed decently itself," she groaned in spirit.

Faith, having spilled ink on her good dress, had serenely put on an old one of faded pink print. A caticornered rent in the skirt had been darned with scarlet tracing cotton and the hem had been let down, showing a bright strip of unfaded pink around the skirt. But Faith was not thinking of her clothes at all. She was feeling suddenly nervous. What had seemed easy in imagination was rather hard in reality. Confronted by all those staring questioning eyes Faith's courage almost failed her. The lights were so bright, the silence so awesome. She thought she could not speak after all. But she *must*—her father *must* be cleared of suspicion. Only—the words would *not* come.

Una's little pearl-pure face gleamed up at her beseechingly from the manse pew. The Blythe children were lost in amazement. Back under the gallery Faith saw the sweet graciousness of Miss Rosemary West's smile and the amusement of Miss Ellen's. But none of these helped her. It was Bertie Shakespeare Drew who saved the situation. Bertie Shakespeare sat in the front seat of the gallery and he made a derisive face at Faith. Faith promptly made a dreadful one back at him, and, in her anger over being grimaced at by Bertie Shakespeare, forgot her stage fright. She found her voice and spoke out clearly and bravely.

"I want to explain something," she said, "and I want to do it now because everybody will hear it that heard the other. People are saying that Una and I stayed home last Sunday and cleaned house instead of going to Sunday School. Well, we did—but we didn't mean to. We had got mixed up in the days of the week. It was all Elder Baxter's fault"—sensation in the Baxter pew—"because he went and changed the prayer meeting to Wednesday night and then we thought Thursday was Friday and so on till we thought Saturday was Sunday. Carl was laid up sick and so was Aunt Martha, so they couldn't put us right. We went to Sunday School in all that rain on Saturday and nobody came. And then we thought we'd clean house on Monday and stop old cats from talking about how dirty the manse was"—general sensation all over church—"and we did. I shook the rugs in the Methodist graveyard because it was such a convenient place and not because I meant to be disrespectful to the dead. It isn't the dead folks who have made the fuss over this—it's the living folks. And it isn't right for any of you to blame my father for this, because he was away and didn't know, and anyhow we thought it was Monday. He's just the best father that ever lived in the world and we love him with all our hearts."

Faith's bravado ebbed out in a sob. She ran down the steps and flashed out of the side door of the church. There the friendly starlit, summer night comforted her and the ache went out of her eyes and throat. She felt very happy. The dreadful explanation was over and everybody knew now that her father wasn't to blame and that she and Una were not so wicked as to have cleaned house knowingly on Sunday.

Inside the church people gazed blankly at each other, but Thomas Douglas rose and walked up the aisle with a set face. *His* duty was clear; the collection must be taken if the skies fell. Taken it was; the choir sang the anthem, with a dismal conviction that it fell terribly flat, and Dr. Cooper gave out the concluding hymn and pronounced the benediction with considerably less unction than usual. The Reverend Doctor had a sense of humor and Faith's performance tickled him. Besides, John Meredith was well known in Presbyterian circles.

Mr. Meredith returned home the next afternoon, but before his coming Faith contrived to scandalize Glen St. Mary again. In the reaction from Sunday evening's intensity and strain she was especially full of what Miss Cornelia would have called "devilment" on Monday. This led her to dare Walter Blythe to ride through Main Street on a pig, while she rode another one.

The pigs in question were two tall, lank animals, supposed to belong to Bertie Shakespeare Drew's father, which had been haunting the roadside by the manse for a couple of weeks. Walter did not want to ride a pig through Glen St. Mary, but whatever Faith Meredith dared him to do must be done. They tore down the hill and through the village, Faith bent double with laughter over her terrified courser, Walter crimson with shame. They tore past the minister himself, just coming home from the station; he, being a little less dreamy and abstracted than usual—owing to having had a talk on the train with Miss Cornelia who always wakened him up temporarily—noticed them, and thought he really must speak to Faith about it and tell her that such conduct was not seemly. But he had forgotten the trifling incident by the time he reached home. They passed Mrs. Alec Davis, who shrieked in horror, and they passed Miss Rosemary West who laughed and sighed. Finally, just before the pigs swooped into Bertie Shakespeare Drew's back yard, never to emerge therefrom again, so great had been the shock to their nerves—Faith and Walter jumped off, as Dr. and Mrs. Blythe drove swiftly by.

"So that is how you bring up your boys," said Gilbert with mock severity.

"Perhaps I do spoil them a little," said Anne contritely, "but, oh, Gilbert, when I think of my own childhood before I came to Green Gables I haven't the heart to be very strict. How hungry for love and fun I was—an unloved little drudge with never a chance to play! They do have such good times with the manse children."

"What about the poor pigs?" asked Gilbert.

Anne tried to look sober and failed.

"Do you really think it hurt them?" she said. "I don't think anything could hurt those animals. They've been the plague of the neighbourhood this summer and the Drews *won't* shut them up. But I'll talk to Walter—if I can keep from laughing when I do it."

Miss Cornelia came up to Ingleside that evening to relieve her feelings over Sunday night. To her surprise she found that Anne did not view Faith's performance in quite the same light as she did.

"I thought there was something brave and pathetic in her getting up there before that churchful of people, to confess," she said. "You could see she was frightened to death—yet she was bound to clear her father. I loved her for it."

"Oh, of course, the poor child meant well," sighed Miss Cornelia, "but just the same it was a terrible thing to do, and is making more talk than the house-cleaning on Sunday. *That* had begun to die away, and this has started it all up again. Rosemary West is like you—she said last night as she left the church that it was a plucky thing for Faith to do, but it made her feel sorry for the child, too. Miss Ellen thought it all a good joke, and said she hadn't had as much fun in church for years. Of course *they* don't care—they are Episcopalians. But we Presbyterians feel it. And there were so many hotel people there that night and scores of Methodists. Mrs. Leander Crawford cried, she felt so bad. And Mrs. Alec Davis said the little hussy ought to be well spanked."

"Mrs. Leander Crawford is always crying in church," said Susan contemptuously. "She cries over every affecting thing the minister says. But you do not often see her name on a subscription list, Mrs. Dr. dear. Tears come cheaper. She tried to talk to me one day about Aunt Martha being such a dirty housekeeper; and I wanted to say, 'Every one knows that *you* have been seen mixing up cakes in the kitchen wash-pan, Mrs. Leander Crawford!' But I did *not* say it, Mrs. Dr. dear, because I have too much respect for myself to condescend to argue with the likes of her. But I could tell worse things than *that* of Mrs. Leander Crawford, if I was disposed to gossip. And as for Mrs. Alec Davis, if she had said that to me, Mrs. Dr. dear, do you know what I would have said? I would have said, 'I have no doubt you would like to spank Faith, Mrs. Davis, but you will never have the chance to spank a minister's daughter either in this world or in that which is to come.' "

"If poor Faith had only been decently dressed,"

lamented Miss Cornelia again, "it wouldn't have been quite so bad. But that dress looked dreadful, as she stood there upon the platform."

"It was clean, though, Mrs. Dr. dear," said Susan. "They *are* clean children. They may be very heedless and reckless, Mrs. Dr. dear, and I am not saying they are not, but they *never* forget to wash behind their ears."

"The idea of Faith forgetting what day was Sunday," persisted Miss Cornelia. "She will grow up just as careless and impractical as her father, believe *me.* I suppose Carl would have known better if he hadn't been sick. I don't know what was wrong with him, but I think it very likely he had been eating those blueberries that grew in the graveyard. No wonder they made him sick. If I was a Methodist I'd try to keep my graveyard cleaned up at least."

"I am of the opinion that Carl only ate the sours that grow on the dyke," said Susan hopefully. "I do not think *any* minister's son would eat blueberries that grew on the graves of dead people. You know it would not be so bad, Mrs. Dr. dear, to eat things that grew on the dyke."

"The worst of last night's performance was the face Faith made at somebody in the congregation before she started in," said Miss Cornelia. "Elder Clow declares she made it at him. And *did* you hear that she was seen riding on a pig to-day?"

"I saw her. Walter was with her. I gave him a

little—a *very* little—scolding about it. He did not say much, but he gave me the impression that it had been his idea and that Faith was not to blame."

"I do not believe *that*, Mrs. Dr. dear," cried Susan, up in arms. "That is just Walter's way—to take the blame on himself. But you know as well as I do, Mrs. Dr. dear, that that blessed child would never have thought of riding on a pig, even if he does write poetry."

"Oh, there's no doubt the notion was hatched in Faith Meredith's brain," said Miss Cornelia. "And I don't say that I'm sorry that Amos Drew's old pigs did get their come-uppance for once. But the minister's daughter!"

"*And* the doctor's son!" said Anne, mimicking Miss Cornelia's tone. Then she laughed. "Dear Miss Cornelia, they're only little children. And you *know* they've never yet done anything bad—they're just heedless and impulsive—as I was myself once. They'll grow sedate and sober—as I've done."

Miss Cornelia laughed, too.

"There are times, Anne dearie, when I know by your eyes that *your* soberness is put on like a garment and you're really aching to do something wild and young again. Well, I feel encouraged. Somehow, a talk with you always does have that effect on me. Now, when I go to see Barbara Samson, it's just the opposite. She makes me feel that everything's wrong and always will be. But of course living all your life with a man like Joe Samson wouldn't be exactly cheering."

"It is a very strange thing to think that she married Joe Samson after all her chances," remarked Susan. "She was much sought after when she was a girl. She used to boast to me that she had twenty-one beaus and Mr. Pethick."

"What was Mr. Pethick?"

"Well, he was a sort of hanger-on, Mrs. Dr. dear, but you could not exactly call him a beau. He did not really have any intentions. Twenty-one beaus—and me that never had one! But Barbara went through the woods and picked up the crooked stick after all. And yet they say her husband can make better baking powder biscuits than she can, and she always gets him to make them when company comes to tea."

"Which reminds *me* that I have company coming to tea to-morrow and I must go home and set my bread," said Miss Cornelia. "Mary said she could set it and no doubt she could. But while I live and move and have my being *I* set my own bread, believe me."

"How is Mary getting on?" asked Anne.

"I've no fault to find with Mary," said Miss Cornelia rather gloomily. "She's getting some flesh on her bones and she's clean and respectful—though there's more in her than *I* can fathom. She's a sly puss. If you dug for a thousand years you couldn't get to the bottom of that child's mind, believe *me!* As for work, I never saw anything like her. She *eats* it up. Mrs. Wiley may have been cruel to her, but folks needn't say she made Mary work. Mary's a born worker. Sometimes I wonder which will wear out first—her legs or her tongue. I don't have enough to do to keep me out of mischief these days. I'll be real glad when school opens, for then I'll have something to do again. Mary doesn't want to go to school, but I put my foot down and said that go she must. I shall *not* have the Methodists saying that I kept her out of school while I lolled in idleness."

CHAPTER XIII

The House on the Hill

THERE was a little unfailing spring, always icy cold and crystal pure in a certain birch-screened hollow of Rainbow Valley in the lower corner near the marsh. Not a great many people knew of its existence. The manse and Ingleside children knew, of course, as they knew everything else about the magic valley. Occasionally they went there to get a drink, and it figured in many of their plays as a fountain of old romance. Anne knew of it and loved it because it somehow reminded her of the beloved Dryad's Bubble at Green Gables. Rosemary West knew of it; it was her fountain of romance, too. Eighteen years ago she had sat beside it one spring twilight and heard young Martin Crawford stammer out a confession of fervent, boyish love. She had whispered her own secret in return, and they had kissed and promised by the wild wood spring. They had never stood together by it again—Martin had sailed on his fatal voyage soon after; but to Rosemary West it was always a sacred spot, hallowed by that immortal hour of youth and love. Whenever she passed near it she turned aside to hold a secret tryst with an old dream—a dream from which the pain had long gone, leaving only its unforgettable sweetness.

The spring was a hidden thing. You might have passed within ten feet of it and never have suspected its existence. Two generations past a huge old pine had fallen almost across it. Nothing was left of the tree but its crumbling trunk out of which the ferns grew thickly, making a green roof and a lacy screen for the water. A maple tree grew beside it with a curiously gnarled and twisted trunk, creeping along the ground for a little way before shooting up into the air, and so forming a quaint seat; and September had flung a scarf of pale smoke-blue asters around the hollow.

John Meredith, taking the cross-lots road through Rainbow Valley on his way home from some pastoral visitations around the Harbour head one evening, turned aside to drink of the little spring. Walter Blythe had shown it to him one afternoon only a few days before, and they had had a long talk together on the maple seat. John Meredith, under all his shyness and aloofness, had the heart of a boy. He had been called Jack in his youth, though nobody in Glen St. Mary would ever have believed it. Walter and he had taken to each other and had talked unreservedly. Mr. Meredith found his way into some sealed and sacred chambers of the lad's soul wherein not even Di had ever looked. They were to be chums from that friendly hour and Walter knew that he would never be frightened of the minister again.

"I never believed before that it was possible to get

really acquainted with a minister," he told his mother that night.

John Meredith drank from his slender white hand, whose grip of steel always surprised people who were unacquainted with it, and then sat down on the maple seat. He was in no hurry to go home; this was a beautiful spot and he was mentally weary after a round of rather uninspiring conversations with many good and stupid people. The moon was rising. Rainbow Valley was wind-haunted and star-sentinelled only where he was, but afar from the upper end came the gay notes of children's laughter and voices.

The ethereal beauty of the asters in the moonlight, the glimmer of the little spring, the soft croon of the brook, the wavering grace of the brackens all wove a white magic round John Meredith. He forgot congregational worries and spiritual problems; the years slipped away from him; he was a young divinity student again and the roses of June were blooming red and fragrant on the dark, queenly head of his Cecilia. He sat there and dreamed like any boy. And it was at this propitious moment that Rosemary West stepped aside from the by-path and stood beside him in that dangerous, spell-weaving place. John Meredith stood up as she came in and saw her—*really* saw her—for the first time.

He had met her in his church once or twice and shaken hands with her abstractedly as he did with any one he happened to encounter on his way down the aisle. He had never met her elsewhere, for the Wests were Episcopalians, with church affinities in Lowbridge, and no occasion for calling upon them had ever arisen. Before to-night, if any one had asked John Meredith what Rosemary West looked like he would not have had the slightest notion. But he was never to forget her, as she appeared to him in the glamour of kind moonlight by the spring.

She was certainly not in the least like Cecilia, who had always been his ideal of womanly beauty. Cecilia had been small and dark and vivacious—Rosemary West was tall and fair and placid, yet John Meredith thought he had never seen so beautiful a woman.

She was bareheaded and her golden hair—hair of a warm gold, "molasses taffy" colour as Di Blythe had said—was pinned in sleek, close coils over her head; she had large, tranquil, blue eyes that always seemed full of friendliness, a high white forehead and a finely shaped face.

Rosemary West was always called a "sweet woman." She was so sweet that even her high-bred, stately air had never gained for her the reputation of being "stuck-up," which it would inevitably have done in the case of any one else in Glen St. Mary. Life had taught her to be brave, to be patient, to love, to forgive. She had watched the ship on which her lover went sailing out of Four Winds Harbour into the sunset. But, though she watched long, she had never seen it coming sailing back. That vigil had taken girlhood from her eyes, yet she kept her youth to a marvellous degree. Perhaps this was because she always seemed to preserve that attitude of delighted surprise towards life which most of us leave behind in childhood—an attitude which not only made Rosemary herself seem young, but flung a pleasing illusion of youth over the consciousness of every one who talked to her.

John Meredith was startled by her loveliness and Rosemary was startled by his presence. She had never thought she would find any one by that remote spring, least of all the recluse of Glen St. Mary manse. She almost dropped the heavy armful of books she was carrying home from the Glen lending library, and then, to cover her confusion, she told one of those small fibs which even the best of women do tell at times.

"I—I came for a drink," she said, stammering a little, in answer to Mr. Meredith's grave "good-evening, Miss West." She felt that she was an unpardonable goose and she longed to shake herself. But John Meredith was not a vain man and he knew she would likely have been as much startled had she met old Elder Clow in that unexpected fashion. Her confusion put him at ease and he forgot to be shy; besides, even the shyest of men can sometimes be quite audacious in moonlight.

"Let me get you a cup," he said smiling. There *was* a cup nearby, if he had only known it, a cracked, handleless blue cup secreted under the maple by the Rainbow Valley children; but he did not know it, so he stepped out to one of the birch trees and stripped a bit of its white skin away. Deftly he fashioned this into a three-cornered cup, filled it from the spring, and handed it to Rosemary.

Rosemary took it and drank every drop to punish herself for her fib, for she was not in the least thirsty, and to drink a fairly large cupful of water when you are not thirsty is something of an ordeal. Yet the memory of that draught was to be very pleasant to Rosemary. In after years it seemed to her that there was something sacramental about it. Perhaps this was because of what the minister did when she handed him back the cup. He stooped again and filled it and drank of it himself. It was only by accident that he put his lips just where Rosemary had put hers, and Rosemary knew it. Nevertheless, it had a curious significance for her. They two had drunk of the same cup. She remembered idly that an old aunt of hers used to say that when two people did this their after-lives would be linked in some fashion, whether for good or ill.

John Meredith held the cup uncertainly. He did not know what to do with it. The logical thing would have been to toss it away, but somehow he was disinclined to do this. Rosemary held out her hand for it.

"Will you let me have it?" she said. "You made it so knackily. I never saw any one make a birch cup so since my little brother used to make them long ago—before he died."

"I learned how to make them when *I* was a boy,

camping out one summer. An old hunter taught me," said Mr. Meredith. "Let me carry your books, Miss West."

Rosemary was startled into another fib and said oh, they were not heavy. But the minister took them from her with quite a masterful air and they walked away together. It was the first time Rosemary had stood by the valley spring without thinking of Martin Crawford. The mystic tryst had been broken.

The little by-path wound around the marsh and then struck up the long wooded hill on the top of which Rosemary lived. Beyond, through the trees, they could see the moonlight shining across the level summer fields. But the little path was shadowy and narrow. Trees crowded over it, and trees are never quite as friendly to human beings after nightfall as they are in daylight. They wrap themselves away from us. They whisper and plot furtively. If they reach out a hand to us it has a hostile, tentative touch. People walking amid trees after night always draw closer together instinctively and involuntarily, making an alliance, physical and mental, against certain alien powers around them. Rosemary's dress brushed against John Meredith as they walked. Not even an absent minded minister, who was after all a young man still, though he firmly believed he had outlived romance, could be insensible to the charm of the night and the path and the companion.

It is never quite safe to think we have done with

life. When we imagine we have finished our story fate has a trick of turning the page and showing us yet another chapter. These two people each thought their hearts belonged irrevocably to the past; but they both found their walk up that hill very pleasant. Rosemary thought the Glen minister was by no means as shy and tongue-tied as he had been represented. He seemed to find no difficulty in talking easily and freely. Glen housewives would have been amazed had they heard him. But then so many Glen housewives talked only of gossip and the price of eggs, and John Meredith was not interested in either. He talked to Rosemary of books and music and wide-world doings and something of his own history, and found that she could understand and respond. Rosemary, it appeared, possessed a book which Mr. Meredith had not read and wished to read. She offered to lend it to him and when they reached the old homestead on the hill he went in to get it.

The house itself was an old-fashioned gray one, hung with vines, through which the light in the sitting room winked in friendly fashion. It looked down the Glen, over the harbour, silvered in the moonlight, to the sand-dunes and the moaning ocean. They walked in through a garden that always seemed to smell of roses, even when no roses were in bloom. There was a sisterhood of lilies at the gate and a ribbon of asters on either side of the broad walk, and a lacery of fir trees on the hill's edge beyond the house.

"You have the whole world at your doorstep here," said John Meredith, with a long breath. "What a view —what an outlook! At times I feel stifled down there in the Glen. You can breathe up here."

"It is calm to-night," said Rosemary laughing. "If there were a wind it would blow your breath away. We get 'a' the airts the wind can blow' up here. This place should be called Four Winds instead of the Harbour."

"I like wind," he said. "A day when there is no wind seems to me *dead*. A windy day wakes me up." He gave a conscious laugh. "On a calm day I fall into day dreams. No doubt you know my reputation, Miss West. If I cut you dead the next time we meet don't put it down to bad manners. Please understand that it is only abstraction and forgive me—and speak to me."

They found Ellen West in the sitting room when they went in. She laid her glasses down on the book she had been reading and looked at them in an amazement tinctured with something else. But she shook hands amiably with Mr. Meredith and he sat down and talked to her, while Rosemary hunted out his book.

Ellen West was ten years older than Rosemary, and so different from her that it was hard to believe they were sisters. She was dark and massive, with black hair, thick, black eyebrows and eyes of the clear, slaty blue of the gulf water in a north wind. She had a rather stern, forbidding look, but she was in reality very jolly, with a hearty, gurgling laugh and a deep, mellow, pleasant voice with a suggestion of masculinity about it. She had once remarked to Rosemary that she would really like to have a talk with that Presbyterian minister at the Glen, to see if he could find a word to say to a woman when he was cornered. She had her chance now and she tackled him on world politics. Miss Ellen, who was a great reader, had been devouring a book on the Kaiser of Germany, and she demanded Mr. Meredith's opinion of him.

"A dangerous man," was his answer.

"I believe you!" Miss Ellen nodded. "Mark my words, Mr. Meredith, that man is going to fight somebody yet. He's *aching* to. He is going to set the world on fire."

"If you mean that he will wantonly precipitate a great war I hardly think so," said Mr. Meredith. "The day has gone by for that sort of thing."

"Bless you, it hasn't," rumbled Ellen. "The day never goes by for men and nations to make asses of themselves and take to the fists. The millennium isn't *that* near, Mr. Meredith, and *you* don't think it is any more than I do. As for this Kaiser, mark my words, he is going to make a heap of trouble"—and Miss Ellen prodded her book emphatically with her long finger. "Yes, if he isn't nipped in the bud he's going to make trouble. *We*'ll live to see it—you and I will live to see it, Mr. Meredith. And who is going to nip him? England should, but she won't. *Who* is going to nip him? Tell me that, Mr. Meredith."

Mr. Meredith couldn't tell her, but they plunged into a discussion of German militarism that lasted long after Rosemary had found the book. Rosemary said nothing, but sat in a little rocker behind Ellen and stroked an important black cat meditatively. John Meredith hunted big game in Europe with Ellen, but he looked oftener at Rosemary than at Ellen, and Ellen noticed it. After Rosemary had gone to the door with him and come back Ellen rose and looked at her accusingly.

"Rosemary West, that man has a notion of courting you."

Rosemary quivered. Ellen's speech was like a blow to her. It rubbed all the bloom off the pleasant evening. But she would not let Ellen see how it hurt her.

"Nonsense," she said, and laughed, a little too carelessly. "You see a beau for me in every bush, Ellen. Why he told me all about his wife to-night—how much she was to him—how empty her death had left the world."

"Well, that may be *his* way of courting," retorted Ellen. "Men have all kinds of ways, I understand. But don't forget your promise, Rosemary."

"There is no need of my either forgetting or remembering it," said Rosemary, a little wearily. "*You* forget that I'm an old maid, Ellen. It is only your sisterly delusion that I am still young and blooming and dangerous. Mr. Meredith merely wants to be a friend—if he wants that much itself. He'll forget us both long before he gets back to the manse."

"I've no objection to your being friends with him," conceded Ellen, "but it mustn't go beyond friendship, remember. I'm always suspicious of widowers. *They* are not given to romantic ideas about friendship. They're apt to mean business. As for this Presbyterian man, what do they call him shy for? He's not a bit shy, though he may be absent-minded—so absent-minded that he forgot to say goodnight to *me* when you started to go to the door with him. He's got brains, too. There's so few men round here that can talk sense to a body. I've enjoyed the evening. I wouldn't mind seeing more of him. But no philandering, Rosemary, mind you—no philandering."

Rosemary was quite used to being warned by Ellen from philandering if she so much as talked five minutes to any marriageable man under eighty or over eighteen. She had always laughed at the warning with unfeigned amusement. This time it did not amuse her—it irritated her a little. Who wanted to philander?

"Don't be such a goose, Ellen," she said with unaccustomed shortness as she took her lamp. She went upstairs without saying goodnight.

Ellen shook her head dubiously and looked at the black cat.

"What is she so cross about, St. George?" she asked.

"When you howl you're hit, I've always heard, George. But she promised, Saint—she promised, and we Wests always keep our word. So it won't matter if he does want to philander, George. She promised. I won't worry."

Upstairs, in her room, Rosemary sat for a long while looking out of the window across the moonlit garden to the distant, shining harbour. She felt vaguely upset and unsettled. She was suddenly tired of outworn dreams. And in the garden the petals of the last red rose were scattered by a sudden little wind. Summer was over—it was autumn.

CHAPTER XIV

Mrs. Alec Davis Makes a Call

JOHN MEREDITH walked slowly home. At first he thought a little about Rosemary, but by the time he reached Rainbow Valley he had forgotten all about her and was meditating on a point regarding German theology which Ellen had raised. He passed through Rainbow Valley and knew it not. The charm of Rainbow Valley had no potency against German theology. When he reached the manse he went to his study and took down a bulky volume in order to see which had been right, he or Ellen. He remained immersed in its mazes until dawn, struck a new trail of speculation and pursued it like a sleuth hound for the next week, utterly lost to the world, his parish and his family. He read day and night; he forgot to go to his meals when Una was not there to drag him to them; he never thought about Rosemary or Ellen again. Old Mrs. Marshall, over-harbour, was very ill and sent for him, but the message lay unheeded on his desk and gathered dust. Mrs. Marshall recovered but never forgave him. A young couple came to the manse to be married and Mr. Meredith, with unbrushed hair, in carpet slippers and faded dressing gown, married them. To be sure, he began by reading the funeral service to them and got along as far as "ashes to ashes and dust to dust" before he vaguely suspected that something was wrong.

"Dear me," he said absently, "that is strange—very strange."

The bride, who was very nervous, began to cry. The bridegroom, who was not in the least nervous, giggled.

"Please, sir, I think you're burying us instead of marrying us," he said.

"Excuse me," said Mr. Meredith, as if it did not matter much. He turned up the marriage service and got through with it, but the bride never felt quite properly married for the rest of her life.

He forgot his prayer meeting again—but that did not matter, for it was a wet night and nobody came. He might even have forgotten his Sunday service if it had not been for Mrs. Alec Davis. Aunt Martha came in on Saturday afternoon and told him that Mrs. Davis was in the parlour and wanted to see him. Mr. Meredith sighed. Mrs. Davis was the only woman in Glen St. Mary church whom he positively detested. Unfortunately, she was also the richest, and his board of managers had warned Mr. Meredith against offending her. Mr. Meredith seldom thought of such a worldly matter as his stipend; but the managers were more practical. Also, they were astute. Without mentioning money, they contrived to instil into Mr. Meredith's mind a conviction that he should not offend Mrs. Davis. Otherwise, he would likely have forgotten all about her as soon as Aunt Martha had gone out. As it was, he turned down his Ewald with a feeling of annoyance and went across the hall to the parlour.

Mrs. Davis was sitting on the sofa, looking about her with an air of scornful disapproval.

What a scandalous room! There were no curtains on the window. Mrs. Davis did not know that Faith and Una had taken them down the day before to use as court trains in one of their plays and had forgotten to put them up again, but she could not have accused those windows more fiercely if she had known. The blinds were cracked and torn. The pictures on the walls were crooked; the rugs were awry; the vases were full of faded flowers; the dust lay in heaps—literally in heaps.

"What are we coming to?" Mrs. Davis asked herself, and then primmed up her unbeautiful mouth.

Jerry and Carl had been whooping and sliding down the bannisters as she came through the hall. They did not see her and continued whooping and sliding, and Mrs. Davis was convinced they did it on purpose. Faith's pet rooster ambled through the hall, stood in the parlour doorway and looked at her. Not liking her looks, he did not venture in. Mrs. Davis gave a scornful sniff. A pretty manse, indeed, where roosters paraded the halls and stared people out of countenance.

"Shoo, there," commanded Mrs. Davis, poking her flounced, changeable-silk parasol at him.

Adam shooed. He was a wise rooster and Mrs. Davis had wrung the necks of so many roosters with her own fair hands in the course of her fifty years that an air of the executioner seemed to hang around her. Adam scuttled through the hall as the minister came in.

Mr. Meredith still wore slippers and dressing gown, and his dark hair still fell in uncared-for locks over his high brow. But he looked the gentleman he was; and Mrs. Alec Davis, in her silk dress and be-plumed bonnet, and kid gloves and gold chain looked the vulgar, coarse-souled woman she was. Each felt the antagonism of the other's personality. Mr. Meredith shrank, but Mrs. Davis girded up her loins for the fray. She had come to the manse to propose a certain thing to the minister and she meant to lose no time in proposing it. She was going to do him a favour—a great favour—and the sooner he was made aware of it the better. She had been thinking about it all summer and had come to a decision at last. This was all that mattered, Mrs. Davis thought. When she decided a thing it *was* decided. Nobody else had any say in the matter. That had always been her attitude. When she had made up her mind to marry Alec Davis she had married him and that was the end to it. Alec had never known how it happened, but what odds? So in this case—Mrs. Davis had arranged everything to her own satisfaction. Now it only remained to inform Mr. Meredith.

"Will you please shut that door?" said Mrs. Davis, unprimming her mouth slightly to say it, but speaking with asperity. "I have something important to say, and I can't say it with that racket in the hall."

Mr. Meredith shut the door meekly. Then he sat down before Mrs. Davis. He was not wholly aware of her yet. His mind was still wrestling with Ewald's arguments. Mrs. Davis sensed this detachment and it annoyed her.

"I have come to tell you, Mr. Meredith," she said aggressively, "that I have decided to adopt Una."

"To—adopt—Una!" Mr. Meredith gazed at her blankly, not understanding in the least.

"Yes. I've been thinking it over for some time. I have often thought of adopting a child, since my husband's death. But it seemed so hard to get a suitable one. It is very few children I would want to take into *my* home. I wouldn't think of taking a home-child—some outcast of the slums in all probability. And there is hardly ever any other child to be got. One of the fishermen down at the harbour mouth died last fall and left six youngsters. They tried to get me to take one, but I soon gave them to understand I had no idea of adopting trash like that. Their grandfather stole a horse. Besides, they were all boys and I wanted a girl—a quiet, obedient girl that I could train up to be a lady. Una will suit me exactly. She would be a nice little thing if she was properly looked after—so different from Faith. I would never dream of adopting Faith. But I'll take Una and I'll give her a good home, and up-bringing, Mr. Meredith, and if she behaves herself I'll leave her all my money when I die. Not one of my own relatives shall have a cent of it in any case, I'm determined on that. It was the idea of aggravating them that set me to thinking of adopting a child as much as anything in the first place. Una shall be well dressed and educated and trained, Mr. Meredith, and I shall give her music and painting lessons and treat her as if she was my own."

Mr. Meredith was wide enough awake by this time. There was a faint flush in his pale cheek and a dangerous light in his fine dark eyes. Was this woman, whose vulgarity and consciousness of money oozed out of her at every pore, actually asking him to give her Una—his dear little wistful Una with Cecilia's own dark blue eyes—the child whom the dying mother had clasped to her heart after the other children had been led weeping from the room. Cecilia had clung to her baby until the gates of death shut between them. She had looked over the little dark head to her husband.

"Take good care of her, John," she had entreated. "She is so small—and sensitive. The others can fight their way—but the world will hurt *her*. Oh, John, I don't know what you and she are going to do. You both need me so much. But keep her close to you—keep her close to you."

These had been almost her last words except a few unforgettable ones for him alone. And it was this child whom Mrs. Davis had coolly announced her intention of taking from him. He sat up straight and looked at Mrs. Davis. In spite of the worn dressing gown and the frayed slippers there was something about him that made Mrs. Davis feel a little of the old reverence for "the cloth" in which she had been brought up. After all, there *was* a certain divinity hedging a minister, even a poor, unworldly, abstracted one.

"I thank you for your kind intentions, Mrs. Davis," said Mr. Meredith with a gentle, final, quite awful courtesy, "but I cannot give you my child."

Mrs. Davis looked blank. She had never dreamed of his refusing.

"Why, Mr. Meredith," she said in astonishment. "You must be cr—— you can't mean it. You must think it over—think of all the advantages I can give her."

"There is no need to think it over, Mrs. Davis. It is entirely out of the question. All the worldly advantages it is in your power to bestow on her could not compensate for the loss of a father's love and care. I thank you again—but it is not to be thought of."

Disappointment angered Mrs. Davis beyond the power of old habit to control. Her broad red face turned purple and her voice trembled.

"I thought you'd be only too glad to let me have her," she sneered.

"Why did you think that?" asked Mr. Meredith quietly.

"Because nobody ever supposed you cared anything about any of your children," retorted Mrs. Davis contemptuously. "You neglect them scandalously. It is the talk of the place. They aren't fed or dressed properly, and they're not trained at all. They have no more manners than a pack of wild Indians. You never think of doing your duty as a father. You let a stray child come here among them for a fortnight and never took any notice of her—a child that swore like a trooper I'm told. *You* wouldn't have cared if they'd caught small-pox from her. And Faith made an exhibition of herself getting up in preaching and making that speech! And she rid a pig down the street—under your very eyes I understand. The way they act is past belief and you never lift a finger to stop them or try to teach them anything. And now when I offer one of them a good home and good prospects you refuse it and insult me. A pretty father you, to talk of loving and caring for your children!"

"That will do, woman!" said Mr. Meredith. He stood up and looked at Mrs. Davis with eyes that made her quail. "That will do," he repeated. "I desire to hear no more, Mrs. Davis. You have said too much. It may be that I have been remiss in some respects in my duty as a parent, but it is not for you to remind me of it in such terms as you have used. Let us say good afternoon."

Mrs. Davis did not say anything half so amiable as good afternoon, but she took her departure. As she swept past the minister a large, plump toad, which Carl had secreted under the lounge, hopped out almost under her feet. Mrs. Davis gave a shriek and in trying to avoid treading on the awful thing, lost her balance and her parasol. She did not exactly fall, but she staggered and reeled across the room in a very undignified fashion and brought up against the door with a thud that jarred her from head to foot. Mr. Meredith, who had not seen the toad, wondered if she had been attacked with some kind of apoplectic or paralytic seizure, and ran in alarm to her assistance. But Mrs. Davis, recovering her feet, waved him back furiously.

"Don't you dare to touch me," she almost shouted. "This is some more of your children's doings, I suppose. This is no fit place for a decent woman. Give me my umbrella and let me go. I'll never darken the doors of your manse or your church again."

Mr. Meredith picked up the gorgeous parasol meekly enough and gave it to her. Mrs. Davis seized it and marched out. Jerry and Carl had given up bannister sliding and were sitting on the edge of the veranda with Faith. Unfortunately, all three were singing at the tops of their healthy young voices "There'll be a hot time in the old town to-night." Mrs. Davis believed the song was meant for her and her only. She stopped and shook her parasol at them.

"Your father is a fool," she said, "and you are three young varmints that ought to be whipped within an inch of your lives."

"He isn't," cried Faith. "We're not," cried the boys. But Mrs. Davis was gone.

"Goodness, isn't she mad!" said Jerry. "And what is a 'varmint' anyhow?"

John Meredith paced up and down the parlour for a few minutes; then he went back to his study and sat down. But he did not return to his German theology. He was too grievously disturbed for that. Mrs. Davis had wakened him up with a vengeance. *Was* he such a remiss, careless father as she had accused him of being? *Had* he so scandalously neglected the bodily and spiritual welfare of the four little motherless creatures dependent on him? *Were* his people talking of it as harshly as Mrs. Davis had declared? It must be so, since Mrs. Davis had come to ask for Una in the full and confident belief that he would hand the child over to her as unconcernedly and gladly as one might hand over a strayed, unwelcome kitten. And, if so, what then?

John Meredith groaned and resumed his pacing up and down the dusty, disordered room. What could he do? He loved his children as deeply as any father could and he knew, past the power of Mrs. Davis or any of her ilk, to disturb his conviction, that they loved him devotedly. But *was* he fit to have charge of them? He knew—none better—his weaknesses and limitations. What was needed was a good woman's presence and influence and common sense. But how could that be arranged? Even were he able to get such a housekeeper it would cut Aunt Martha to the quick. She believed she could still do all that was meet and necessary. He could not so hurt and insult the poor old woman who had been so kind to him and his. How devoted she had been to Cecilia! And Cecilia had asked him to be very considerate of Aunt Martha. To be sure, he suddenly remembered that Aunt Martha had once hinted that he ought to marry again. He felt she would not resent a wife as she would a housekeeper. But that was out of the question. He did not wish to marry—he did not and could not care for any one. Then what could he do? It suddenly occurred to him that he would go over to Ingleside and talk over his difficulties with Mrs. Blythe. Mrs. Blythe was one of the few women he never felt shy or tongue-tied with. She was always so sympathetic and refreshing. It might be that she could suggest some solution of his problems. And even if she could not Mr. Meredith felt that he needed a little decent human companionship after his dose of Mrs. Davis—something to take the taste of her out of his soul.

He dressed hurriedly and ate his supper less abstractedly than usual. It occurred to him that it was a poor meal. He looked at his children; they were rosy and healthy looking enough—except Una, and she had never been very strong even when her mother was alive. They were all laughing and talking—certainly they seemed happy. Carl was especially happy because he had two most beautiful spiders crawling around his supper plate. Their voices were pleasant, their manners did not seem bad, they were considerate of and gentle to one another. Yet Mrs. Davis had said their behaviour was the talk of the congregation.

As Mr. Meredith went through his gate Dr. Blythe and Mrs. Blythe drove past on the road that led to Lowbridge. The minister's face fell. Mrs. Blythe was going away—there was no use in going to Ingleside. And he craved a little companionship more than ever. As he gazed rather hopelessly over the landscape the sunset light struck on a window of the old West homestead on the hill. It flared out rosily like a beacon of good hope. He suddenly remembered Rosemary and Ellen West. He thought that he would relish some of Ellen's pungent conversation. He thought it would be pleasant to see Rosemary's slow, sweet smile and calm, heavenly blue eyes again. What did that old poem of Sir Philip Sidney's say?—"continual comfort in a face"—that just suited her. And he needed comfort. Why not go and call? He remembered that Ellen had asked him to drop in sometimes and there was Rosemary's book to take back—he ought to take it back before he forgot. He had an uneasy suspicion that there were a great many books in his library which he had borrowed at sundry times and in divers places and had forgotten to take back. It was surely his duty to guard against that in this case. He went back into his study, got the book, and plunged downward into Rainbow Valley.

CHAPTER XV

More Gossip

On the evening after Mrs. Myra Murray of the over-harbour section had been buried Miss Cornelia and Mary Vance came up to Ingleside. There were several things concerning which Miss Cornelia wished to unburden her soul. The funeral had to be all talked over, of course. Susan and Miss Cornelia thrashed this out between them; Anne took no part or delight in such ghoulish conversations. She sat a little apart and watched the autumnal flame of dahlias in the garden, and the dreaming, glamorous harbour of the September sunset. Mary Vance sat beside her, knitting meekly. Mary's heart was down in Rainbow Valley, whence came sweet, distance-softened sounds of children's laughter, but her fingers were under Miss Cornelia's eye. She had to knit so many rounds of her stocking before she might go to the valley. Mary knit and held her tongue, but used her ears.

"I never saw a nicer looking corpse," said Miss Cornelia judicially. "Myra Murray was always a pretty woman—she was a Corey from Lowbridge and the Coreys were noted for their good looks."

"I said to the corpse as I passed it, 'poor woman, I hope you are as happy as you look,' " sighed Susan. "She had not changed much. That dress she wore was the black satin she got for her daughter's wedding fourteen years ago. Her aunt told her then to keep it for her funeral, but Myra laughed and said, 'I may wear it to my funeral, Aunty, but I will have a good time out of it first.' And I may say she did. Myra Murray was not a woman to attend her own funeral before she died. Many a time afterwards when I saw her enjoying herself out in company I thought to myself, 'You are a handsome woman, Myra Murray, and that dress becomes you, but it will likely be your shroud at last.' And you see my words have come true, Mrs. Marshall Elliott."

Susan sighed again heavily. She was enjoying herself hugely. A funeral was really a delightful subject of conversation.

"I always liked to meet Myra," said Miss Cornelia. "She was always so gay and cheerful—she made you feel better just by her handshake. Myra always made the best of things."

"That is true," asserted Susan. "Her sister-in-law told me that when the doctor told her at last that he could do nothing for her and she would never rise from that bed again, Myra said quite cheerfully, 'Well, if that is so, I'm thankful the preserving is all done, and I will not have to face the fall housecleaning. I always liked housecleaning in spring,' she says, 'but I always hated it in the fall. I will get clear of it this year, thank goodness.' There are people who would call that levity, Mrs. Marshall Elliott, and I think her sister-in-law was a little ashamed of it. She said perhaps her sickness had made Myra a little light-headed. But I said, 'No, Mrs. Murray, do not worry over it. It was just Myra's way of looking at the bright side.' "

"Her sister Luella was just the opposite," said Miss Cornelia. "There was no bright side for Luella—there was just black and shades of gray. For years she used always to be declaring she was going to die in a week or so. 'I won't be here to burden you long,' she would tell her family with a groan. And if any of them ventured to talk about their little future plans she'd groan also and say, 'Ah, *I* won't be here then.' When I went to see her I always agreed with her and it made her so mad that she was always quite a lot better for several days afterward. She has better health now but no more cheerfulness. Myra was so different. She was always doing or saying something to make someone feel good. Perhaps the men they married had something to do with it. Luella's man was a Tartar, believe *me,* while Jim Murray was decent, as men go. He looked heart-broken to-day. It isn't often I feel sorry for a man at his wife's funeral, but I did feel for Jim Murray."

"No wonder he looked sad. He will not get a wife like Myra again in a hurry," said Susan. "Maybe he will not try, since his children are all grown up and Mirabel is able to keep house. But there is no predicting what a widower may or may not do and I, for one, will not try."

"We'll miss Myra terrible in church," said Miss Cornelia. "She was such a worker. Nothing ever stumped *her*. If she couldn't get over a difficulty she'd get around it, and if she couldn't get around it she'd pretend it wasn't there—and generally it wasn't. 'I'll keep a stiff upper lip to my journey's end,' said she to me once. Well, she has ended her journey."

"Do you think so?" asked Anne suddenly, coming back from dreamland. "I can't picture *her* journey as being ended. Can *you* think of her sitting down and folding her hands—that eager, asking spirit of hers, with its fine adventurous outlook? No, I think in death she just opened a gate and went through—on—on—to new, shining adventures."

"Maybe—maybe," assented Miss Cornelia. "Do you know, Anne dearie, I never was much taken with this everlasting rest doctrine myself—though I hope it isn't heresy to say so. I want to bustle round in heaven the same as here. And I hope there'll be a celestial substitute for pies and doughnuts—something that has to be *made*. Of course, one does get awful tired at times—and the older you are the tireder you get. But the very tiredest could get rested in something short of eternity, you'd think—except, perhaps, a lazy man."

"When I meet Myra Murray again," said Anne, "I want to see her coming towards me, brisk and laughing, just as she always did here."

"Oh, Mrs. Dr. dear," said Susan, in a shocked tone,

"you surely do not think that Myra will be laughing in the world to come?"

"Why not, Susan? Do you think we will be crying there?"

"No, no, Mrs. Dr. dear, do not misunderstand me. I do not think we shall be either crying or laughing."

"What then?"

"Well," said Susan, driven to it, "it is my opinion, Mrs. Dr. dear, that we shall just look solemn and holy."

"And do you really think, Susan," said Anne, looking solemn enough, "that either Myra Murray or I could look solemn and holy all the time—*all* the time, Susan?"

"Well," admitted Susan reluctantly, "I might go so far as to say that you both would have to smile now and again, but I can never admit that there will be laughing in heaven. The idea seems really irreverent, Mrs. Dr. dear."

"Well, to come back to earth," said Miss Cornelia, "who can we get to take Myra's class in Sunday School? Julia Clow has been teaching it since Myra took ill, but she's going to town for the winter and we'll have to get somebody else."

"I heard that Mrs. Laurie Jamieson wanted it," said Anne. "The Jamiesons have come to church very regularly since they moved to the Glen from Lowbridge."

"New brooms!" said Miss Cornelia dubiously. "Wait till they've gone regularly for a year."

"You cannot depend on Mrs. Jamieson a bit, Mrs. Dr. dear," said Susan solemnly. "She died once and when they were measuring her for her coffin, after laying her out just beautiful, did she not go and come back to life! Now, Mrs. Dr. dear, you know you *cannot* depend on a woman like that."

"She might turn Methodist at any moment," said Miss Cornelia. "They tell me they went to the Methodist Church at Lowbridge quite as often as to the Presbyterian. I haven't caught them at it here yet, but I would not approve of taking Mrs. Jamieson into the Sunday School. Yet we must not offend them. We are losing too many people, by death or bad temper. Mrs. Alec Davis has left the church, no one knows why. She told the managers that she would never pay another cent to Mr. Meredith's salary. Of course, most people say that the children offended her, but somehow I don't think so. I tried to pump Faith, but all I could get out of her was that Mrs. Davis had come, seemingly in high good humour, to see her father, and had left in an awful rage, calling them all 'varmints!' "

"Varmints, indeed!" said Susan furiously. "Does Mrs. Alec Davis forget that her uncle on her mother's side was suspected of poisoning his wife? Not that it was ever proved, Mrs. Dr. dear, and it does not do to believe all you hear. But if *I* had an uncle whose wife died without any satisfactory reason, *I* would not go about the country calling innocent children varmints."

"The point is," said Miss Cornelia, "that Mrs. Davis paid a large subscription, and how its loss is going to be made up is a problem. And if she turns the other Douglases against Mr. Meredith, as she will certainly try to do, he will just have to go."

"I do not think Mrs. Alec Davis is very well liked by the rest of the clan," said Susan. "It is not likely she will be able to influence them."

"But those Douglases all hang together so. If you touch one, you touch all. We can't do without them, so much is certain. They pay half the salary. They are not mean, whatever else may be said of them. Norman Douglas used to give a hundred a year long ago before he left."

"What did he leave for?" asked Anne.

"He declared a member of the session cheated him in a cow deal. He hasn't come to church for twenty years. His wife used to come regular while she was alive, poor thing, but he never would let her pay anything, except one red cent every Sunday. She felt dreadfully humiliated. I don't know that he was any too good a husband to her, though she was never heard to complain. But she always had a cowed look. Norman Douglas didn't get the woman he wanted thirty years ago and the Douglases never liked to put up with second best."

"Who was the woman he did want."

"Ellen West. They weren't engaged exactly, I believe, but they went about together for two years. And then they just broke off—nobody ever knew why. Just some silly quarrel, I suppose. And Norman went and married Hester Reese before his temper had time to cool—married her just to spite Ellen, I haven't a doubt. So like a man! Hester was a nice little thing, but she never had much spirit and he broke what little she had. She was too meek for Norman. He needed a woman who could stand up to him. Ellen would have kept him in fine order and he would have liked her all the better for it. He despised Hester, that is the truth, just because she always gave in to him. I used to hear him say many a time, long ago when he was a young fellow, 'Give me a spunky woman—spunk for me every time.' And then he went and married a girl who couldn't say bo to a goose—man-like. That family of Reeses were just vegetables. They went through the motions of living, but they didn't *live*."

"Russell Reese used his first wife's wedding ring to marry his second," said Susan reminiscently. "That was *too* economical in my opinion, Mrs. Dr. dear. And his brother John has his own tombstone put up in the over-harbour graveyard, with everything on it but the date of death, and he goes and looks at it every Sunday. Most folks would not consider that much fun, but it is plain he does. People do have such different ideas of enjoyment. As for Norman Douglas, he is a perfect heathen. When the last minister asked him why he never went to church he said 'Too many ugly women there, parson—too many ugly women!' I should like to go to such a man, Mrs. Dr. dear, and say to him solemnly, 'There is a hell!' "

"Oh, Norman doesn't believe there is such a place," said Miss Cornelia. "I hope he'll find out his mistake when he comes to die. There, Mary, you've knit your three inches and you can go and play with the children for half an hour."

Mary needed no second bidding. She flew to Rainbow Valley with a heart as light as her heels, and in the course of conversation told Faith Meredith all about Mrs. Alec Davis.

"And Mrs. Elliott says that she'll turn all the Douglases against your father and then he'll have to leave the Glen because his salary won't be paid," concluded Mary. "*I* don't know what is to be done, honest to goodness. If only old Norman Douglas would come back to church and pay, it wouldn't be so bad. But he won't—and the Douglases will leave—and you all will have to go."

Faith carried a heavy heart to bed with her that night. The thought of leaving the Glen was unbearable. Nowhere else in the world were there such chums as the Blythes. Her little heart had been wrung when they had left Maywater—she had shed many bitter tears when she parted with Maywater chums and the old manse there where her mother had lived and died. She could not contemplate calmly the thought of such another and harder wrench. She *couldn't* leave Glen St. Mary and dear Rainbow Valley and that delicious graveyard.

"It's awful to be a minister's family," groaned Faith into her pillow. "Just as soon as you get fond of a place you are torn up by the roots. I'll never, never, *never* marry a minister, no matter how nice he is."

Faith sat up in bed and looked out of the little vine-hung window. The night was very still, the silence broken only by Una's soft breathing. Faith felt terribly alone in the world. She could see Glen St. Mary lying under the starry blue meadows of the autumn night. Over the valley a light shone from the girls' room at Ingleside, and another from Walter's room. Faith wondered if poor Walter had toothache again. Then she sighed, with a little passing sigh of envy of Nan and Di. They had a mother and a settled home—*they* were not at the mercy of people who got angry without any reason and called you a varmint. Away beyond the Glen, amid fields that were very quiet with sleep, another light was burning. Faith knew it shone in the house where Norman Douglas lived. He was reputed to sit up all hours of the night reading. Mary had said if he could only be induced to return to the church all would be well. And why not? Faith looked at a big, low star hanging over the tall, pointed spruce at the gate of the Methodist Church and had an inspiration. She knew what ought to be done and she, Faith Meredith, would do it. She would make everything right. With a sigh of satisfaction she turned from the lonely, dark world and cuddled down beside Una.

CHAPTER XVI

Tit for Tat

WITH Faith, to decide was to act. She lost no time in carrying out her idea. As soon as she came home from school the next day she left the manse and made her way down the Glen. Walter Blythe joined her as she passed the post office.

"I'm going to Mrs. Elliott's on an errand for mother," he said. "Where are you going, Faith?"

"I am going somewhere on church business," said Faith loftily. She did not volunteer any further information and Walter felt rather snubbed. They walked on in silence for a little while. It was a warm, windy evening with a sweet, resinous air. Beyond the sand dunes were gray seas, soft and beautiful. The Glen brook bore down a freight of gold and crimson leaves, like fairy shallops. In Mr. James Reese's buckwheat stubble-land, with its beautiful tones of red and brown, a crow parliament was being held, whereat solemn deliberations regarding the welfare of crowland were in progress. Faith cruelly broke up the august assembly by climbing up on the fence and hurling a broken rail at it. Instantly the air was filled with flapping black wings and indignant caws.

"Why did you do that?" said Walter reproachfully. "They were having such a good time."

"Oh, I hate crows," said Faith airily. "They are so black and sly I feel sure they're hypocrites. They steal little birds' eggs out of their nests, you know. I saw one do it on our lawn last spring. Walter, what makes you so pale to-day? Did you have the toothache again last night?"

Walter shivered.

"Yes—a raging one. I couldn't sleep a wink—so I just paced up and down the floor and imagined I was an early Christian martyr being tortured at the command of Nero. That helped ever so much for a while—and then I got so bad I couldn't imagine anything."

"Did you cry?" asked Faith anxiously.

"No—but I lay down on the floor and groaned," admitted Walter. "Then the girls came in and Nan put cayenne pepper in it—and that made it worse—and Di made me hold a swallow of cold water in my mouth—and I couldn't stand it, so they called Susan. Susan said it served me right for sitting up in the cold garret yesterday writing poetry trash. But she started up the kitchen fire and got me a hot water bottle and it stopped the toothache. As soon as I felt better I told Susan my poetry wasn't trash and she wasn't any judge. And she said no, thank goodness she was not and she did not know anything about poetry except that it was mostly a lot of lies. Now, you know, Faith, that isn't so. That is one reason why I like writing poetry—you can say so many things in it that are true in poetry but wouldn't be true in prose. I told Susan so, but she said to stop my jawing and go to sleep before the water got cold, or she'd leave me to see if rhyming would cure toothache, and she hoped it would be a lesson to me."

"Why don't you go to the dentist at Lowbridge and get the tooth out?"

Walter shivered again.

"They want me to—but I can't. It would hurt so."

"Are you afraid of a little pain?" asked Faith contemptuously.

Walter flushed.

"It would be a *big* pain. I hate being hurt. Father said he wouldn't insist on my going—he'd wait until I'd made up my own mind to go."

"It wouldn't hurt as long as the toothache," argued Faith. "You've had five spells of toothache. If you'd just go and have it out there'd be no more bad nights. *I* had a tooth out once. I yelled for a moment, but it was all over then—only the bleeding."

"The bleeding is worst of all—it's so ugly," cried Walter. "It just made me sick when Jem cut his foot last summer. Susan said I looked more like fainting than Jem did. But I couldn't bear to see Jem hurt, either. Somebody is always getting hurt, Faith—and it's awful. I just can't *bear* to see things hurt. It makes me just want to run—and run—and run—till I can't hear or see them."

"There's no use making a fuss over any one getting hurt," said Faith, tossing her curls. "Of course, if you're hurt yourself very bad, you have to yell—and blood *is* messy—and I don't like seeing other people hurt, either. But I don't want to run—I want to go to work and help them. Your father *has* to hurt people lots of times to cure them. What would they do if *he* ran away?"

"I didn't say I *would* run. I said I *wanted* to run. That's a different thing. I want to help people, too. But oh, I wish there weren't any ugly, dreadful things in the world. I wish everything was glad and beautiful."

"Well, don't let's think of what isn't," said Faith. "After all, there's lots of fun in being alive. You wouldn't have toothache if you were dead, but still, wouldn't you lots rather be alive than dead? I would, a hundred times. Oh, here's Dan Reese. He's been down to the harbour for fish."

"I hate Dan Reese," said Walter.

"So do I. All us girls do. I'm just going to walk past and never take the least notice of him. You watch me!"

Faith accordingly stalked past Dan with her chin out and an expression of scorn that bit into his soul. He turned and shouted after her.

"Pig-girl! Pig-girl!! Pig-girl!!!" in a crescendo of insult.

Faith walked on, seemingly oblivious. But her lip trembled slightly with a sense of outrage. She knew she was no match for Dan Reese when it came to an exchange of epithets. She wished Jem Blythe had been with her instead of Walter. If Dan Reese had dared to call her a pig-girl in Jem's hearing Jem would have wiped up the dust with him. But it never occurred to Faith to expect Walter to do it, or blame him for not doing it. Walter, she knew, never fought other boys. Neither did Charlie Clow of the north road. The strange part was that, while she despised Charlie for a coward, it never occurred to her to disdain Walter. It was simply that he seemed to her an inhabitant of a world of his own, where different traditions prevailed. Faith would as soon have expected a starry-eyed young angel to pummel dirty, freckled Dan Reese for her as Walter Blythe. She would not have blamed the angel and she did not blame Walter Blythe. But she wished that sturdy Jem or Jerry had been there and Dan's insult continued to rankle in her soul.

Walter was pale no longer. He had flushed crimson and his beautiful eyes were clouded with shame and anger. He knew that he ought to have avenged Faith. Jem would have sailed right in and made Dan eat his words with bitter sauce. Ritchie Warren would have overwhelmed Dan with worse "names" than Dan had called Faith. But Walter could not—simply could not—"call names." He knew he would get the worst of it. He could never conceive or utter the vulgar, ribald insults of which Dan Reese had unlimited command. And as for the trial by fist, Walter couldn't fight. He hated the idea. It was rough and painful—and, worst of all, it was ugly. He never could understand Jem's exultation in an occasional conflict. But he wished he *could* fight Dan Reese. He was horribly ashamed because Faith Meredith had been insulted in his presence and he had not tried to punish her insulter. He felt sure she must despise him. She had not even spoken to him since Dan had called her pig-girl. He was glad when they came to the parting of the ways.

Faith, too, was relieved, though for a different reason. She wanted to be alone because she suddenly felt rather nervous about her errand. Impulse had cooled, especially since Dan had bruised her self-respect. She must go through with it, but she no longer had enthusiasm to sustain her. She was going to see Norman Douglas and ask him to come back to church, and she began to be afraid of him. What had seemed so easy and simple up at the Glen seemed very different down here. She had heard a good deal about Norman Douglas, and she knew that even the biggest boys in school were afraid of him. Suppose he called her something nasty—she had heard he was given to that. Faith could not endure being called names—they subdued her far more quickly than a physical blow. But she would go on—Faith Meredith always went on. If she did not her father might have to leave the Glen.

At the end of the long lane Faith came to the house—a big, old-fashioned one with a row of soldierly Lombardies marching past it. On the back veranda

Norman Douglas himself was sitting, reading a newspaper. His big dog was beside him. Behind, in the kitchen, where his housekeeper, Mrs. Wilson, was getting supper, there was a clatter of dishes—an angry clatter, for Norman Douglas had just had a quarrel with Mrs. Wilson, and both were in a very bad temper over it. Consequently, when Faith stepped on the veranda and Norman Douglas lowered his newspaper she found herself looking into the choleric eyes of an irritated man.

Norman Douglas was rather a fine looking personage in his way. He had a sweep of long red beard over his broad chest and a mane of red hair, ungrizzled by the years, on his massive head. His high, white forehead was unwrinkled and his blue eyes could flash still with all the fire of his tempestuous youth. He could be very amiable when he liked, and he could be very terrible. Poor Faith, so anxiously bent on retrieving the situation in regard to the church, had caught him in one of his terrible moods.

He did not know who she was and he gazed at her with disfavour. Norman Douglas liked girls of spirit and flame and laughter. At this moment Faith was very pale. She was of the type to which colour means everything. Lacking her crimson cheeks she seemed meek and even insignificant. She looked apologetic and afraid, and the bully in Norman Douglas' heart stirred.

"Who the dickens are you? And what do you want

here?" he demanded in his great resounding voice, with a fierce scowl.

For once in her life Faith had nothing to say. She had never supposed Norman Douglas was like *this.* She was paralyzed with terror of him. He saw it and it made him worse.

"What's the matter with you?" he boomed. "You look as if you wanted to say something and was scared to say it. What's troubling you? Confound it, speak up, can't you?"

No. Faith could not speak up. No words would come. But her lips began to tremble.

"For heaven's sake, don't cry," shouted Norman. "I can't stand snivelling. If you've anything to say, say it and have done. Great Kitty, is the girl possessed of a dumb spirit? Don't look at me like that—I'm human—I haven't got a tail! Who are you—who are you, I say?"

Norman's voice could have been heard at the harbour. Operations in the kitchen were suspended. Mrs. Wilson was listening open-eared and eyed. Norman put his huge brown hands on his knees and leaned forward, staring into Faith's pallid, shrinking face. He seemed to loom over her like some evil giant out of a fairy tale. She felt as if he would eat her up next thing, body and bones.

"I—am—Faith—Meredith," she said, in little more than a whisper.

"Meredith, hey? One of the parson's youngsters,

hey? I've heard of you—I've heard of you! Riding on pigs and breaking the Sabbath! A nice lot! What do you want here, hey? What do you want of the old pagan, hey? *I* don't ask favours of parsons—and I don't give any. What do you want, I say?"

Faith wished herself a thousand miles away. She stammered out her thought in its naked simplicity.

"I came—to ask you—to go to church—and pay—to the salary."

Norman glared at her. Then he burst forth again.

"You impudent young hussy—you! Who put you up to it, jade? Who put you up to it?"

"Nobody," said poor Faith.

"That's a lie. Don't lie to me! Who sent you here? It wasn't your father—he hasn't the smeddum of a flea—but he wouldn't send you to do what he dassn't do himself. I suppose it was some of them confounded old maids at the Glen, was it—was it, hey?"

"No—I—I just came myself."

"Do you take me for a fool?" shouted Norman.

"No—I thought you were a gentleman," said Faith faintly, and certainly without any thought of being sarcastic.

Norman bounced up.

"Mind your own business. I don't want to hear another word from you. If you wasn't such a kid I'd teach you to interfere in what doesn't concern you. When I want parsons or pill-dosers I'll send for them.

Till I do I'll have no truck with them. Do you understand? Now, get out, cheese-face."

Faith got out. She stumbled blindly down the steps, out of the yard gate and into the lane. Half way up the lane her daze of fear passed away and a reaction of tingling anger possessed her. By the time she reached the end of the lane she was in such a furious temper as she had never experienced before. Norman Douglas' insults burned in her soul, kindling a scorching flame. She shut her teeth and clenched her fists. Go home! Not she! She would go straight back and tell that old ogre just what she thought of him—she would show him—oh, wouldn't she! Cheese-face, indeed!

Unhesitatingly she turned and walked back. The veranda was deserted and the kitchen door shut. Faith opened the door without knocking, and went in. Norman Douglas had just sat down at the supper table, but he still held his newspaper. Faith walked inflexibly across the room, caught the paper from his hand, flung it on the floor and stamped on it. Then she faced him, with her flashing eyes and scarlet cheeks. She was such a handsome young fury that Norman Douglas hardly recognized her.

"What's brought you back?" he growled, but more in bewilderment than rage.

Unquailingly she glared back into the angry eyes against which so few people could hold their own.

"I have come back to tell you exactly what I think

of you," said Faith in clear, ringing tones. "I am not afraid of you. You are a rude, unjust, tyrranical, disagreeable old man. Susan says you are sure to go to hell, and I was sorry for you, but I am not now. Your wife never had a new hat for ten years—no wonder she died. I am going to make faces at you whenever I see you after this. Every time I am behind you you will know what is happening. Father has a picture of the devil in a book in his study, and I mean to go home and write your name under it. You are an old vampire and I hope you'll have the Scotch fiddle!"

Faith did not know what a vampire meant any more than she knew what the Scotch fiddle was. She had heard Susan use the expressions and gathered from her tone that both were dire things. But Norman Douglas knew what the latter meant at least. He had listened in absolute silence to Faith's tirade. When she paused for breath, with a stamp of her foot, he suddenly burst into loud laughter. With a mighty slap of hand on knee he exclaimed,

"I vow you've got spunk, after all—I like spunk. Come, sit down—sit down!"

"I will not." Faith's eyes flashed still more passionately. She thought she was being made fun of—treated contemptuously. She would have enjoyed another explosion of rage, but this cut deep. "I will not sit down in your house. I am going home. But I am glad I came back here and told you exactly what my opinion of you is."

"So am I—so am I," chuckled Norman. "I like you—you're fine—you're great. Such roses—such vim! Did I call her cheese-face? Why, she never smelt a cheese. Sit down. If you'd looked like that at the first, girl! So you'll write my name under the devil's picture, will you? But he's black, girl, he's black—and I'm red. It won't do—it won't do! And you hope I'll have the Scotch fiddle, do you? Lord love you, girl, I had *it* when I was a boy. Don't wish it on me again. Sit down—sit in. We'll tak' a cup o' kindness."

"No, thank you," said Faith haughtily.

"Oh, yes, you will. Come, come now, I apologize, girl—I apologize. I made a fool of myself and I'm sorry. Man can't say fairer. Forget and forgive. Shake hands, girl,—shake hands. She won't—no, she won't! But she must! Look-a-here, girl, if you'll shake hands and break bread with me I'll pay what I used to to the salary and I'll go to church the first Sunday in every month and I'll make Kitty Alec hold her jaw. I'm the only one in the clan can do it. Is it a bargain, girl?"

It seemed to be a bargain. Faith found herself shaking hands with the ogre and then sitting at his board. Her temper was over—Faith's tempers never lasted very long—but its excitement still sparkled in her eyes and crimsoned her cheeks. Norman Douglas looked at her admiringly.

"Go, get some of your best preserves, Wilson,"

he ordered, "and stop sulking, woman, stop sulking. What if we did have a quarrel, woman? A good squall clears the air and briskens things up. But no drizzling and fogging afterwards—no drizzling and fogging, woman. I can't stand that. Temper in a woman but no tears for me. Here, girl, is some messed up meat and potatoes for you. Begin on that. Wilson has some fancy name for it, but I call it macanaccady. Anything I can't analyze in the eating line I call macanaccady and anything wet that puzzles me I call shallamagouslem. Wilson's tea is shallamagouslem. I swear she makes it out of burdocks. Don't take any of the ungodly black liquid—here's some milk for you. What did you say your name was?"

"Faith."

"No name that—no name that! I can't stomach such a name. Got any other?"

"No, sir."

"Don't like the name, don't like it. There's no smeddum to it. Besides, it makes me think of my Aunt Jinny. She called her three girls Faith, Hope and Charity. Faith didn't believe in anything—Hope was a born pessimist—and Charity was a miser. You ought to be called Red Rose—you look like one when you're mad. *I'll* call you Red Rose. And you've roped me into promising to go to church? But only once a month, remember—only once a month. Come now, girl, will you let me off? I used to pay a hundred to the salary every year and go to church. If I promise to pay two hundred a year will you let me off going to church? Come now!"

"No, no, sir," said Faith, dimpling roguishly. "I want you to go to church, too."

"Well, a bargain is a bargain. I reckon I can stand it twelve times a year. What a sensation it'll make the first Sunday I go! And old Susan Baker says I'm going to hell, hey? Do you believe I'll go there—come, now, do you?"

"I hope not, sir," stammered Faith in some confusion.

"*Why* do you hope not? Come, now, *why* do you hope not? Give us a reason, girl—give us a reason."

"It—it must be a very—uncomfortable place, sir."

"Uncomfortable? All depends on your taste in company, girl. I'd soon get tired of angels. Fancy old Susan in a halo, now!"

Faith did fancy it, and it tickled her so much that she had to laugh. Norman eyed her approvingly.

"See the fun of it, hey? Oh, I like you—you're great. About this church business now—can your father preach?"

"He is a splendid preacher," said loyal Faith.

"He is, hey? I'll see—I'll watch out for flaws. He'd better be careful what he says before *me*. I'll catch him—I'll trip him up—I'll keep tabs on his arguments. I'm bound to have some fun out of this church going business. Does he ever preach hell?"

"No—o—o—I don't think so."

"Too bad. I like sermons on that subject. You tell him that if he wants to keep me in good humour to preach a good rip-roaring sermon on hell once every six months—and the more brimstone the better. I like 'em smoking. And think of all the pleasure he'd give the old maids, too. They'd all keep looking at old Norman Douglas and thinking, 'That's for you, you old reprobate. That's what's in store for *you!*' I'll give an extra ten dollars every time you get your father to preach on hell. Here's Wilson and the jam. Like that, hey? *It* isn't macanaccady. Taste!"

Faith obediently swallowed the big spoonful Norman held out to her. Luckily it *was* good.

"Best plum jam in the world," said Norman, filling a large saucer and plumping it down before her. "Glad you like it. I'll give you a couple of jars to take home with you. There's nothing mean about me—never was. The devil can't catch me at *that* corner, anyhow. It wasn't my fault that Hester didn't have a new hat for ten years. It was her own—she pinched on hats to save money to give yellow fellows over in China. *I* never gave a cent to missions in my life—never will. Never you try to bamboozle me into that! A hundred a year to the salary and church once a month—but no spoiling good heathen to make poor Christians! Why, girl, they wouldn't be fit for heaven or hell—clean spoiled for either place—clean spoiled. Hey, Wilson, haven't you got a smile on yet? Beats all how you women can sulk! *I* never sulked in my life—it's just one big flash and crash with me and then—pouf—the squall's over and the sun is out and you could eat out of my hand."

Norman insisted on driving Faith home after supper and he filled the buggy up with apples, cabbages, potatoes and pumpkins and jars of jam.

"There's a nice little tom-pussy out in the barn. I'll give you that too, if you'd like it. Say the word," he said.

"No, thank, you," said Faith, decidedly. "I don't like cats, and, besides, I have a rooster."

"Listen to her. You can't cuddle a rooster as you can a kitten. Who ever heard of petting a rooster? Better take little Tom. I want to find a good home for him."

"No. Aunt Martha has a cat and he would kill a strange kitten."

Norman yielded the point rather reluctantly. He gave Faith an exciting drive home, behind his wild two-year old, and when he had let her out at the kitchen door of the manse and dumped his cargo on the back veranda he drove away shouting,

"It's only once a month—only once a month, mind!"

Faith went up to bed, feeling a little dizzy and breathless, as if she had just escaped from the grasp of a genial whirlwind. She was happy and thankful. No fear now that they would have to leave the Glen and the graveyard and Rainbow Valley. But she fell asleep troubled by a disagreeable subconsciousness that

Dan Reese had called her pig-girl and that, having stumbled on such a congenial epithet, he would continue to call her so whenever opportunity offered.

CHAPTER XVII

A Double Victory

NORMAN DOUGLAS came to church the first Sunday in November and made all the sensation he desired. Mr. Meredith shook hands with him absently on the church steps and hoped dreamily that Mrs. Douglas was well.

"She wasn't very well just before I buried her ten years ago, but I reckon she has better health now," boomed Norman, to the horror and amusement of every one except Mr. Meredith, who was absorbed in wondering if he had made the last head of his sermon as clear as he might have, and hadn't the least idea what Norman had said to him or he to Norman.

Norman intercepted Faith at the gate.

"Kept my word, you see—kept my word, Red Rose. I'm free now till the first Sunday in December. Fine sermon, girl—fine sermon. Your father has more in his head than he carries on his face. But he contradicted himself once—tell him he contradicted himself. And tell him I want that brimstone sermon in December. Great way to wind up the old year—with a taste of hell, you know. And what's the matter with a nice tasty discourse on heaven for New Year's? Though it wouldn't be half as interesting as hell, girl—not half. Only I'd like to know what your father thinks about heaven—he *can* think—rarest thing in the world—a parson who can think. But he *did* contradict himself. Ha, ha! Here's a question you might ask him sometime when he's awake, girl. 'Can God make a stone so big He couldn't lift it Himself?' Don't forget now. I want to hear his opinion of it. I've stumped many a minister with that, girl."

Faith was glad to escape him and run home. Dan Reese, standing among the crowd of boys at the gate, looked at her and shaped his mouth into "pig-girl," but dared not utter it aloud just there. Next day in school was a different matter. At noon recess Faith encountered Dan in the little spruce plantation behind the school and Dan shouted once more,

"Pig-girl! Pig-girl! *Rooster-girl!*"

Walter Blythe suddenly rose from a mossy cushion behind a little clump of firs where he had been reading. He was very pale, but his eyes blazed.

"You hold your tongue, Dan Reese!" he said.

"Oh, hello, Miss Walter," retorted Dan, not at all abashed. He vaulted airily to the top of the rail fence and chanted insultingly,

"Cowardy, cowardy-custard
Stole a pot of mustard,
Cowardy, cowardy-custard!"

"You are a coincidence!" said Walter scornfully, turning still whiter. He had only a very hazy idea what a coincidence was, but Dan had none at all and thought it must be something peculiarly opprobrious.

"Yah! Cowardy!" he yelled again. "Your mother writes lies—lies—lies! And Faith Meredith is a pig-girl—a—pig-girl—a pig-girl! And she's a rooster-girl—a rooster-girl—a rooster-girl! Yah! Cowardy—cowardy—cust—"

Dan got no further. Walter had hurled himself across the intervening space and knocked Dan off the fence backward with one well-directed blow. Dan's sudden inglorious sprawl was greeted with a burst of laughter and a clapping of hands from Faith. Dan sprang up, purple with rage, and began to climb the fence. But just then the school bell rang and Dan knew what happened to boys who were late during Mr. Hazard's regime.

"We'll fight this out," he howled. "Cowardy!"

"Any time you like," said Walter.

"Oh, no, no, Walter," protested Faith. "Don't fight him. *I* don't mind what he says—I wouldn't condescend to mind the like of *him*."

"He insulted you and he insulted my mother," said Walter, with the same deadly calm. "To-night after school, Dan."

"I've got to go right home from school to pick taters after the harrows, dad says," answered Dan sulkily. "But to-morrow night'll do."

"All right—here to-morrow night," agreed Walter.

"And I'll smash your sissy-face for you," promised Dan.

Walter shuddered—not so much from fear of the

threat as from repulsion over the ugliness and vulgarity of it. But he held his head high and marched into school. Faith followed in a conflict of emotions. She hated to think of Walter fighting that little sneak, but oh, he had been splendid! And he was going to fight for *her*—Faith Meredith—to punish her insulter! Of course he would win—such eyes spelled victory.

Faith's confidence in her champion had dimmed a little by evening, however. Walter had seemed so very quiet and dull the rest of the day in school.

"If it were only Jem," she sighed to Una, as they sat on Hezekiah Pollock's tombstone in the graveyard. "*He* is such a fighter—he could finish Dan off in no time. But Walter doesn't know much about fighting."

"I'm so afraid he'll be hurt," sighed Una, who hated fighting and couldn't understand the subtle, secret exultation she divined in Faith.

"He oughtn't to be," said Faith uncomfortably. "He's every bit as big as Dan."

"But Dan's so much older," said Una. "Why, he's nearly a year older."

"Dan hasn't done much fighting when you come to count up," said Faith. "I believe he's really a coward. He didn't think Walter would fight, or he wouldn't have called names before him. Oh, if you could just have seen Walter's face when he looked at him, Una! It made me shiver—with a nice shiver. He looked just like Sir Galahad in that poem father read us on Saturday."

"I hate the thought of them fighting and I wish it could be stopped," said Una.

"Oh, it's got to go on now," cried Faith. "It's a matter of honor. Don't you *dare* tell any one, Una. If you do I'll never tell you secrets again!"

"I won't tell," agreed Una. "But I won't stay to-morrow to watch the fight. I'm coming right home."

"Oh, all right. *I* have to be there—it would be mean not to, when Walter is fighting for me. I'm going to tie my colours on his arm—that's the thing to do when he's my knight. How lucky Mrs. Blythe gave me that pretty blue hair ribbon for my birthday! I've only worn it twice so it will be almost new. But I wish I was sure Walter would win. It will be so—so *humiliating* if he doesn't."

Faith would have been yet more dubious if she could have seen her champion just then. Walter had gone home from school with all his righteous anger at a low ebb and a very nasty feeling in its place. He had to fight Dan Reese the next night—and he didn't want to—he hated the thought of it. And he kept thinking of it all the time. Not for a minute could he get away from the thought. Would it hurt much? He was terribly afraid that it would hurt. And would he be defeated and shamed?

He could not eat any supper worth speaking of. Susan had made a big batch of his favourite monkey-faces, but he could choke only one down. Jem ate four. Walter wondered how he could. How could *anybody* eat? And how could they all talk gaily as they were doing? There was mother, with her shining eyes and pink cheeks. *She* didn't know her son had to fight next day. Would she be so gay if she knew, Walter wondered darkly. Jem had taken Susan's picture with his new camera and the result was passed around the table and Susan was terribly indignant over it.

"I am no beauty, Mrs. Dr. dear, and well I know it, and have always known it," she said in an aggrieved tone, "but that I am as ugly as that picture makes me out I will never, no, never believe."

Jem laughed over this and Anne laughed again with him. Walter couldn't endure it. He got up and fled to his room.

"That child has got something on his mind, Mrs. Dr. dear," said Susan. "He has et next to nothing. Do you suppose he is plotting another poem?"

Poor Walter was very far removed in spirit from the starry realms of poesy just then. He propped his elbow on his open window sill and leaned his head drearily on his hands.

"Come on down to the shore, Walter," cried Jem, bursting in. "The boys are going to burn the sand-hill grass to-night. Father says we can go. Come on."

At any other time Walter would have been delighted. He gloried in the burning of the sand-hill grass. But now he flatly refused to go, and no arguments or entreaties could move him. Disappointed Jem, who did not care for the long dark walk to Four Winds Point alone, retreated to his museum in the garret and buried himself in a book. He soon forgot his disappointment, revelling with the heroes of old romance, and pausing occasionally to picture himself a famous general, leading his troops to victory on some great battlefield.

Walter sat at his window until bedtime. Di crept in, hoping to be told what was wrong, but Walter could not talk of it, even to Di. Talking of it seemed to give it a reality from which he shrank. It was torture enough to think of it. The crisp, withered leaves rustled on the maple trees outside his window. The glow of rose and flame had died out of the hollow, silvery sky, and the full moon was rising gloriously over Rainbow Valley. Afar off, a ruddy wood fire was painting a page of glory on the horizon beyond the hills. It was a sharp, clear evening when far-away sounds were heard distinctly. A fox was barking across the pond; an engine was puffing down at the Glen station; a blue jay was screaming madly in the maple grove; there was laughter over on the manse lawn. How could people laugh? How could foxes and blue jays and engines behave as if nothing were going to happen on the morrow?

"Oh, I wish it was over," groaned Walter.

He slept very little that night and had hard work choking down his porridge in the morning. Susan *was* rather lavish in her platefuls. Mr. Hazard found him an unsatisfactory pupil that day. Faith Meredith's wits seemed to be wool-gathering, too. Dan Reese kept drawing surreptitious pictures of girls, with pig or rooster heads, on his slate and holding them up for all to see. The news of the coming battle had leaked out and most of the boys and many of the girls were in the spruce plantation when Dan and Walter sought it after school. Una had gone home, but Faith was there, having tied her blue ribbon around Walter's arm. Walter was thankful that neither Jem nor Di nor Nan were among the crowd of spectators. Somehow they had not heard of what was in the wind and had gone home, too. Walter faced Dan quite undauntedly now. At the last moment all his fear had vanished, but he still felt disgust at the idea of fighting. Dan, it was noted, was really paler under his freckles than Walter was. One of the older boys gave the word and Dan struck Walter in the face.

Walter reeled a little. The pain of the blow tingled through all his sensitive frame for a moment. Then he felt pain no longer. Something, such as he had never experienced before, seemed to roll over him like a flood. His face flushed crimson, his eyes burned like flame. The scholars of Glen St. Mary school had never dreamed that "Miss Walter" could look like that. He hurled himself forward and closed with Dan like a young wildcat.

There were no particular rules in the fights of the

Glen school boys. It was catch-as-catch can, and get your blows in anyhow. Walter fought with a savage fury and a joy in the struggle against which Dan could not hold his ground. It was all over very speedily. Walter had no clear consciousness of what he was doing until suddenly the red mist cleared from his sight and he found himself kneeling on the body of the prostrate Dan whose nose—oh, horror!—was spouting blood.

"Have you had enough?" demanded Walter through his clenched teeth.

Dan sulkily admitted that he had.

"My mother doesn't write lies?"

"No."

"Faith Meredith isn't a pig-girl?"

"No."

"Nor a rooster-girl?"

"No."

"And I'm not a coward?"

"No."

Walter had intended to ask, "And you are a liar?" but pity intervened and he did not humiliate Dan further. Besides, that blood was so horrible.

"You can go, then," he said contemptuously.

There was a loud clapping from the boys who were perched on the rail fence, but some of the girls were crying. They were frightened. They had seen schoolboy fights before, but nothing like Walter as he had grappled with Dan. There had been something terrifying about him. They thought he would kill Dan. Now that all was over they sobbed hysterically—except Faith, who still stood tense and crimson cheeked.

Walter did not stay for any conqueror's meed. He sprang over the fence and rushed down the spruce hill to Rainbow Valley. He felt none of the victor's joy, but he felt a certain calm satisfaction in duty done and honour avenged—mingled with a sickish qualm when he thought of Dan's gory nose. It had been so ugly, and Walter hated ugliness.

Also, he began to realize that he himself was somewhat sore and battered up. His lip was cut and swollen and one eye felt very strange. In Rainbow Valley he encountered Mr. Meredith, who was coming home from an afternoon call on the Miss Wests. That reverend gentleman looked gravely at him.

"It seems to me that you have been fighting, Walter?"

"Yes, sir," said Walter, expecting a scolding.

"What was it about?"

"Dan Reese said my mother wrote lies and that Faith was a pig-girl," answered Walter bluntly.

"Oh—h! Then you were certainly justified, Walter."

"Do you think it's right to fight, sir?" asked Walter curiously.

"Not always—and not often—but sometimes—yes, sometimes," said John Meredith. "When womenkind are insulted for instance—as in your case. My motto,

Walter, is, don't fight till you're sure you ought to, and *then* put every ounce of you into it. In spite of sundry discolorations I infer that you came off best."

"Yes. I made him take it all back."

"Very good—very good, indeed. I didn't think you were such a fighter, Walter."

"I never fought before—and I didn't want to right up to the last—and then," said Walter, determined to make a clean breast of it, "I liked it while I was at it."

The Rev. John's eyes twinkled.

"You were—a little frightened—at first?"

"I was a whole lot frightened," said honest Walter. "But I'm not going to be frightened any more, sir. Being frightened of things is worse than the things themselves. I'm going to ask father to take me over to Lowbridge to-morrow to get my tooth out."

"Right again. 'Fear is more pain than is the pain it fears.' Do you know who wrote that, Walter? It was Shakespeare. Was there any feeling or emotion or experience of the human heart that that wonderful man did not know? When you go home tell your mother I am proud of you."

Walter did not tell her that, however; but he told her all the rest, and she sympathized with him and told him she was glad he had stood up for her and Faith, and she anointed his sore spots and rubbed cologne on his aching head.

"Are all mothers as nice as you?" asked Walter, hugging her. "You're *worth* standing up for."

Miss Cornelia and Susan were in the living room when Anne came downstairs, and listened to the story with much enjoyment. Susan in particular was highly gratified.

"I am real glad to hear he has had a good fight, Mrs. Dr. dear. Perhaps it may knock that poetry nonsense out of him. And I never, no, never could bear that little viper of a Dan Reese. Will you not sit nearer to the fire, Mrs. Marshall Elliott? These November evenings are very chilly."

"Thank you, Susan, I'm not cold. I called at the manse before I came here and got quite warm—though I had to go to the kitchen to do it, for there was no fire anywhere else. The kitchen looked as if it had been stirred up with a stick, believe *me*. Mr. Meredith wasn't home. I couldn't find out where he was, but I have an idea he was up at the Wests'. Do you know, Anne dearie, they say he has been going there frequently all the fall and people are beginning to think he is going to see Rosemary."

"He would get a very charming wife if he married Rosemary," said Anne, piling driftwood on the fire. "She is one of the most delightful girls I've ever known—truly one of the race of Joseph."

"Ye—s—only she is an Episcopalian," said Miss Cornelia doubtfully. "Of course, that is better than if she was a Methodist—but I do think Mr. Meredith could find a good enough wife in his own denomination. However, very likely there is nothing in it. It's only a month ago that I said to him, 'You ought to marry again, Mr. Meredith.' He looked as shocked as if I had suggested something improper. 'My wife is in her grave, Mrs. Elliott,' he said, in that gentle, saintly way of his. 'I supposed so,' I said, 'or I wouldn't be advising you to marry again.' Then he looked more shocked than ever. So I doubt if there is much in this Rosemary story. If a single minister calls twice at a house where there is a single woman all the gossips have it he is courting her."

"It seems to me—if I may presume to say so—that Mr. Meredith is too shy to go courting a second wife," said Susan solemnly.

"He *isn't* shy, believe *me,*" retorted Miss Cornelia. "Absent-minded,—yes—but shy, no. And for all he is so abstracted and dreamy he has a very good opinion of himself, man-like, and when he is really awake he wouldn't think it much of a chore to ask any woman to have him. No, the trouble is, he's deluding himself into believing that his heart is buried, while all the time it's beating away inside of him just like anybody else's. He may have a notion of Rosemary West and he may not. If he has, we must make the best of it. She is a sweet girl and a fine housekeeper, and would make a good mother for those poor, neglected children. And," concluded Miss Cornelia resignedly, "my own grandmother was an Episcopalian."

CHAPTER XVIII

MARY BRINGS EVIL TIDINGS

MARY VANCE, whom Mrs. Elliott had sent up to the manse on an errand, came tripping down Rainbow Valley on her way to Ingleside where she was to spend the afternoon with Nan and Di as a Saturday treat. Nan and Di had been picking spruce gum with Faith and Una in the manse woods and the four of them were now sitting on a fallen pine by the brook, all, it must be admitted, chewing rather vigorously. The Ingleside twins were not allowed to chew spruce gum anywhere but in the seclusion of Rainbow Valley, but Faith and Una were quite unrestricted by such rules of etiquette and cheerfully chewed it everywhere, at home and abroad, to the very proper horror of the Glen. Faith had been seen chewing it in church one day; but Jerry had realized the enormity of *that*, and had given her such an older-brotherly scolding that she never did it again.

"I was so hungry I just felt as if I had to chew something," she protested. "You know well enough what breakfast was like, Jerry Meredith. I *couldn't* eat scorched porridge and my stomach just felt so queer and empty. The gum helped a lot—and I didn't chew *very* hard. I didn't make any noise and I never cracked the gum once."

"You mustn't chew gum in church, anyhow," insisted Jerry. "Don't let me catch you at it again."

"You chewed yourself in prayer meeting last week," cried Faith.

"*That's* different," said Jerry loftily. "Prayer meeting isn't on Sunday. Besides, I sat away at the back in a dark seat and nobody saw me. You were sitting right up in front where every one saw you. And I took the gum out of my mouth for the last hymn and stuck it on the back of the pew in front of me. Then I came away and forgot it. I went back to get it next morning, but it was gone. I suppose Rod Warren swiped it. And it was a dandy chew."

Mary Vance walked down the Valley with her head held high. She had on a new blue velvet cap with a scarlet rosette in it, a coat of navy blue cloth and a little squirrel-fur muff. She was very conscious of her new clothes and very well pleased with herself. Her hair was elaborately crimped, her face was quite plump, her cheeks rosy, her white eyes shining. She did not look much like the forlorn and ragged waif the Merediths had found in the old Taylor barn. Una tried not to feel envious. Here was Mary with a new velvet cap, but she and Faith had to wear their shabby old gray tams again this winter. Nobody ever thought of getting them new ones and they were afraid to ask their father for them for fear that he might be short of money and then he would feel badly. Mary had told them once that ministers were always short of money, and found it "awful hard" to make ends meet. Since then Faith and Una would have gone in rags rather than ask their father for anything if they could help it. They did not worry a great deal over their shabbiness; but it was rather trying to see Mary Vance coming out in such style and putting on such airs about it, too. The new squirrel muff was really the last straw. Neither Faith nor Una had ever had a muff, counting themselves lucky if they could compass mittens without holes in them. Aunt Martha could not see to darn holes and though Una tried to, she made sad cobbling. Somehow, they could not make their greeting of Mary very cordial. But Mary did not mind or notice that; she was not overly sensitive. She vaulted lightly to a seat on the pine tree, and laid the offending muff on a bough. Una saw that it was lined with shirred red satin and had red tassels. She looked down at her own rather purple, chapped, little hands and wondered if she would ever, *ever* be able to put them into a muff like that.

"Give us a chew," said Mary companionably. Nan, Di and Faith all produced an amber-hued knot or two from their pockets and passed them to Mary. Una sat very still. She had four lovely big knots in the pocket of her tight, thread-bare little jacket, but she wasn't going to give one of them to Mary Vance—not one. Let Mary pick her own gum! People with squirrel muffs needn't expect to get everything in the world.

"Great day, isn't it?" said Mary, swinging her legs, the better, perhaps, to display new boots with very smart cloth tops. Una tucked *her* feet under her. There was a hole in the toe of one of her boots and both laces were much knotted. But they were the best she had. Oh, this Mary Vance! Why hadn't they left her in the old barn?

Una never felt badly because the Ingleside twins were better dressed than she and Faith were. *They* wore their pretty clothes with careless grace and never seemed to think about them at all. Somehow, they did not make other people feel shabby. But when Mary Vance was dressed up she seemed fairly to exude clothes—to walk in an atmosphere of clothes—to make everybody else feel and think clothes. Una, as she sat there in the honey-tinted sunshine of the gracious December afternoon, was acutely and miserably conscious of everything she had on—the faded tam, which was yet her best, the skimpy jacket she had worn for three winters, the holes in her skirt and her boots, the shivering insufficiency of her poor little undergarments. Of course, Mary was going out for a visit and she was not. But even if she had been she had nothing better to put on and in this lay the sting.

"Say, this is great gum. Listen to me cracking it. There ain't any gum spruces down at Four Winds," said Mary. "Sometimes I just hanker after a chew. Mrs. Elliott won't let me chew gum if she sees me. She says it ain't lady-like. This lady-business puzzles me. I can't get on to all its kinks. Say, Una, what's the matter with you? Cat got your tongue?"

"No," said Una, who could not drag her fascinated eyes from that squirrel muff. Mary leaned past her, picked it up and thrust it into Una's hands.

"Stick your paws in that for a while," she ordered. "They look sorter pinched. Ain't that a dandy muff? Mrs. Elliott give it to me last week for a birthday present. I'm to get the collar at Christmas. I heard her telling Mr. Elliott that."

"Mrs. Elliott is very good to you," said Faith.

"You bet she is. And *I'm* good to her, too," retorted Mary. "I work like a nigger to make it easy for her and have everything just as she likes it. We was made for each other. 'Tisn't every one could get along with her as well as I do. She's pizen neat, but so am I, and so we agree fine."

"I told you she would never whip you."

"So you did. She's never tried to lay a finger on me and I ain't never told a lie to her—not one, true's you live. She combs me down with her tongue sometimes, though, but that just slips off *me* like water off a duck's back. Say, Una, why didn't you hang on to the muff?"

Una had put it back on the bough.

"My hands aren't cold, thank you," she said stiffly.

"Well, if you're satisfied, *I* am. Say, old Kitty Alec has come back to church as meek as Moses and nobody knows why. But everybody is saying it was Faith brought Norman Douglas out. His housekeeper says you went there and gave him an awful tongue-lashing. Did you?"

"I went and asked him to come to church," said Faith uncomfortably.

"Fancy your spunk!" said Mary admiringly. "*I* wouldn't have dared do that and I'm not so slow. Mrs. Wilson says the two of you jawed something scandalous, but you come off best and then he just turned round and like to eat you up. Say, is your father going to preach here to-morrow?"

"No. He's going to exchange with Mr. Perry from Charlottetown. Father went to town this morning and Mr. Perry is coming out to-night."

"I *thought* there was something in the wind, though old Martha wouldn't give me any satisfaction. But I felt sure she wouldn't have been killing that rooster for nothing."

"What rooster? What do you mean?" cried Faith, turning pale.

"*I* don't know what rooster. I didn't see it. When she took the butter Mrs. Elliott sent up she said she'd been out to the barn killing a rooster for dinner to-morrow."

Faith sprang down from the pine.

"It's Adam—we have no other rooster—she has killed Adam."

"Now, don't fly off the handle. Martha said the butcher at the Glen had no meat this week and she had to have something and the hens were all laying and too poor."

"If she has killed Adam—" Faith began to run up the hill.

Mary shrugged her shoulders.

"She'll go crazy now. She was so fond of that Adam. He ought to have been in the pot long ago—he'll be as tough as sole leather. But *I* wouldn't like to be in Martha's shoes. Faith's just white with rage. Una, you'd better go after her and try to peacify her."

Mary had gone a few steps with the Blythe girls when Una suddenly turned and ran after her.

"Here's some gum for you, Mary," she said, with a little repentant catch in her voice, thrusting all her four knots into Mary's hands, "and I'm glad you have such a pretty muff."

"Why, thanks," said Mary, rather taken by surprise. To the Blythe girls, after Una had gone, she said, "Ain't she a queer little mite? But I've always said she had a good heart."

CHAPTER XIX

Poor Adam!

WHEN Una got home Faith was lying face downwards on her bed, utterly refusing to be comforted. Aunt Martha had killed Adam. He was reposing on a platter in the pantry that very minute, trussed and dressed, encircled by his liver and heart and gizzard. Aunt Martha heeded Faith's passion of grief and anger not a whit.

"We had to have something for the strange minister's dinner," she said. "You're too big a girl to make such a fuss over an old rooster. You knew he'd have to be killed sometime."

"I'll tell father when he comes home what you've done," sobbed Faith.

"Don't you go bothering your poor father. He has troubles enough. And *I*'m housekeeper here."

"Adam was *mine*—Mrs. Johnson gave him to me. You had no business to touch him," stormed Faith.

"Don't you get sassy now. The rooster's killed and there's an end of it. I ain't going to set no strange minister down to a dinner of cold b'iled mutton. I was brought up to know better than that, if I have come down in the world."

Faith would not go down to supper that night and

she would not go to church the next morning. But at dinner time she went to the table, her eyes swollen with crying, her face sullen.

The Rev. James Perry was a sleek, rubicund man, with a bristling white moustache, bushy white eyebrows, and a shining bald head. He was certainly not handsome and he was a very tiresome, pompous sort of person. But if he had looked like the Archangel Michael and talked with the tongues of men and angels Faith would still have utterly detested him. He carved Adam up dexterously, showing off his plump white hands and very handsome diamond ring. Also, he made jovial remarks all through the performance. Jerry and Carl giggled, and even Una smiled wanly, because she thought politeness demanded it. But Faith only scowled darkly. The Rev. James thought her manners shockingly bad. Once, when he was delivering himself of an unctuous remark to Jerry, Faith broke in rudely with a flat contradiction. The Rev. James drew his bushy eyebrows together at her.

"Little girls should not interrupt," he said, "and they should not contradict people who know far more than they do."

This put Faith in a worse temper than ever. To be called "little girl" as if she were no bigger than chubby Rilla Blythe over at Ingleside! It was insufferable. And how that abominable Mr. Perry did eat! He even picked poor Adam's bones. Neither Faith nor Una would touch a mouthful, and looked upon the boys as little better than cannibals. Faith felt that if that awful repast did not soon come to an end she would wind it up by throwing something at Mr. Perry's gleaming head. Fortunately, Mr. Perry found Aunt Martha's leathery apple pie too much even for his powers of mastication and the meal came to an end, after a long grace in which Mr. Perry offered up devout thanks for the food which a kind and beneficent Providence had provided for sustenance and temperate pleasure.

"God hadn't a single thing to do with providing Adam for you," muttered Faith rebelliously under her breath.

The boys gladly made their escape to outdoors, Una went to help Aunt Martha with the dishes—though that rather grumpy old dame never welcomed her timid assistance—and Faith betook herself to the study where a cheerful wood fire was burning in the grate. She thought she would thereby escape from the hated Mr. Perry, who had announced his intention of taking a nap in his room during the afternoon. But scarcely had Faith settled herself in a corner, with a book, when he walked in and, standing before the fire, proceeded to survey the disorderly study with an air of disapproval.

"You father's books seem to be in somewhat deplorable confusion, my little girl," he said severely.

Faith darkled in her corner and said not a word. She would *not* talk to this—this creature.

"You should try to put them in order," Mr. Perry went on, playing with his handsome watch chain and smiling patronizingly on Faith. "You are quite old enough to attend to such duties. *My* little daughter at home is only ten and she is already an excellent little housekeeper and the greatest help and comfort to her mother. She is a very sweet child. I wish you had the privilege of her acquaintance. She could help you in many ways. Of course, you have not had the inestimable privilege of a good mother's care and training. A sad lack—a very sad lack. I have spoken more than once to your father in this connection and pointed out his duty to him faithfully, but so far with no effect. I trust he may awaken to a realization of his responsibility before it is too late. In the meantime, it is your duty and privilege to endeavour to take your sainted mother's place. You might exercise a great influence over your brothers and your little sister—you might be a true mother to them. I fear that you do not think of these things as you should. My dear child, allow me to open your eyes in regard to them."

Mr. Perry's oily, complacent voice trickled on. He was in his element. Nothing suited him better than to lay down the law, patronize and exhort. He had no idea of stopping, and he did not stop. He stood before the fire, his feet planted firmly on the rug, and poured out a flood of pompous platitudes. Faith heard not a word. She was really not listening to him at all. But she was watching his long black coat-tails with impish delight growing in her brown eyes. Mr. Perry was standing *very* near the fire. His coat-tails began to scorch—his coat-tails began to smoke. He still prosed on, wrapped up in his own eloquence. The coat-tails smoked worse. A tiny spark flew up from the burning wood and alighted in the middle of one. It clung and caught and spread into a smouldering flame. Faith could restrain herself no longer and broke into a stifled giggle.

Mr. Perry stopped short, angered over this impertinence. Suddenly he became conscious that a reek of burning cloth filled the room. He whirled round and saw nothing. Then he clapped his hands to his coat-tails and brought them around in front of him. There was already quite a hole in one of them—and this was his new suit. Faith shook with helpless laughter over his pose and expression.

"Did you see my coat-tails burning?" he demanded angrily.

"Yes, sir," said Faith demurely.

"Why didn't you tell me?" he demanded, glaring at her.

"You said it wasn't good manners to interrupt, sir," said Faith, more demurely still.

"If—if I was your father, I would give you a spanking that you would remember all your life, Miss," said a very angry reverend gentleman, as he stalked out of the study. The coat of Mr. Meredith's second best suit would not fit Mr. Perry, so he had to go to the evening service with his singed coat-tail. But he did not walk up the aisle with his usual consciousness of the honour he was conferring on the building. He never would agree to an exchange of pulpits with Mr. Meredith again, and he was barely civil to the latter when they met for a few minutes at the station the next morning. But Faith felt a certain gloomy satisfaction. Adam was partially avenged.

CHAPTER XX

Faith Makes a Friend

NEXT day in school was a hard one for Faith. Mary Vance had told the tale of Adam, and all the scholars, except the Blythes, thought it quite a joke. The girls told Faith, between giggles, that it was too bad, and the boys wrote sardonic notes of condolence to her. Poor Faith went home from school feeling her very soul raw and smarting within her.

"I'm going over to Ingleside to have a talk with Mrs. Blythe," she sobbed. "*She* won't laugh at me, as everybody else does. I've just *got* to talk to somebody who understands how bad I feel."

She ran down through Rainbow Valley. Enchantment had been at work the night before. A light snow had fallen and the powdered firs were dreaming of a spring to come and a joy to be. The long hill beyond was richly purple with leafless beeches. The rosy light of sunset lay over the world like a pink kiss. Of all the airy, fairy places, full of weird, elfin grace, Rainbow Valley that winter evening was the most beautiful. But all its dreamlike loveliness was lost on poor, sore-hearted little Faith.

By the brook she came suddenly upon Rosemary

West, who was sitting on the old pine tree. She was on her way home from Ingleside, where she had been giving the girls their music lesson. She had been lingering in Rainbow Valley quite a little time, looking across its white beauty and roaming some by-ways of dream. Judging from the expression of her face, her thoughts were pleasant ones. Perhaps the faint, occasional tinkle from the bells on the Tree Lovers brought the little lurking smile to her lips. Or perhaps it was occasioned by the consciousness that John Meredith seldom failed to spend Monday evening in the gray house on the white wind-swept hill.

Into Rosemary's dreams burst Faith Meredith full of rebellious bitterness. Faith stopped abruptly when she saw Miss West. She did not know her very well—just well enough to speak to when they met. And she did not want to see any one just then—except Mrs. Blythe. She knew her eyes and nose were red and swollen and she hated to have a stranger know she had been crying.

"Good evening, Miss West," she said uncomfortably.

"What is the matter, Faith?" asked Rosemary gently.

"Nothing," said Faith rather shortly.

"Oh!" Rosemary smiled. "You mean nothing that you can tell to outsiders, don't you?"

Faith looked at Miss West with sudden interest. Here was a person who understood things. And how pretty she was! How golden her hair was under her plumy hat! How pink her cheeks were over her velvet coat! How blue and companionable her eyes were! Faith felt that Miss West could be a lovely friend—if only she were a friend instead of a stranger!

"I—I'm going up to tell Mrs. Blythe," said Faith. "She always understands—she never laughs at us. I always talk things over with her. It helps."

"Dear girlie, I'm sorry to have to tell you that Mrs. Blythe isn't home," said Miss West, sympathetically. "She went to Avonlea to-day and isn't coming back till the last of the week."

Faith's lip quivered.

"Then I might as well go home again," she said miserably.

"I suppose so—unless you think you could bring yourself to talk it over with me instead," said Miss Rosemary gently. "It *is* such a help to talk things over. *I* know. I don't suppose I can be as good at understanding as Mrs. Blythe—but I promise you that I won't laugh."

"You wouldn't laugh outside," hesitated Faith. "But you might—inside."

"No, I wouldn't laugh inside, either. Why should I? Something has hurt you—it never amuses me to see anybody hurt, no matter what hurts them. If you feel that you'd like to tell me what has hurt you I'll be glad to listen. But if you think you'd rather not—that's all right, too, dear."

Faith took another long, earnest look into Miss West's eyes. They were very serious—there was no laughter in them, not even far, far back. With a little sigh she sat down on the old pine beside her new friend and told her all about Adam and his cruel fate.

Rosemary did not laugh or feel like laughing. She understood and sympathized—really, she was almost as good as Mrs. Blythe—yes, quite as good.

"Mr. Perry is a minister, but he should have been a *butcher,*" said Faith bitterly. "He is so fond of carving things up. He *enjoyed* cutting poor Adam to pieces. He just sliced into him as if he were any common rooster."

"Between you and me, Faith, *I* don't like Mr. Perry very well myself," said Rosemary, laughing a little—but at Mr. Perry, not at Adam, as Faith clearly understood. "I never did like him. I went to school with him—he was a Glen boy, you know—and he was a most detestable little prig even then. Oh, how we girls used to hate holding his fat, clammy hands in the ring-around games. But we must remember, dear, that he didn't know that Adam had been a pet of yours. He thought he *was* just a common rooster. We must be just, even when we are terribly hurt."

"I suppose so," admitted Faith. "But why does everybody seem to think it funny that I should have loved Adam so much, Miss West? If it had been a horrid old cat nobody would have thought it queer. When Lottie Warren's kitten had its legs cut off by the binder everybody was sorry for her. She cried two days in school and nobody laughed at her, not even Dan Reese. And all her chums went to the kitten's funeral and helped her bury it—only they couldn't bury its poor little paws with it, because they couldn't find them. It was a horrid thing to have happen, of course, but I don't think it was as dreadful as seeing your pet *eaten up*. Yet everybody laughs at *me*."

"I think it is because the name 'rooster' seems rather a funny one," said Rosemary gravely. "There *is* something in it that is comical. Now, 'chicken' is different. It doesn't sound so funny to talk of loving a chicken."

"Adam was the dearest little chicken, Miss West. He was just a little golden ball. He would run up to me and peck out of my hand. And he was handsome when he grew up, too—white as snow, with such a beautiful curving white tail, though Mary Vance said it was too short. He knew his name and always came when I called him—he was a very intelligent rooster. And Aunt Martha had no right to kill him. He was mine. It wasn't fair, was it, Miss West?"

"No, it wasn't," said Rosemary decidedly. "Not a bit fair. I remember I had a pet hen when I was a little girl. She was such a pretty little thing—all golden brown and speckly. I loved her as much as I ever loved any pet. She was never killed—she died of old age. Mother wouldn't have her killed because she was my pet."

"If *my* mother had been living she wouldn't have let

Adam be killed," said Faith. "For that matter, father wouldn't have either, if he'd been home and known of it. I'm *sure* he wouldn't, Miss West."

"I'm sure, too," said Rosemary. There was a little added flush on her face. She looked rather conscious but Faith noticed nothing.

"Was it *very* wicked of me not to tell Mr. Perry his coat-tails were scorching?" she asked anxiously.

"Oh, terribly wicked," answered Rosemary, with dancing eyes. "But *I* would have been just as naughty, Faith—*I* wouldn't have told him they were scorching—and I don't believe I would ever have been a bit sorry for my wickedness, either."

"Una thought I should have told him because he was a minister."

"Dearest, if a minister doesn't behave as a gentleman we are not bound to respect his coat-tails. I know *I* would just have loved to see Jimmy Perry's coat-tails burning up. It must have been fun."

Both laughed; but Faith ended with a bitter little sigh.

"Well, anyway, Adam is dead and I am *never* going to love anything again."

"Don't say that, dear. We miss so much out of life if we don't love. The more we love the richer life is—even if it is only some little furry or feathery pet. Would you like a canary, Faith—a little golden bit of a canary? If you would I'll give you one. We have two up home."

"Oh, I *would* like that," cried Faith. "I love birds. Only—would Aunt Martha's cat eat it? It's so *tragic* to have your pets eaten. I don't think I could endure it a second time."

"If you hang the cage far enough from the wall I don't think the cat could harm it. I'll tell you just how to take care of it and I'll bring it to Ingleside for you the next time I come down."

To herself, Rosemary was thinking,

"It will give every gossip in the Glen something to talk of, but I *will* not care. I want to comfort this poor little heart."

Faith was comforted. Sympathy and understanding were very sweet. She and Miss Rosemary sat on the old pine until the twilight crept softly down over the white valley and the evening star shone over the gray maple grove. Faith told Rosemary all her small history and hopes, her likes and dislikes, the ins and outs of life at the manse, the ups and downs of school society. Finally they parted firm friends.

Mr. Meredith was, as usual, lost in dreams when supper began that evening, but presently a name pierced his abstraction and brought him back to reality. Faith was telling Una of her meeting with Rosemary.

"She is just lovely, I think," said Faith. "Just as nice as Mrs. Blythe—but different. I felt as if I wanted to hug her. She did hug *me*—such a nice, velvety hug. And she called me 'dearest.' It *thrilled* me. I could tell her *anything*."

"So you liked Miss West, Faith?" Mr. Meredith asked, with a rather odd intonation.

"I love her," cried Faith.

"Ah!" said Mr. Meredith. "Ah!"

CHAPTER XXI

The Impossible Word

JOHN MEREDITH walked meditatively through the clear crispness of a winter night in Rainbow Valley. The hills beyond glistened with the chill, splendid lustre of moonlight on snow. Every little fir tree in the long valley sang its own wild song to the harp of wind and frost. His children and the Blythe lads and lasses were coasting down the eastern slope and whizzing over the glassy pond. They were having a glorious time and their gay voices and gayer laughter echoed up and down the valley, dying away in elfin cadences among the trees. On the right the lights of Ingleside gleamed through the maple grove with the genial lure and invitation which seems always to glow in the beacons of a home where we know there is love and good-cheer and a welcome for all kin, whether of flesh or spirit. Mr. Meredith liked very well on occasion to spend an evening arguing with the doctor by the drift wood fire, where the famous china dogs of Ingleside kept ceaseless watch and ward, as became deities of the hearth, but to-night he did not look that way. Far on the western hill gleamed a paler but more alluring star. Mr. Meredith was on his way to see Rosemary West, and he meant to tell her something which had been slowly blossoming in his heart since their first meeting and had sprung into full flower on the evening when Faith had so warmly voiced her admiration for Rosemary.

He had come to realize that he had learned to care for Rosemary. Not as he had cared for Cecilia, of course. *That* was entirely different. That love of romance and dream and glamour could never, he thought, return. But Rosemary was beautiful and sweet and dear—very dear. She was the best of companions. He was happier in her company than he had ever expected to be again. She would be an ideal mistress for his home, a good mother to his children.

During the years of his widowhood Mr. Meredith had received innumerable hints from brother members of Presbytery and from many parishioners who could not be suspected of any ulterior motive, as well as from some who could, that he ought to marry again. But these hints never made any impression on him. It was commonly thought he was never aware of them. But he was quite acutely aware of them. And in his own occasional visitations of common sense he knew that the common sensible thing for him to do was to marry. But common sense was not the strong point of John Meredith, and to choose out, deliberately and cold-bloodedly, some "suitable" woman, as one might choose a housekeeper or a business partner, was something he was quite incapable of doing. How he hated that word "suitable." It reminded him so strongly of James Perry. "A *suit*able woman of *suit*able age," that unctuous brother of the cloth had said, in his far from subtle hint. For the moment John Meredith had had a perfectly unbelievable desire to rush madly away and propose marriage to the youngest, most unsuitable woman it was possible to discover.

Mrs. Marshall Elliott was his good friend and he liked her. But when she had bluntly told him he should marry again he felt as if she had torn away the veil that hung before some sacred shrine of his innermost life, and he had been more or less afraid of her ever since. He knew there were women in his congregation "of suitable age" who would marry him quite readily. That fact had seeped through all his abstraction very early in his ministry in Glen St. Mary. They were good, substantial, uninteresting women, one or two fairly comely, the others not exactly so; and John Meredith would as soon have thought of marrying any one of them as of hanging himself. He had some ideals to which no seeming necessity could make him false. He could ask no woman to fill Cecilia's place in his home unless he could offer her at least some of the affection and homage he had given to his girlish bride. And where, in his limited feminine acquaintance, was such a woman to be found?

Rosemary West had come into his life on that autumn evening bringing with her an atmosphere in which his spirit recognized native air. Across the gulf of strangerhood they clasped hands of friendship. He knew her better in that ten minutes by the hidden spring than he knew Emmeline Drew or Elizabeth Kirk or Amy Annetta Douglas in a year, or could know them, in a century. He had fled to her for comfort when Mrs. Alec Davis had outraged his mind and soul and had found it. Since then he had gone often to the house on the hill, slipping through the shadowy paths of night in Rainbow Valley so astutely that Glen gossip could never be absolutely certain that he *did* go to see Rosemary West. Once or twice he had been caught in the West living room by other visitors; that was all the Ladies' Aid had to go by. But when Elizabeth Kirk heard it she put away a secret hope she had allowed herself to cherish, without a change of expression on her kind plain face, and Emmeline Drew resolved that the next time she saw a certain old bachelor of Lowbridge she would not snub him as she had done at a previous meeting. Of course, if Rosemary West was out to catch the minister she would catch him; she looked younger than she was and *men* thought her pretty; besides, the West girls had money!

"It is to be hoped that he won't be so absent-minded as to propose to Ellen by mistake," was the only malicious thing she allowed herself to say to a sympathetic sister Drew. Emmeline bore no further grudge towards Rosemary. When all was said and done, an unencumbered bachelor was far better than a widower with four children. It had been only the glamour of the manse that had temporarily blinded Emmeline's eyes to the better part.

A sled with three shrieking occupants sped past Mr. Meredith to the pond. Faith's long curls streamed in the wind and her laughter rang above that of the others. John Meredith looked after them kindly and longingly. He was glad that his children had such chums as the Blythes—glad that they had so wise and gay and tender a friend as Mrs. Blythe. But they needed something more, and that something would be supplied when he brought Rosemary West as a bride to the old manse. There was in her a quality essentially maternal.

It was Saturday night and he did not often go calling on Saturday night, which was supposed to be dedicated to a thoughtful revision of Sunday's sermon. But he had chosen this night because he had learned that Ellen West was going to be away and Rosemary would be alone. Often as he had spent pleasant evenings in the house on the hill he had never, since that first meeting at the spring, seen Rosemary alone. Ellen had always been there.

He did not precisely object to Ellen being there. He liked Ellen West very much and they were the best of friends. Ellen had an almost masculine understanding and a sense of humour which his own shy, hidden appreciation of fun found very agreeable. He liked her interest in politics and world events. There was no man in the Glen, not even excepting Dr. Blythe, who had a better grasp of such things.

"I think it is just as well to be interested in things as long as you live," she had said. "If you're not, it doesn't seem to me that there's much difference between the quick and the dead."

He liked her pleasant, deep, rumbly voice; he liked the hearty laugh with which she always ended up some jolly and well-told story. She never gave him digs about his children as other Glen women did; she never bored him with local gossip; she had no malice and no pettiness. She was always splendidly sincere. Mr. Meredith, who had picked up Miss Cornelia's way of classifying people, considered that Ellen belonged to the race of Joseph. Altogether, an admirable woman for a sister-in-law. Nevertheless, a man did not want even the most admirable of women around when he was proposing to another woman. And Ellen was always around. She did not insist on talking to Mr. Meredith herself all the time. She let Rosemary have a fair share of him. Many evenings, indeed, Ellen effaced herself almost totally, sitting back in the corner with St. George on her lap, and letting Mr. Meredith and Rosemary talk and sing and read books together. Sometimes they quite forgot her presence. But if their conversation or choice of duets ever betrayed the least tendency to what Ellen considered philandering, Ellen promptly nipped that tendency in the bud and blotted Rosemary out for the rest of the evening.

But not even the grimmest of amiable dragons can altogether prevent a certain subtle language of eye and smile and eloquent silence; and so the minister's courtship progressed after a fashion.

But if it was ever to reach a climax that climax must come when Ellen was away. And Ellen was so seldom away, especially in winter. She found her own fireside the pleasantest place in the world, she vowed. Gadding had no attraction for her. She was fond of company but she wanted it at home. Mr. Meredith had almost been driven to the conclusion that he must write to Rosemary what he wanted to say, when Ellen casually announced one evening that she was going to a silver wedding next Saturday night. She had been bridesmaid when the principals were married. Only old guests were invited, so Rosemary was not included. Mr. Meredith pricked up his ears a trifle and a gleam flashed into his dreamy dark eyes. Both Ellen and Rosemary saw it; and both Ellen and Rosemary felt, with a tingling shock, that Mr. Meredith would certainly come up the hill next Saturday night.

"Might as well have it over with, St. George," Ellen sternly told the black cat, after Mr. Meredith had gone home and Rosemary had silently gone upstairs. "He means to ask her, St. George—I'm perfectly sure of that. So he might as well have his chance to do it and find out he can't get her, George. She'd rather like to take him, Saint. I know that—but she promised, and she's got to keep her promise. I'm rather sorry in some ways, St. George. I don't know of a man I'd sooner have for a brother-in-law if a brother-in-law was convenient. I haven't a thing against him, Saint—not a thing except that he won't see and can't be made to see that the Kaiser is a menace to the peace of Europe. That's *his* blind spot. But he's good company and I like him. A woman can say anything she likes to a man with a mouth like John Meredith's and be sure of not being misunderstood. Such a man is more precious than rubies, Saint—and much rarer, George. But he can't have Rosemary—and I suppose when he finds out he can't have her he'll drop us both. And we'll miss him, Saint—we'll miss him something scandalous, George. But she promised, and I'll see that she keeps her promise!"

Ellen's face looked almost ugly in its lowering resolution. Upstairs Rosemary was crying into her pillow.

So Mr. Meredith found his lady alone and looking very beautiful. Rosemary had not made any special toilet for the occasion; she wanted to, but she thought it would be absurd to dress up for a man you meant to refuse. So she wore her plain dark afternoon dress and looked like a queen in it. Her suppressed excitement coloured her face to brilliancy, her great blue eyes were pools of light less placid than usual.

She wished the interview was over. She had looked forward to it all day with dread. She felt quite sure that John Meredith cared a great deal for her after a fashion—and she felt just as sure that he did not care for her as he had cared for his first love. She felt that her refusal would disappoint him considerably, but she did not think it would altogether overwhelm him. Yet she hated to make it; hated for his sake and—Rosemary was quite honest with herself—for her own. She knew she could have loved John Meredith if—if it had been permissible. She knew that life would be a blank thing if, rejected as lover, he refused longer to be a friend. She knew that she could be very happy with him and that she could make him happy. But between her and happiness stood the prison gate of the promise she had made to Ellen years ago.

Rosemary could not remember her father. He had died when she was only three years old. Ellen, who had been thirteen, remembered him, but with no special tenderness. He had been a stern, reserved man many years older than his fair, pretty wife. Five years later their brother of twelve died also; since his death the two girls had always lived alone with their mother. They had never mingled very freely in the social life of the Glen or Lowbridge, though where they went the wit and spirit of Ellen and the sweetness and beauty of Rosemary made them welcome guests. Both had what was called "a disappointment" in their girlhood. The sea had not given up Rosemary's lover; and Norman Douglas, then a handsome, red-haired young giant, noted for wild driving and noisy though harmless escapades, had quarrelled with Ellen and left her in a fit of pique.

There were not lacking candidates for both Martin's and Norman's places, but none seemed to find favour in the eyes of the West girls, who drifted slowly out of youth and bellehood without any seeming regret. They were devoted to their mother, who was a chronic invalid. The three had a little circle of home interests—books and pets and flowers—which made them happy and contented.

Mrs. West's death, which occurred on Rosemary's twenty-fifth birthday, was a bitter grief to them. At first they were intolerably lonely. Ellen, especially, continued to grieve and brood, her long, moody musings broken only by fits of stormy, passionate weeping. The old Lowbridge doctor told Rosemary that he feared permanent melancholy or worse.

Once, when Ellen had sat all day, refusing either to speak or eat, Rosemary had flung herself on her knees by her sister's side.

"Oh, Ellen, you have me yet," she said imploringly. "Am I nothing to you? We have always loved each other so."

"I won't have you always," Ellen had said, breaking her silence with harsh intensity. "You will marry and leave me. I shall be left all alone. I cannot bear the thought—I *cannot*. I would rather die."

"I will never marry," said Rosemary, "never, Ellen."

Ellen bent forward and looked searchingly into Rosemary's eyes.

"Will you promise me that solemnly?" she said. "Promise it on mother's Bible."

Rosemary assented at once, quite willing to humor Ellen. What did it matter? She knew quite well she would never want to marry any one. Her love had gone down with Martin Crawford to the deeps of the sea; and without love she could not marry any one. So she promised readily, though Ellen made rather a fearsome rite of it. They clasped hands over the Bible, in their mother's vacant room, and both vowed to each other that they would never marry and would always live together.

Ellen's condition improved from that hour. She soon regained her normal cheery poise. For ten years she and Rosemary lived in the old house happily, undisturbed by any thought of marrying or giving in marriage. Their promise sat very lightly on them. Ellen never failed to remind her sister of it whenever any eligible male creature crossed their paths, but she had never been really alarmed until John Meredith came home that night with Rosemary. As for Rosemary, Ellen's obsession regarding that promise had always been a little matter of mirth to her—until lately. Now, it was a merciless fetter, self-imposed but never to be shaken off. Because of it to-night she must turn her face from happiness.

It was true that the shy, sweet, rosebud love she

had given to her boy-lover she could never give to another. But she knew now that she could give to John Meredith a love richer and more womanly. She knew that he touched deeps in her nature that Martin had never touched—that had not, perhaps, been in the girl of seventeen to touch. And she must send him away to-night—send him back to his lonely hearth and his empty life and his heart-breaking problems, because she had promised Ellen, ten years before, on their mother's Bible, that she would never marry.

John Meredith did not immediately grasp his opportunity. On the contrary, he talked for two good hours on the least lover-like of subjects. He even tried politics, though politics always bored Rosemary. The latter began to think that she had been altogether mistaken, and her fears and expectations suddenly seemed to her grotesque. She felt flat and foolish. The glow went out of her face and the lustre out of her eyes. John Meredith had not the slightest intention of asking her to marry him.

And then, quite suddenly, he rose, came across the room, and standing by her chair, he asked it. The room had grown terribly still. Even St. George ceased to purr. Rosemary heard her own heart beating and was sure John Meredith must hear it too.

Now was the time for her to say no, gently but firmly. She had been ready for days with her stilted, regretful little formula. And now the words of it had completely vanished from her mind. She had to say no—and she suddenly found she could not say it. It was the impossible word. She knew now that it was not that she *could* have loved John Meredith, but that she *did* love him. The thought of putting him from her life was agony.

She must say *something;* she lifted her bowed golden head and asked him stammeringly to give her a few days for—for consideration.

John Meredith was a little surprised. He was not vainer than any man has a right to be, but he had expected that Rosemary West would say yes. He had been tolerably sure she cared for him. Then why this doubt—this hesitation? She was not a school girl to be uncertain as to her own mind. He felt an ugly shock of disappointment and dismay. But he assented to her request with his unfailing gentle courtesy and went away at once.

"I will tell you in a few days," said Rosemary with downward eyes and burning face.

When the door shut behind him she went back into the room and wrung her hands.

CHAPTER XXII

St. George Knows All About It

AT midnight Ellen West was walking home from the Pollock silver wedding. She had stayed a little while after the other guests had gone to help the gray-haired bride wash the dishes. The distance between the two houses was not far and the road good, so that Ellen was enjoying her walk back home in the moonlight.

The evening had been a pleasant one. Ellen, who had not been to a party for years, found it very pleasant. All the guests had been members of her old set and there was no intrusive youth to spoil the flavour, for the only son of the bride and groom was far away at college and could not be present. Norman Douglas had been there and they had met socially for the first time in years, though she had seen him once or twice in church that winter. Not the least sentiment was awakened in Ellen's heart by their meeting. She was accustomed to wonder, when she thought about it at all, how she could ever have fancied him or felt so badly over his sudden marriage. But she had rather liked meeting him again. She had forgotten how bracing and stimulating he could be. No gathering was ever stagnant when Norman Douglas was present.

Everybody had been surprised when Norman came. It was well known he never went anywhere. The Pollocks had invited him because he had been one of the original guests, but they never thought he would come. He had taken his second cousin, Amy Annetta Douglas, out to supper and seemed rather attentive to her. But Ellen sat across the table from him and had a spirited argument with him—an argument during which all his shouting and banter could not fluster her and in which she came off best, flooring Norman so composedly and so completely that he was silent for ten minutes. At the end of which time he had muttered in his ruddy beard,—"spunky as ever—spunky as ever"—and began to hector Amy Annetta, who giggled foolishly over his sallies where Ellen would have retorted bitingly.

Ellen thought these things over as she walked home, tasting them with reminiscent relish. The moonlit air sparkled with frost. The snow crisped under her feet. Below her lay the Glen with the white harbour beyond. There was a light in the manse study. So John Meredith had gone home. Had he asked Rosemary to marry him? And after what fashion had she made her refusal known? Ellen felt that she would never know this, though she was quite curious. She was sure that Rosemary would never tell her anything about it and she would not dare to ask. She must just be content with the fact of the refusal. After all, that was the only thing that really mattered.

"I hope he'll have sense enough to come back once in a while and be friendly," she said to herself. She disliked so much to be alone that thinking aloud was one of her devices for circumventing unwelcome solitude. "It's awful never to have a man-body with some brains to talk to once in a while. And like as not he'll never come near the house again. There's Norman Douglas, too—I like that man, and I'd like to have a good rousing argument with him now and then. But he'd never dare come up for fear people would think he was courting me again—for fear *I*'d think it, too, most likely—though he's more of a stranger to me now than John Meredith. It seems like a dream that we could ever have been beaus. But there it is—there's only two men in the Glen I'd ever want to talk to—and what with gossip and this wretched love-making business it's not likely I'll ever see either of them again. I could," said Ellen, addressing the unmoved stars with spiteful emphasis, "I could have made a better world myself."

She paused at her gate with a sudden vague feeling of alarm. There was still a light in the living room and to and fro across the window-shades went the shadow of a woman walking restlessly up and down. What was Rosemary doing up at this hour of the night? And why was she striding about like a lunatic?

Ellen went softly in. As she opened the hall door Rosemary came out of the room. She was flushed and breathless. An atmosphere of stress and passion hung about her like a garment.

"Why aren't you in bed, Rosemary?" demanded Ellen.

"Come in here," said Rosemary intensely. "I want to tell you something."

Ellen composedly removed her wraps and overshoes, and followed her sister into the warm, fire-lighted room. She stood with her hand on the table and waited. She was looking very handsome herself, in her own grim, black-browed style. The new black velvet dress, with its train and V-neck, which she had made purposely for the party, became her stately, massive figure. She wore coiled around her neck the rich heavy necklace of amber beads which was a family heirloom. Her walk in the frosty air had stung her cheeks into a glowing scarlet. But her steel-blue eyes were as icy and unyielding as the sky of the winter night. She stood waiting in a silence which Rosemary could break only by a convulsive effort.

"Ellen, Mr. Meredith was here this evening."

"Yes?"

"And—and—he asked me to marry him."

"So I expected. Of course you refused him?"

"No."

"Rosemary." Ellen clenched her hands and took an involuntary step forward. "Do you mean to tell me that you accepted him?"

"No—no."

Ellen recovered her self-command.

"What *did* you do then?"

"I—I asked him to give me a few days to think it over."

"I hardly see why that was necessary," said Ellen, coldly contemptuous, "when there is only the one answer you can make him."

Rosemary held out her hands beseechingly.

"Ellen," she said desperately, "I love John Meredith—I want to be his wife. Will you set me free from that promise?"

"No," said Ellen, merciless, because she was sick from fear.

"Ellen—Ellen—"

"Listen," interrupted Ellen. "I did not ask you for that promise. You offered it."

"I know—I know. But I did not think then that I could ever care for any one again."

"You offered it," went on Ellen unmovably. "You promised it over our mother's Bible. It was more than a promise—it was an oath. Now you want to break it."

"I only asked you to set me free from it, Ellen."

"I will not do it. A promise is a promise in my eyes. I will not do it. Break your promise—be forsworn if you will—but it shall not be with any assent of mine."

"You are very hard on me, Ellen."

"Hard on you! And what of me? Have you ever given a thought to what my loneliness would be here if you left me? I could not bear it—I would go crazy. I *cannot* live alone. Haven't I been a good sister to you? Have I ever opposed any wish of yours? Haven't I indulged you in everything?"

"Yes—yes."

"Then why do you want to leave me for this man whom you hadn't even seen a year ago?"

"I love him, Ellen."

"Love! You talk like a school miss instead of a middle-aged woman. He doesn't love you. He wants a housekeeper and a governess. You don't love him. You want to be 'Mrs.'—you are one of those weak-minded women who thinks it's a disgrace to be ranked as an old maid. That's all there is to it."

Rosemary quivered. Ellen could not, or would not, understand. There was no use arguing with her.

"So you won't release me, Ellen?"

"No, I won't. And I won't talk of it again. You promised and you've got to keep your word. That's all. Go to bed. Look at the time! You're all romantic and worked up. To-morrow you'll be more sensible. At any rate, don't let me hear any more of this nonsense. Go."

Rosemary went without another word, pale and spiritless. Ellen walked stormily about the room for a few minutes, then paused before the chair where St. George had been calmly sleeping through the whole evening. A reluctant smile overspread her dark face. There had been only one time in her life—the time of her mother's death—when Ellen had not been able to temper tragedy with comedy. Even in that long ago bitterness, when Norman Douglas had, after a fashion, jilted her, she had laughed at herself quite as often as she had cried.

"I expect there'll be some sulking, St. George. Yes, Saint, I expect we are in for a few unpleasant foggy days. Well, we'll weather them through, George. We've dealt with foolish children before now, Saint. Rosemary'll sulk a while—and then she'll get over it—and all will be as before, George. She promised—and she's got to keep her promise. And that's the last word on the subject I'll say to you or her or any one, Saint."

But Ellen lay savagely awake till morning.

There was no sulking, however. Rosemary was pale and quiet the next day, but beyond that Ellen could detect no difference in her. Certainly, she seemed to bear Ellen no grudge. It was stormy, so no mention was made of going to church. In the afternoon Rosemary shut herself in her room and wrote a note to John Meredith. She could not trust herself to say no in person. She felt quite sure that if he suspected she was saying "no" reluctantly he would not take it for an answer, and she could not face pleading or entreaty. She must make him think she cared nothing at all for him and she could do that only by letter. She wrote him the stiffest, coolest little refusal imaginable. It was barely courteous; it certainly left no loophole of hope for the boldest lover—and John Meredith was anything but that. He shrank into himself, hurt and mortified, when he read Rosemary's letter next day in his dusty study. But under his mortification a dreadful realization presently made itself felt. He had thought he did not love Rosemary as deeply as he had loved Cecilia. Now, when he had lost her, he knew that he did. She was everything to him—everything! And he must put her out of his life completely. Even friendship was impossible now. Life stretched before him in intolerable dreariness. He must go on—there was his work—his children—but the heart had gone out of him. He sat alone all that evening in his dark, cold, comfortless study with his head bowed on his hands. Up on the hill Rosemary had a headache and went early to bed, while Ellen remarked to St. George, purring his disdain of foolish humankind, who did not know that a soft cushion was the only thing that really mattered,

"What would women do if headaches had never been invented, St. George? But never mind, Saint. We'll just wink the other eye for a few weeks. I admit I don't feel comfortable myself, George. I feel as if I had drowned a kitten. But she promised, Saint—and she was the one to offer it, George. Bismillah!"

CHAPTER XXIII

The Good-Conduct Club

A LIGHT rain had been falling all day—a little, delicate, beautiful spring rain, that somehow seemed to hint and whisper of mayflowers and wakening violets. The harbour and the gulf and the low-lying shore fields had been dim with pearl-gray mists. But now in the evening the rain had ceased and the mists had blown out to sea. Clouds sprinkled the sky over the harbour like little fiery roses. Beyond it the hills were dark against a spendthrift splendour of daffodil and crimson. A great silvery evening star was watching over the bar. A brisk, dancing, new-sprung wind was blowing up from Rainbow Valley, resinous with the odours of fir and damp mosses. It crooned in the old spruces around the graveyard and ruffled Faith's splendid curls as she sat on Hezekiah Pollock's tombstone with her arms round Mary Vance and Una. Carl and Jerry were sitting opposite them on another tombstone and all were rather full of mischief after being cooped up all day.

"The air just *shines* to-night, doesn't it? It's been washed so clean, you see," said Faith happily.

Mary Vance eyed her gloomily. Knowing what

she knew, or fancied she knew, Mary considered that Faith was far too light-hearted. Mary had something on her mind to say and she meant to say it before she went home. Mrs. Elliott had sent her up to the manse with some new-laid eggs, and had told her not to stay longer than half an hour. The half hour was nearly up so Mary uncurled her cramped legs from under her and said abruptly,

"Never mind about the air. Just you listen to me. You manse young ones have just got to behave better than you've been doing this spring—that's all there is to it. I just come up to-night a-purpose to tell you so. The way people are talking about you is awful."

"What have we been doing now?" cried Faith in amazement, pulling her arm away from Mary. Una's lip trembled and her sensitive little soul shrank within her. Mary was always so brutally frank. Jerry began to whistle out of bravado. He meant to let Mary see he didn't care for *her* tirades. Their behaviour was no business of *hers* anyway. What right had *she* to lecture them on their conduct?

"Doing now! You're doing *all* the time," retorted Mary. "Just as soon as the talk about one of your didos fades away you do something else to start it up again. It seems to me you haven't any idea of how manse children ought to behave!"

"Maybe *you* can tell us," said Jerry, killingly sarcastic.

Sarcasm was quite thrown away on Mary.

"*I* can tell you what will happen if you don't learn to behave yourselves. The session will ask your father to resign. There now, Master Jerry-know-it-all. Mrs. Alec Davis said so to Mrs. Elliott. I heard her. I always have my ears pricked up when Mrs. Alec Davis comes to tea. She said you were all going from bad to worse and that though it was only what was to be expected when you had nobody to bring you up, still the congregation couldn't be expected to put up with it much longer, and something would have to be done. The Methodists just laugh and laugh at you, and that hurts the Presbyterian feelings. *She* says you all need a good dose of birch tonic. Lor', if that would make folks good *I* oughter be a young saint. I'm not telling you this because I want to hurt *your* feelings. I'm sorry for you"—Mary was past mistress in the gentle art of condescension. "*I* understand that you haven't much chance, the way things are. But other people don't make as much allowance as *I* do. Miss Drew says Carl had a frog in his pocket in Sunday School last Sunday and it hopped out while she was hearing the lesson. She says she's going to give up the class. Why don't you keep your insecks home?"

"I popped it right back in again," cried Carl. "It didn't hurt anybody—a poor little frog! And I wish old Jane Drew *would* give up our class. I hate her. Her own nephew had a dirty plug of tobacco in his pocket and offered us fellows a chew when Elder Clow was praying. I guess that's worse than a frog."

"No, 'cause frogs are more unexpected-like. They make more of a sensation. 'Sides, he wasn't caught at it. And then that praying competition you had last week has made a fearful scandal. Everybody is talking about it."

"Why, the Blythes were in that as well as us," cried Faith, indignantly. "It was Nan Blythe who suggested it in the first place. And Walter took the prize."

"Well, you get the credit of it any way. It wouldn't have been so bad if you hadn't had it in the graveyard."

"I should think a graveyard was a very good place to pray in," retorted Jerry.

"Deacon Hazard drove past when *you* were praying," said Mary, "and he saw and heard you, with your hands folded over your stomach, and groaning after every sentence. He thought you were making fun of *him*."

"So I was," declared unabashed Jerry. "Only I didn't know he was going by, of course. That was just a mean accident. *I* wasn't praying in real earnest—I knew I had no chance of winning the prize. So I was just getting what fun I could out of it. Walter Blythe can pray bully. Why, he can pray as well as dad."

"Una is the only one of *us* who really likes praying," said Faith pensively.

"Well, if praying scandalizes people so much we mustn't do it any more," sighed Una.

"Shucks, you can pray all you want to, only not in

the graveyard—and don't make a game of it. That was what made it so bad—that, and having a tea-party on the tombstones."

"We hadn't."

"Well, a soap-bubble party then. You had *something.* The over-harbour people swear you had a tea-party, but *I'm* willing to take your word. And you used this tombstone for a table."

"Well, Martha wouldn't let us blow bubbles in the house. She was awful cross that day," explained Jerry. "And this old slab made such a jolly table."

"Weren't they pretty?" cried Faith, her eyes sparkling over the remembrance. "They reflected the trees and the hills and the harbour like little fairy worlds, and when we shook them loose they floated away down to Rainbow Valley."

"All but one and it went over and bust up on the Methodist spire," said Carl.

"I'm glad we did it once, anyhow, before we found out it was wrong," said Faith.

"It wouldn't have been wrong to blow them on the lawn," said Mary impatiently. "Seems like I can't knock any sense into your heads. You've been told often enough you shouldn't play in the graveyard. The Methodists are sensitive about it."

"We forget," said Faith dolefully. "And the lawn is so small—and so caterpillary—and so full of shrubs and things. We can't be in Rainbow Valley all the time—and where are we to go?"

"It's the things you *do* in the graveyard. It wouldn't matter if you just sat here and talked quiet, same as we're doing now. Well, I don't know what is going to come of it all, but I *do* know that Elder Warren is going to speak to your pa about it. Deacon Hazard is his cousin."

"I wish they wouldn't bother father about us," said Una.

"Well, people think he ought to bother himself about you a little more. *I* don't—*I* understand him. He's a child in some ways hisself—that's what he is, and needs some one to look after him as bad as you do. Well, perhaps he'll have some one before long, if all tales is true."

"What do you mean?" asked Faith.

"Haven't you got any idea—honest?" demanded Mary.

"No, no. What *do* you mean?"

"Well, you are a lot of innocents, upon my word. Why, *every*body is talking of it. Your pa goes to see Rosemary West. *She* is going to be your step-ma."

"I don't believe it," cried Una, flushing crimson.

"Well, *I* dunno. I just go by what folks say. *I* don't give it for a fact. But it would be a good thing. Rosemary West'd make you toe the mark if she came here, I'll bet a cent, for all she's so sweet and smiley on the face of her. They're always that way till they've caught them. But you need some one to bring you up. You're disgracing your pa and I feel for him. I've always thought an awful lot of your pa ever since that night he talked to me so nice. I've never said a single swear word since, or told a lie. And I'd like to see him happy and comfortable, with his buttons on and his meals decent, and you young ones licked into shape, and that old cat of a Martha put in *her* proper place. The way she looked at the eggs I brought her to-night. 'I hope they're fresh,' says she. I just wished they *was* rotten. But you just mind that she gives you all one for breakfast, including your pa. Make a fuss if she doesn't. That was what they was sent up for—but I don't trust old Martha. She's quite capable of feeding 'em to her cat."

Mary's tongue being temporarily tired, a brief silence fell over the graveyard. The manse children did not feel like talking. They were digesting the new and not altogether palatable ideas Mary had suggested to them. Jerry and Carl were somewhat startled. But, after all, what did it matter? And it wasn't likely there was a word of truth in it. Faith, on the whole, was pleased. Only Una was seriously upset. She felt that she would like to get away and cry.

"Will there be any stars in my crown?" sang the Methodist choir, beginning to practice in the Methodist church.

"*I* want just three," said Mary, whose theological knowledge had increased notably since her residence with Mrs. Elliott. "Just three—setting up on my head, like a corrownet, a big one in the middle and a small one each side."

"Are there different sizes in souls?" asked Carl.

"Of course. Why, little babies must have smaller ones than big men. Well, it's getting dark and I must scoot home. Mrs. Elliott doesn't like me to be out after dark. Laws, when I lived with Mrs. Wiley the dark was just the same as the daylight to me. I didn't mind it no more'n a gray cat. Them days seem a hundred years ago. Now, you mind what I've said and try to behave yourselves, for your pa's sake. *I'll* always back you up and defend you—you can be dead sure of that. Mrs. Elliott says she never saw the like of me for sticking up for my friends. I was real sassy to Mrs. Alec Davis about you and Mrs. Elliott combed me down for it afterwards. The fair Cornelia has a tongue of her own and no mistake. But she was pleased underneath for all, 'cause she hates old Kitty Alec and she's real fond of you. *I* can see through folks."

Mary sailed off, excellently well pleased with herself, leaving a rather depressed little group behind her.

"Mary Vance always says something that makes us feel bad when she comes up," said Una resentfully.

"I wish we'd left her to starve in the old barn," said Jerry vindictively.

"Oh, that's wicked, Jerry," rebuked Una.

"May as well have the game as the name," retorted

unrepentant Jerry. "If people say we're so bad let's *be* bad."

"But not if it hurts father," pleaded Faith.

Jerry squirmed uncomfortably. He adored his father. Through the unshaded study window they could see Mr. Meredith at his desk. He did not seem to be either reading or writing. His head was in his hands and there was something in his whole attitude that spoke of weariness and dejection. The children suddenly felt it.

"I dare say somebody's been worrying him about us to-day," said Faith. "I wish we *could* get along without making people talk. Oh—Jem Blythe! How you scared me!"

Jem Blythe had slipped into the graveyard and sat down beside the girls. He had been prowling about Rainbow Valley and had succeeded in finding the first little star-white cluster of arbutus for his mother. The manse children were rather silent after his coming. Jem was beginning to grow away from them somewhat this spring. He was studying for the entrance examination of Queen's Academy and stayed after school with the older pupils for extra lessons. Also, his evenings were so full of work that he seldom joined the others in Rainbow Valley now. He seemed to be drifting away into grown-up land.

"What is the matter with you all to-night?" he asked. "There's no fun in you."

"Not much," agreed Faith dolefully. "There

wouldn't be much fun in *you* either if you knew you were disgracing your father and making people talk about you."

"Who's been talking about you now?"

"Everybody—so Mary Vance says." And Faith poured out her troubles to sympathetic Jem. "You see," she concluded dolefully, "we've nobody to bring us up. And so we get into scrapes and people think we're bad."

"Why don't you bring yourselves up?" suggested Jem. "I'll tell you what to do. Form a Good-Conduct Club and punish yourselves every time you do anything that's not right."

"That's a good idea," said Faith, struck by it. "But," she added doubtfully, "things that don't seem a bit of harm to *us* seem simply dreadful to other people. How can we tell? We can't be bothering father all the time—and he has to be away a lot, anyhow."

"You could mostly tell if you stopped to think a thing over before doing it and ask yourselves what the congregation would say about it," said Jem. "The trouble is you just rush into things and don't think them over at all. Mother says you're all too impulsive, just as she used to be. The Good-Conduct Club would help you to think, if you were fair and honest about punishing yourselves when you broke the rules. You'd have to punish in some way that really *hurt,* or it wouldn't do any good."

"Whip each other?"

"Not exactly. You'd have to think up different ways of punishment to suit the person. You wouldn't punish each other—you'd punish *yourselves.* I read all about such a club in a story-book. You try it and see how it works."

"Let's," said Faith; and when Jem was gone they agreed they would. "If things aren't right we've just got to make them right," said Faith, resolutely.

"We've got to be fair and square, as Jem says," said Jerry. "This is a club to bring ourselves up, seeing there's nobody else to do it. There's no use in having many rules. Let's just have one and any of us that breaks it has got to be punished hard."

"But *how.*"

"We'll think that up as we go along. We'll hold a session of the club here in the graveyard every night and talk over what we've done through the day, and if we think we've done anything that isn't right or that would disgrace dad the one that does it, or is responsible for it, must be punished. That's the rule. We'll all decide on the kind of punishment—it must be made to fit the crime, as Mr. Flagg says. And the one that's guilty will be bound to carry it out and no shirking. There's going to be fun in this," concluded Jerry, with a relish.

"You suggested the soap-bubble party," said Faith.

"But that was before we'd formed the club," said Jerry hastily. "Everything starts from to-night."

"But what if we can't agree on what's right, or what the punishment ought to be? S'pose two of us thought one thing and two another. There ought to be five in a club like this."

"We can ask Jem Blythe to be umpire. He is the squarest boy in Glen St. Mary. But I guess we can settle our own affairs mostly. We want to keep this as much of a secret as we can. Don't breathe a word to Mary Vance. She'd want to join and do the bringing up.

"*I* think," said Faith, "that there's no use in spoiling every day by dragging punishments in. Let's have a punishment day."

"We'd better choose Saturday because there is no school to interfere," suggested Una.

"And spoil the one holiday in the week," cried Faith. "Not much! No, let's take Friday. That's fish day, anyhow, and we all hate fish. We may as well have all the disagreeable things in one day. Then other days we can go ahead and have a good time."

"Nonsense," said Jerry authoritatively. "Such a scheme wouldn't work at all. We'll just punish ourselves as we go along and keep a clear slate. Now, we all understand, don't we? This is a Good-Conduct Club, for the purpose of bringing ourselves up. We agree to punish ourselves for bad conduct, and always to stop before we do anything, no matter what, and ask ourselves if it is likely to hurt dad in any way, and any one who shirks is to be cast out of the club and never allowed to play with the rest of us in Rainbow Valley again. Jem Blythe to be umpire in case of disputes. No more taking bugs to Sunday School, Carl, and no more chewing gum in public, if you please, Miss Faith."

"No more making fun of elders praying or going to the Methodist prayer meeting," retorted Faith.

"Why, it isn't any harm to go to the Methodist prayer meeting," protested Jerry in amazement.

"Mrs. Elliott says it is. She says manse children have no business to go anywhere but to Presbyterian things."

"Darn it, I won't give up going to the Methodist prayer meeting," cried Jerry. "It's ten times more fun than ours is."

"You said a naughty word," cried Faith. *"Now,* you've got to punish yourself."

"Not till it's all down in black and white. We're only talking the club over. It isn't really formed until we've written it out and signed it. There's got to be a constitution and by-laws. And you *know* there's nothing wrong in going to a prayer meeting."

"But it's not only the wrong things we're to punish ourselves for, but anything that might hurt father."

"It won't hurt anybody. You know Mrs. Elliott is cracked on the subject of Methodists. Nobody else makes any fuss about my going. I always behave myself. You ask Jem or Mrs. Blythe and see what they say. I'll abide by their opinion. I'm going for the paper now and I'll bring out the lantern and we'll all sign."

Fifteen minutes later the document was solemnly signed on Hezekiah Pollock's tombstone, on the centre of which stood the smoky manse lantern, while the children knelt around it. Mrs. Elder Clow was going past at the moment and next day all the Glen heard that the manse children had been having another praying competition and had wound it up by chasing each other all over the graves with a lantern. This piece of embroidery was probably suggested by the fact that, after the signing and sealing was completed, Carl had taken the lantern and had walked circumspectly to the little hollow to examine his ant-hill. The others had gone quietly into the manse and to bed.

"Do you think it is true that father is going to marry Miss West?" Una had tremulously asked of Faith, after their prayers had been said.

"I don't know, but I'd like it," said Faith.

"Oh, I wouldn't," said Una, chokingly. "She is nice the way she is. But Mary Vance says it changes people *altogether* to be made stepmothers. They get horrid cross and mean and hateful then, and turn your father against you. She says they're *sure* to do that. She never knew it to fail in a single case."

"I don't believe Miss West would *ever* try to do that," cried Faith.

"Mary says *anybody* would. She knows *all* about stepmothers, Faith—she says she's seen hundreds of them—and you've never seen one. Oh, Mary has told me blood-curdling things about them. She says she knew of one who whipped her husband's little girls on their bare shoulders till they bled, and then shut them up in a cold, dark, coal cellar all night. She says they're *all* aching to do things like that."

"I don't believe Miss West would. You don't know her as well as I do, Una. Just think of that sweet little bird she sent me. I love it far more even than Adam."

"It's just being a stepmother changes them. Mary says they can't help it. I wouldn't mind the whippings so much as having father hate us."

"You know nothing could make father hate us. Don't be silly, Una. I daresay there's nothing to worry over. Likely if we run our club right and bring ourselves up properly father won't think of marrying any one. And if he does, I *know* Miss West will be lovely to us."

But Una had no such conviction and she cried herself to sleep.

CHAPTER XXIV

A Charitable Impulse

FOR a fortnight things ran smoothly in the Good-Conduct Club. It seemed to work admirably. Not once was Jem Blythe called in as umpire. Not once did any of the manse children set the Glen gossips by the ears. As for their minor peccadilloes at home, they kept sharp tabs on each other and gamely underwent their self-imposed punishment—generally a voluntary absence from some gay Friday night frolic in Rainbow Valley, or a sojourn in bed on some spring evening when all young bones ached to be out and away. Faith, for whispering in Sunday School, condemned herself to pass a whole day without speaking a single word, unless it was absolutely necessary, and accomplished it. It was rather unfortunate that Mr. Baker from over-harbour should have chosen that evening for calling at the manse, and that Faith should have happened to go to the door. Not one word did she reply to his genial greeting, but went silently away to call her father briefly. Mr. Baker was slightly offended and told his wife when he went home that that biggest Meredith girl seemed a very shy, sulky little thing, without manners enough to speak when she was spoken to. But nothing worse came of it, and generally their penances did no harm to themselves or anybody else. All of them were beginning to feel quite cocksure that, after all, it was a very easy matter to bring yourself up.

"I guess people will soon see that we can behave ourselves properly as well as anybody," said Faith jubilantly. "It isn't hard when we put our minds to it."

She and Una were sitting on the Pollock tombstone. It had been a cold, raw, wet day of spring storm and Rainbow Valley was out of the question for girls, though the manse and the Ingleside boys were down there fishing. The rain had held up, but the east wind blew mercilessly in from the sea, cutting to bone and marrow. Spring was late in spite of its early promise, and there was even yet a hard drift of old snow and ice in the northern corner of the graveyard. Lida Marsh, who had come up to bring the manse a mess of herring, slipped in through the gate, shivering. She belonged to the fishing village at the harbour mouth and her father had, for thirty years, made a practice of sending a mess from his first spring catch to the manse. He never darkened a church door; he was a hard drinker and a reckless man, but as long as he sent those herring up to the manse every spring, as his father had done before him, he felt comfortably sure that his account with the Powers That Govern was squared for the year. He would not have expected a good mackerel catch if he had not so sent the first fruits of the season.

Lida was a mite of ten and looked younger, because she was such a small, wizened little creature. To-night, as she sidled boldly enough up to the manse girls, she looked as if she had never been warm since she was born. Her face was purple and her pale-blue, bold little eyes were red and watery. She wore a tattered print dress and a ragged woollen comforter, tied across her thin shoulders and under her arms. She had walked the three miles from the harbour mouth barefooted, over a road where there was still snow and slush and mud. Her feet and legs were as purple as her face. But Lida did not mind this much. She was used to being cold, and she had been going barefooted for a month already, like all the other swarming young fry of the fishing village. There was no self-pity in her heart as she sat down on the tombstone and grinned cheerfully at Faith and Una. Faith and Una grinned cheerfully back. They knew Lida slightly, having met her once or twice the preceding summer when they had gone down the harbour with the Blythes.

"Hello!" said Lida, "ain't this a fierce kind of a night? 'Taint fit for a dog to be out, is it?"

"Then why are you out?" asked Faith.

"Pa made me bring you up some herring," returned Lida. She shivered, coughed, and stuck out her bare feet. Lida was not thinking about herself or her feet. She was used to being cold and was making no bid for sympathy. She held her feet out instinctively to keep them from the wet grass around the tombstone. But Faith and Una were instantly swamped with a wave of pity for her. She looked so cold—so miserable.

"Oh, why are you barefooted such a cold night?" cried Faith. "Your feet must be almost frozen."

"Pretty near," said Lida proudly. "I tell you it was fierce walking up that harbour road."

"Why didn't you put on your shoes and stockings?" asked Una.

"Hain't none to put on. All I had was wore out by the time winter was over," said Lida indifferently.

For a moment Faith stared in horror. This was terrible. Here was a little girl, almost a neighbour, half frozen because she had no shoes or stockings in this cruel spring weather. Impulsive Faith thought of nothing but the dreadfulness of it. In a moment she was pulling off her own shoes and stockings.

"Here, take these and put them right on," she said, forcing them into the hands of the astonished Lida. "Quick now. You'll catch your death of cold. I've got others. Put them right on."

Lida, recovering her wits, snatched at the offered gift, with a sparkle in her dull eyes. Sure she would put them on, and that mighty quick, before any one appeared with authority to recall them. In a minute she had pulled the stockings over her scrawny little legs and slipped Faith's shoes over her thick little ankles.

"I'm obliged to you," she said, "but won't your folks be cross?"

"No—and I don't care if they are," said Faith. "Do you think I could see any one freezing to death without helping them if I could? It wouldn't be right, especially when my father's a minister."

"Will you want them back? It's awful cold down at the harbour mouth—long after it's warm up here," said Lida slyly.

"No, you're to keep them, of course. That is what I meant when I gave them. I have another pair of shoes and plenty of stockings."

Lida had meant to stay awhile and talk to the girls about many things. But now she thought she had better get away before somebody came and made her yield up her booty. So she shuffled off through the bitter twilight, in the noiseless, shadowy way she had slipped in. As soon as she was out of sight of the manse she sat down, took off the shoes and stockings, and put them in her herring basket. She had no intention of keeping them on down that dirty harbour road. They were to be kept good for gala occasions. Not another little girl down at the harbour mouth had such fine black cashmere stockings and such smart, almost new shoes. Lida was furnished forth for the summer. She had no qualms in the matter. In her eyes the manse people were quite fabulously rich, and no doubt those girls had slathers of shoes and stockings. Then Lida ran down to the Glen village and played for an hour with the boys before Mr. Flagg's store, splashing about in a pool of slush with the maddest of them, until Mrs. Elliott came along and bade her begone home.

"I don't think, Faith, that you should have done that," said Una, a little reproachfully, after Lida had gone. "You'll have to wear your good boots every day now, and they'll soon scuff out."

"I don't care," cried Faith, still in the fine glow of having done a kindness to a fellow creature. "It isn't fair that I should have two pairs of shoes and poor little Lida Marsh not have any. *Now* we both have a pair. You know perfectly well, Una, that father said in his sermon last Sunday that there was no real happiness in getting or having—only in giving. And it's true. I feel *far* happier now than I ever did in my whole life before. Just think of Lida walking home this very minute with her poor little feet all nice and warm and comfy."

"You know you haven't another pair of black cashmere stockings," said Una. "Your other pair were so full of holes that Aunt Martha said she couldn't darn them any more and she cut the legs up for stove dusters. You've nothing but those two pairs of striped stockings you hate so."

All the glow and uplift went out of Faith. Her

gladness collapsed like a pricked balloon. She sat for a few dismal minutes in silence, facing the consequences of her rash act.

"Oh, Una, I never thought of that," she said dolefully. "I didn't stop to think at all."

The striped stockings were thick, heavy, coarse, ribbed stockings of blue and red which Aunt Martha had knit for Faith in the winter. They were undoubtedly hideous. Faith loathed them as she had never loathed anything before. Wear them she certainly would not. They were still unworn in her bureau drawer.

"You'll have to wear the striped stockings after this," said Una. "Just think how the boys in school will laugh at you. You know how they laugh at Mamie Warren for her striped stockings and call her barber pole and yours are far worse."

"I won't wear them," said Faith. "I'll go barefooted first, cold as it is."

"You can't go barefooted to church to-morrow. Think what people would say."

"Then I'll stay home."

"You can't. You know very well Aunt Martha will make you go."

Faith did know this. The one thing on which Aunt Martha troubled herself to insist was that they must all go to church, rain or shine. How they were dressed, or if they were dressed at all, never concerned her. But go they must. That was how Aunt Martha had been brought up, seventy years ago, and that was how she meant to bring them up.

"Haven't you got a pair you can lend me, Una?" said poor Faith piteously.

Una shook her head. "No, you know I only have the one black pair. And they're so tight I can hardly get them on. They wouldn't go on you. Neither would my gray ones. Besides, the legs of *them* are all darned *and* darned."

"I won't wear those striped stockings," said Faith stubbornly. "The feel of them is even worse than the looks. They make me feel as if my legs were as big as barrels and they're so *scratchy.*"

"Well, I don't know what you're going to do."

"If father was home I'd go and ask him to get me a new pair before the store closes. But he won't be home till too late. I'll ask him Monday—and I won't go to church to-morrow. I'll pretend I'm sick and Aunt Martha'll *have* to let me stay home."

"That would be acting a lie, Faith," cried Una. "You *can't* do that. You know it would be dreadful. What would father say if he knew? Don't you remember how he talked to us after mother died and told us we must always be *true,* no matter what else we failed in. He said we must never tell or act a lie—he said he'd *trust* us not to. You *can't* do it, Faith. Just wear the striped stockings. It'll only be for once. Nobody will notice them in church. It isn't like school.

And your new brown dress is so long they won't show much. Wasn't it lucky Aunt Martha made it big, so you'd have room to grow in it, for all you hated it so when she finished it?"

"I won't wear those stockings," repeated Faith. She uncoiled her bare, white legs from the tombstone and deliberately walked through the wet, cold grass to the bank of snow. Setting her teeth, she stepped upon it and stood there.

"What are you doing?" cried Una aghast. "You'll catch your death of cold, Faith Meredith."

"I'm trying to," answered Faith. "I hope I'll catch a fearful cold and be *awful* sick to-morrow. Then I won't be acting a lie. I'm going to stand here as long as I can bear it."

"But, Faith, you might really die. You might get pneumonia. Please, Faith, don't. Let's go into the house and get *something* for your feet. Oh, here's Jerry. I'm so thankful. Jerry, *make* Faith get off that snow. Look at her feet."

"Holy cats! Faith, what *are* you doing?" demanded Jerry. "Are you crazy?"

"No. Go away!" snapped Faith.

"Then are you punishing yourself for something? It isn't right, if you are. You'll be sick."

"I want to be sick. I'm not punishing myself. Go away."

"Where's her shoes and stockings?" asked Jerry of Una.

"She gave them to Lida Marsh."

"Lida Marsh? What for?"

"Because Lida had none—and her feet were so cold. And now she wants to be sick so that she won't have to go to church to-morrow and wear her striped stockings. But, Jerry, she may die."

"Faith," said Jerry, "get off that ice bank or I'll pull you off."

"Pull away," dared Faith.

Jerry sprang at her and caught her arms. He pulled one way and Faith pulled another. Una ran behind Faith and pushed. Faith stormed at Jerry to leave her alone. Jerry stormed back at her not to be a dizzy idiot; and Una cried. They made no end of noise and they were close to the road fence of the graveyard. Henry Warren and his wife drove by and heard and saw them. Very soon the Glen heard that the manse children had been having an awful fight in the graveyard and using most improper language. Meanwhile, Faith had allowed herself to be pulled off the ice because her feet were aching so sharply that she was ready to get off any way. They all went in amiably and went to bed. Faith slept like a cherub and woke in the morning without a trace of a cold. She felt that she couldn't feign sickness and act a lie, after remembeing that long-ago talk with her father. But she was still as fully determined as ever that she would not wear those abominable stockings to church.

CHAPTER XXV

Another Scandal and Another "Explanation"

FAITH went early to Sunday School and was seated in the corner of her class pew before any one came. Therefore the dreadful truth did not burst upon any one until Faith left the class pew near the door to walk up to the manse pew after Sunday School. The church was already half filled and all who were sitting near the aisle saw that the minister's daughter had boots on but no stockings!

Faith's new brown dress, which Aunt Martha had made from an ancient pattern, was absurdly long for her, but even so it did not meet her boot tops. Two good inches of bare white leg showed plainly.

Faith and Carl sat alone in the manse pew. Jerry had gone into the gallery to sit with a chum and the Blythe girls had taken Una with them. The Meredith children were given to "sitting all over the church" in this fashion and a great many people thought it very improper. The gallery especially, where irresponsible lads congregated and were known to whisper and suspected of chewing tobacco during service, was no place for a son of the manse. But Jerry hated the manse pew at the very top of the church, under the eyes of Elder Clow and his family. He escaped from it whenever he could.

Carl, absorbed in watching a spider spinning its web at the window, did not notice Faith's legs. She walked home with her father after church and he never noticed them. She got on the hated striped stockings before Jerry and Una arrived, so that for the time being none of the occupants of the manse knew what she had done. But nobody else in Glen St. Mary was ignorant of it. The few who had not seen soon heard. Nothing else was talked of on the way home from church. Mrs. Alec Davis said it was only what she expected, and the next thing you would see some of those young ones coming to church with no clothes at all on. The president of the Ladies' Aid decided that she would bring the matter up at the next Aid meeting, and suggest that they wait in a body on the minister and protest. Miss Cornelia said that she, for her part, gave up. There was no use worrying over the manse fry any longer. Even Mrs. Dr. Blythe felt a little shocked, though she attributed the occurrence solely to Faith's forgetfulness. Susan could not immediately begin knitting stockings for Faith because it was Sunday, but she had one set up before any one else was out of bed at Ingleside the next morning.

"You need not tell me anything but that it was old Martha's fault, Mrs. Dr. dear," she told Anne. "I suppose that poor little child had no decent stockings to wear. I suppose every stocking she had was in holes, as you know very well they generally are. And *I* think, Mrs. Dr. dear, that the Ladies' Aid would be better employed in knitting some for them than in fighting over the new carpet for the pulpit platform. *I* am not a Ladies' Aider, but I shall knit Faith two pairs of stockings, out of this nice black yarn, as fast as my fingers can move and that you may tie to. Never shall I forget my sensations, Mrs. Dr. dear, when I saw a minister's child walking up the aisle of our church with no stockings on. I really did not know what way to look."

"And the church was just full of Methodists yesterday, too," groaned Miss Cornelia, who had come up to the Glen to do some shopping and run into Ingleside to talk the affair over. "I don't know how it is, but just as sure as those manse children do something especially awful the church is sure to be crowded with Methodists. I thought Mrs. Deacon Hazard's eyes would drop out of her head. When she came out of church she said, 'Well, that exhibition was no more than decent. I do pity the Presbyterians.' And we just had to *take* it. There was nothing one could say."

"There was something *I* could have said, Mrs. Dr. dear, if I had heard her," said Susan grimly. "I would have said, for one thing, that in my opinion clean bare legs were quite as decent as holes. And I would have said, for another, that the Presbyterians did not feel greatly in need of pity seeing that they had a minister who could *preach* and the Methodists had *not*. *I* could have squelched Mrs. Deacon Hazard, Mrs. Dr. dear, and that you may tie to."

"I wish Mr. Meredith didn't preach quite so well and looked after his family a little better," retorted Miss Cornelia. "He could at least glance over his children before they went to church and see that they were quite properly clothed. I'm tired making excuses for him, believe *me*."

Meanwhile, Faith's soul was being harrowed up in Rainbow Valley. Mary Vance was there and, as usual, in a lecturing mood. She gave Faith to understand that she had disgraced herself and her father beyond redemption and that she, Mary Vance, was done with her. "Everybody" was talking, and "everybody" said the same thing.

"I simply feel that I can't associate with you any longer," she concluded.

"*We* are going to associate with her then," cried Nan Blythe. Nan secretly thought Faith *had* done a rather awful thing, but she wasn't going to let Mary Vance run matters in this high-handed fashion. "And if *you* are not you needn't come any more to Rainbow Valley, *Miss* Vance."

Nan and Di both put their arms around Faith and glared defiance at Mary. The latter suddenly crumpled up, sat down on a stump and began to cry.

"It ain't that I don't want to," she wailed. "But if I keep in with Faith people'll be saying I put her up to doing things. Some are saying it now, true's you live.

I can't afford to have such things said of me, now that I'm in a respectable place and trying to be a lady. And *I* never went bare-legged to church in my toughest days. I'd never have thought of doing such a thing. But that hateful old Kitty Alec says Faith has never been the same girl since that time I stayed in the manse. She says Cornelia Elliott will live to rue the day she took me in. It hurts my feelings, I tell you. But it's Mr. Meredith I'm really worried over."

"I think you needn't worry about him," said Di scornfully. "It isn't likely necessary. Now, Faith darling, stop crying and tell us why you did it."

Faith explained tearfully. The Blythe girls sympathized with her, and even Mary Vance agreed that it was a hard position to be in. But Jerry, on whom the thing came like a thunderbolt, refused to be placated. So *this* was what some mysterious hints he had got in school that day meant! He marched Faith and Una home without ceremony, and the Good-Conduct Club held an immediate session in the graveyard to sit in judgment on Faith's case.

"I don't see that it was any harm," said Faith defiantly. "Not *much* of my legs showed. It wasn't *wrong* and it didn't hurt anybody."

"It will hurt dad. You *know* it will. You know people blame him whenever we do anything queer."

"I didn't think of that," muttered Faith.

"That's just the trouble. You didn't think and you *should* have thought. That's what our Club is for—

to bring us up and *make* us think. We promised we'd always stop and think before doing things. You didn't and you've got to be punished, Faith—and real hard, too. You'll wear those striped stockings to school for a week for punishment."

"Oh, Jerry. Won't a day do—two days? Not a whole week!"

"Yes, a whole week," said inexorable Jerry. "It is fair—ask Jem Blythe if it isn't."

Faith felt she would rather submit than ask Jem Blythe about such a matter. She was beginning to realize that her offence was a quite shameful one.

"I'll do it, then," she muttered, a little sulkily.

"You're getting off easy," said Jerry severely. "And no matter how we punish you it won't help father. People will always think you just did it for mischief, and they'll blame father for not stopping it. We can never explain it to everybody."

This aspect of the case weighed on Faith's mind. Her own condemnation she could bear, but it tortured her that her father should be blamed. If people knew the true facts of the case they would not blame him. But how could she make them known to all the world? Getting up in church, as she had once done, and explaining the matter was out of the question. Faith had heard from Mary Vance how the congregation had looked upon that performance and realized that she must not repeat it. Faith worried over the problem for half a week. Then she had an inspiration and promptly acted upon it. She spent that evening in the garret, with a lamp and an exercise book, writing busily, with flushed cheeks and shining eyes. It was the very thing! How clever she was to have thought of it! It would put everything right and explain everything and yet cause no scandal. It was eleven o'clock when she had finished to her satisfaction and crept down to bed, dreadfully tired, but perfectly happy.

In a few days the little weekly published in the Glen under the name of *The Journal* came out as usual, and the Glen had another sensation. A letter signed "Faith Meredith" occupied a prominent place on the front page and ran as follows:—

"To whom it may concern:

I want to explain to everybody how it was I came to go to church without stockings on, so that everybody will know that father was not to blame one bit for it, and the old gossips need not say he is, because it is not true. I gave my only pair of black stockings to Lida Marsh, because she hadn't any and her poor little feet were awful cold and I was so sorry for her. No child ought to have to go without shoes and stockings in a Christian community before the snow is all gone, and I think the W. F. M. S. ought to have given her stockings. Of course, I know they are sending things to the little heathen children, and that is all right and a kind thing to do. But the little heathen children have lots more warm weather than we have, and I think the women of our church ought to look after Lida and not leave it all to me. When I gave her my stockings I forgot they were the only black pair I had without holes, but I am glad I did give them to her, because my conscience would have been uncomfortable if I hadn't. When she had gone away, looking so proud and happy, the poor little thing, I remembered that all I had to wear were the horrid red and blue things Aunt Martha knit last winter for me out of some yarn that Mrs. Joseph Burr of Upper Glen sent us. It was dreadfully coarse yarn and all knots, and I never saw any of Mrs. Burr's own children wearing things made of such yarn. But Mary Vance says Mrs. Burr gives the minister stuff that she can't use or eat herself, and thinks it ought to go as part of the salary her husband signed to pay, but never does.

I just couldn't bear to wear those hateful stockings. They were so ugly and rough and felt so scratchy. Everybody would have made fun of me. I thought at first I'd pretend I was sick and not go to church next day, but I decided I couldn't do that, because it would be acting a lie, and father told us after mother died that was something we must never, never do. It is just as bad to act a lie as to tell one, though I know some people, right here in the Glen, who act them, and never seem to feel a bit bad about it. I will not mention any names, but I know who they are and so does father.

Then I tried my best to catch cold and really be sick by standing on the snowbank in the Methodist graveyard with my bare feet until Jerry pulled me off. But it didn't hurt me a bit and so I couldn't get out of going to church. So I just decided I would put my boots on and go that way. I can't see why it was so wrong and I was so careful to wash my legs just as clean as my face, but, anyway, father wasn't to blame for it. He was in the study thinking of his sermon and other heavenly things, and I kept out of his way before I went to Sunday school. Father does not look at people's legs in church, so of course he did not notice mine, but all the gossips did and talked about it, and that is why I am writing this letter to the *Journal* to explain. I suppose I did very wrong, since everybody says so, and I am sorry and I am wearing those awful stockings to punish myself, although father bought me two nice new black pairs as soon as

Mr. Flagg's store opened on Monday morning. But it was all my fault, and if people blame father for it after they read this they are not Christians and so I do not mind what they say.

There is another thing I want to explain about before I stop. Mary Vance told me that Mr. Evan Boyd is blaming the Lew Baxters for stealing potatoes out of his field last fall. They did not touch his potatoes. They are very poor, but they are honest. It was us did it—Jerry and Carl and I. Una was not with us at the time. We never thought it was stealing. We just wanted a few potatoes to cook over a fire in Rainbow Valley one evening to eat with our fried trout. Mr. Boyd's field was the nearest, just between the valley and the village, so we climbed over his fence and pulled up some stalks. The potatoes were awful small, because Mr. Boyd did not put enough fertilizer on them and we had to pull up a lot of stalks before we got enough, and then they were not much bigger than marbles. Walter and Di Blythe helped us eat them, but they did not come along until we had them cooked and did not know where we got them, so they were not to blame at all, only us. We didn't mean any harm, but if it was stealing we are very sorry and we will pay Mr. Boyd for them if he will wait until we grow up. We never have any money now because we are not big enough to earn any, and Aunt Martha says it takes every cent of poor father's salary, even when it is paid up regularly—and it isn't often—to run this house. But Mr. Boyd must not blame the Lew Baxters any more, when they were quite innocent, and give them a bad name.

Yours respectfully,

FAITH MEREDITH."

CHAPTER XXVI

Miss Cornelia Gets a New Point of View

"SUSAN, after I'm dead I'm going to come back to earth every time when the daffodils blow in this garden," said Anne rapturously. "Nobody may see me, but I'll be here. If anybody is in the garden at the time—I *think* I'll come on an evening just like this, but it *might* be just at dawn—a lovely, pale-pinky spring dawn—they'll just see the daffodils nodding wildly as if an extra gust of wind had blown past them, but it will be *I*."

"Indeed, Mrs. Dr. dear, you will not be thinking of flaunting worldly things like daffies after you are dead," said Susan. "And I do *not* believe in ghosts, seen or unseen."

"Oh, Susan, I shall not be a ghost! That has such a horrible sound. I shall just be *me*. And I shall run around in the twilight, whether it is of morn or eve, and see all the spots I love. Do you remember how badly I felt when I left our little House of Dreams, Susan? I thought I could never love Ingleside so well. But I do. I love every inch of the ground and every stick and stone on it."

"I am rather fond of the place myself," said Susan,

who would have died if she had been removed from it, "but we must not set our affections too much on earthly things, Mrs. Dr. dear. There are such things as fires and earthquakes. We should always be prepared. The Tom McAllisters over-harbour were burned out three nights ago. Some say Tom McAllister set the house on fire himself to get the insurance. That may or may not be. But I advise the doctor to have our chimneys seen to at once. An ounce of prevention is worth a pound of cure. But I see Mrs. Marshall Elliott coming in at the gate, looking as if she had been sent for and couldn't go."

"Anne, dearie, have you seen the *Journal* to-day?"

Miss Cornelia's voice was trembling, partly from emotion, partly from the fact that she had hurried up from the store too fast and lost her breath.

Anne bent over the daffodils to hide a smile. She and Gilbert had laughed heartily and heartlessly over the front page of the *Journal* that day, but she knew that to dear Miss Cornelia it was almost a tragedy, and she must not wound her feelings by any display of levity.

"Isn't it dreadful? What *is* to be done?" asked Miss Cornelia despairingly. Miss Cornelia had vowed that she was done with worrying over the pranks of the manse children, but she went on worrying just the same.

Anne led the way to the veranda, where Susan was knitting, with Shirley and Rilla conning their primers on either side. Susan was already on her second pair of stockings for Faith. Susan never worried over poor humanity. She did what in her lay for its betterment and serenely left the rest to the Higher Powers.

"Cornelia Elliott thinks she was born to run this world, Mrs. Dr. dear," she had once said to Anne, "and so she is always in a stew over something. I have never thought *I* was, and so I go calmly along. Not but what it has sometimes occurred to me that things might be run a little better than they are. But it is not for us poor worms of the dust to nourish such thoughts. They only make us uncomfortable and do not get us anywhere."

"I don't see that anything can be done—now—" said Anne, pulling out a nice, cushiony chair for Miss Cornelia. "But how in the world did Mr. Vickers allow that letter to be printed? Surely he should have known better."

"Why, he's away, Anne, dearie,—he's been away to New Brunswick for a week. And that young scalawag of a Joe Vickers is editing the *Journal* in his absence. Of course, Mr. Vickers would never have put it in, even if he is a Methodist, but Joe would just think it a good joke. As you say, I don't suppose there is anything to be done now, only live it down. But if I ever get Joe Vickers cornered somewhere I'll give him a talking to he won't forget in a hurry. I wanted Marshall to stop our subscription to the *Journal* instantly, but he only laughed and said that to-day's issue was the only one that had had anything readable in it for a year. Marshall never will take anything seriously—just like a man. Fortunately, Evan Boyd is like that, too. He takes it as a joke and is laughing all over the place about it. And he's another Methodist! As for Mrs. Burr of the Upper Glen, of course she will be furious and they will leave the church. Not that it will be a great loss from any point of view. The Methodists are quite welcome to *them*."

"It serves Mrs. Burr right," said Susan, who had an old feud with the lady in question and had been hugely tickled over the reference to her in Faith's letter. "She will find that she will not be able to cheat the Methodist parson out of *his* salary with bad yarn."

"The worst of it is, there's not much hope of things getting any better," said Miss Cornelia gloomily. "As long as Mr. Meredith was going to see Rosemary West I did hope the manse would soon have a proper mistress. But that is all off. I suppose she wouldn't have him on account of the children—at least, everybody seems to think so."

"I do not believe that he ever asked her," said Susan, who could not conceive of any one refusing a minister.

"Well, nobody knows anything about *that*. But one thing is certain, he doesn't go there any longer. And Rosemary didn't look well all the spring. I hope her visit to Kingsport will do her good. She's been gone for a month and will stay another month, I understand. I can't remember when Rosemary was away from home before. She and Ellen could never bear to be parted. But I understand Ellen insisted on her going this time. And meanwhile Ellen and Norman Douglas are warming up the old soup."

"Is that really so?" asked Anne, laughing. "I heard a rumour of it, but I hardly believed it."

"Believe it! You may believe it all right, Anne dearie. Nobody is in ignorance of it. Norman Douglas never left anybody in doubt as to his intentions in regard to anything. He always did his courting before the public. He told Marshall that he hadn't thought about Ellen for years, but the first time he went to church last fall he saw her and fell in love with her all over again. He said he'd clean forgot how handsome she was. He hadn't seen her for twenty years, if you can believe it. Of course he never went to church, and Ellen never went anywhere else round here. Oh, we all know what Norman means, but what Ellen means is a different matter. I shan't take it upon me to predict whether it will be a match or not."

"He jilted her once—but it seems that does not count with some people, Mrs. Dr. dear," Susan remarked rather acidly.

"He jilted her in a fit of temper and repented it all his life," said Miss Cornelia. "That is different from a cold-blooded jilting. For my part, I never detested Norman as some folks do. He could never over-crow *me*. I *do* wonder what started him coming to church. I have never been able to believe Mrs. Wilson's story that Faith Meredith went there and bullied him into it. I've always intended to ask Faith herself, but I've never happened to think of it just when I saw her. What influence could *she* have over Norman Douglas? He was in the store when I left, bellowing with laughter over that scandalous letter. You could have heard him at Four Winds Point. 'The greatest girl in the world,' he was shouting. 'She's that full of spunk she's bursting with it. And all the old grannies want to tame her, darn them. But they'll never be able to do it—never! They might as well try to drown a fish. Boyd, see that you put more fertilizer on your potatoes next year. Ho, ho, ho!' And then he laughed till the roof shook."

"Mr. Douglas pays well to the salary, at least," remarked Susan.

"Oh, Norman isn't mean in some ways. He'd give a thousand without blinking a lash, and roar like a Bull of Bashan if he had to pay five cents too much for anything. Besides, he likes Mr. Meredith's sermons, and Norman Douglas was always willing to shell out if he got his brains tickled up. There is no more Christianity about him than there is about a black, naked heathen in Africa and never will be. But he's clever and well read and he judges sermons as he would lectures. Anyhow, it's well he backs up Mr. Meredith and the children as he does, for they'll need friends more than ever after this. I am tired of making excuses for them, believe *me*."

"Do you know, dear Miss Cornelia," said Anne seriously, "I think we have all been making too many excuses. It is very foolish and we ought to stop it. I am going to tell you what I'd *like* to do. I shan't do it, of course"—Anne had noted a glint of alarm in Susan's eye—"it would be too unconventional, and we must be conventional or die, after we reach what is supposed to be a dignified age. But I'd *like* to do it. I'd like to call a meeting of the Ladies' Aid and W. M. S. and the Girls' Sewing Society, and include in the audience all and any Methodists who have been criticising the Merediths—although I do think if we Presbyterians stopped criticising and excusing we would find that other denominations would trouble themselves very little about our manse folks. I would say to them, 'Dear Christian friends'—with marked emphasis on 'Christian'—I have something to say to you and I want to say it good and hard, that you may take it home and repeat it to your families. You Methodists need not pity us, and we Presbyterians need not pity ourselves. We are not going to do it any more. And we are going to say, boldly and truthfully, to all critics and sympathizers, 'We are *proud* of our minister and his family. Mr. Meredith is the best preacher Glen St. Mary Church ever had. Moreover, he is a sincere, earnest teacher of truth and Christian charity. He is a faithful friend, a judicious pastor in all essentials, and a refined, scholarly, well-bred man. His family are worthy of him. Gerald Meredith is the cleverest pupil in the Glen school, and Mr. Hazard says that he is destined to a brilliant career. He is a manly, honourable, truthful little fellow. Faith Meredith is a beauty, and as inspiring and original as she is beautiful. There is nothing commonplace about her. All the other girls in the Glen put together haven't the vim, and wit, and joyousness and 'spunk' she has. She has not an enemy in the world. Every one who knows her loves her. Of how many, children or grown-ups, can that be said? Una Meredith is sweetness personified. She will make a most lovable woman. Carl Meredith, with his love for ants and frogs and spiders, will some day be a naturalist whom all Canada—nay, all the world, will delight to honour. Do you know of any other family in the Glen, or out of it, of whom all these things can be said? Away with shamefaced excuses and apologies. We *rejoice* in our minister and his splendid boys and girls!"

Anne stopped, partly because she was out of breath after her vehement speech and partly because she could not trust herself to speak further in view of Miss Cornelia's face. That good lady was staring helplessly at Anne, apparently engulfed in billows of new ideas. But she came up with a gasp and struck out for shore gallantly.

"Anne Blythe, I wish you *would* call that meeting and say just that! You've made me ashamed of myself, for one, and far be it from me to refuse to admit it. *Of course,* that is how we should have talked—

especially to the Methodists. And it's every word of it true—every word. We've just been shutting our eyes to the big worth-while things and squinting them on the little things that don't really matter a pin's worth. Oh, Anne, dearie, I can see a thing when it's hammered into my head. No more apologizing for Cornelia Marshall! *I* shall hold *my* head up after this, believe *me,*—though I *may* talk things over with *you* as usual just to relieve my feelings if the Merediths do any more startling stunts. Even that letter I felt so bad about—why, it's only a good joke after all, as Norman says. Not many girls would have been cute enough to think of writing it—and all punctuated so nicely and not one word misspelled. Just let me hear any Methodist say one word about it—though all the same I'll never forgive Joe Vickers—believe *me!* Where are the rest of your small fry to-night?"

"Walter and the twins are in Rainbow Valley. Jem is studying in the garret."

"They are all crazy about Rainbow Valley. Mary Vance thinks it's the only place in the world. She'd be off up here every evening if I'd let her. But I don't encourage her in gadding. Besides, I miss the creature when she isn't around, Anne dearie. I never thought I'd get so fond of her. Not but what I see her faults and try to correct them. But she has never said one saucy word to me since she came to my house and she is a *great* help—for when all is said and done, Anne dearie, I am not so young as I once was, and there is no sense in denying it. I was fifty-nine my last birthday. I don't *feel* it, but there is no gainsaying the Family Bible."

CHAPTER XXVII

A Sacred Concert

IN spite of Miss Cornelia's new point of view she could not help feeling a little disturbed over the next performance of the manse children. In public she carried off the situation splendidly, saying to all the gossips the substance of what Anne had said in daffodil time, and saying it so pointedly and forcibly that her hearers found themselves feeling rather foolish and began to think that, after all, they were making too much of a childish prank. But in private Miss Cornelia allowed herself the relief of bemoaning it to Anne.

"Anne, dearie, they had a *concert in the graveyard* last Thursday evening, while the Methodist prayer meeting was going on. There they sat, on Hezekiah Pollock's tombstone, and sang for a solid hour. Of course, I understand it was mostly hymns they sang, and it wouldn't have been quite so bad if they'd done nothing else. But I'm told they finished up with *Polly Wolly Doodle* at full length—and that just when Deacon Baxter was praying."

"I was there that night," said Susan, "and, although I did not say anything about it to you, Mrs. Dr. dear,

I could not help thinking that it was a great pity they picked that particular evening. It was truly blood-curdling to hear them sitting there in that abode of the dead, shouting that frivolous song at the tops of their lungs."

"I don't know what *you* were doing in a Methodist prayer meeting," said Miss Cornelia acidly.

"I have never found that Methodism was catching," retorted Susan stiffly. "And, as I was going to say when I was interrupted, badly as I felt, I did *not* give in to the Methodists. When Mrs. Deacon Baxter said, as we came out, 'What a disgraceful exhibition!' *I* said, looking her fairly in the eye, 'They are all beautiful singers and none of *your* choir, Mrs. Baxter, ever bother themselves coming out to your prayer meeting, it seems. Their voices appear to be in tune only on Sundays!' She was quite meek and I felt that I had snubbed her properly. But I could have done it much more thoroughly, Mrs. Dr. dear, if only they had left out *Polly Wolly Doodle*. It is truly terrible to think of that being sung in a graveyard."

"Some of those dead folks sang *Polly Wolly Doodle* when they were living, Susan. Perhaps they like to hear it yet," suggested Gilbert.

Miss Cornelia looked at him reproachfully and made up her mind that, on some future occasion, she would hint to Anne that the doctor should be admonished not to say such things. They might injure his practice. People might get it into their heads that he wasn't orthodox. To be sure, Marshall said even worse things habitually, but then *he* was not a public man.

"I understand that their father was in his study all the time, with his windows open, but never noticed them at all. Of course, he was lost in a book as usual. But *I* spoke to him about it yesterday, when he called.

"How could you dare, Mrs. Marshall Elliott?" asked Susan rebukingly.

"Dare! It's time somebody dared something. Why, they say he knows nothing about that letter of Faith's to the *Journal* because nobody liked to mention it to him. He never looks at a *Journal* of course. But I thought he ought to know of this to prevent any such performances in future. He said he would 'discuss it with them.' But of course he'd never think of it again after he got out of our gate. That man has no sense of humour, Anne, believe *me.* He preached last Sunday on 'How to Bring up Children.' A beautiful sermon it was, too—and everybody in church thinking 'what a pity you can't practice what you preach.'"

Miss Cornelia did Mr. Meredith an injustice in thinking he would so soon forget what she had told him. He went home much disturbed and when the children came from Rainbow Valley that night, at a much later hour than they should have been prowling in it, he called them into his study.

They went in, somewhat awed. It was such an unusual thing for their father to do. What could he be going to say to them? They racked their memories for any recent transgression of sufficient importance, but could not recall any. Carl had spilled a saucerful of jam on Mrs. Peter Flagg's silk dress two evenings before, when, at Aunt Martha's invitation, she had stayed to supper. But Mr. Meredith had not noticed it, and Mrs. Flagg, who was a kindly soul, had made no fuss. Besides, Carl had been punished by having to wear Una's dress all the rest of the evening.

Una suddenly thought that perhaps her father meant to tell them that he was going to marry Miss West. Her heart began to beat violently and her legs trembled. Then she saw that Mr. Meredith looked very stern and sorrowful. No, it could not be that.

"Children," said Mr. Meredith, "I have heard something that has pained me very much. Is it true that you sat out in the graveyard all last Thursday evening and sang ribald songs while a prayer meeting was being held in the Methodist church?"

"Great Cesær, dad, we forgot all about it being their prayer meeting night," exclaimed Jerry in dismay.

"Then it is true—you did do this thing?"

"Why, dad, I don't know what you mean by ribald songs. We sang hymns—it was a sacred concert, you know. What harm was that? I tell you we never thought about it's being Methodist prayer meeting night. They used to have their meeting Tuesday nights and since they've changed to Thursdays it's hard to remember."

"Did you sing nothing but hymns?"

"Why," said Jerry, turning red, "we *did* sing *Polly Wolly Doodle* at the last. Faith said, 'Let's have something cheerful to wind up with.' But we didn't mean any harm, father—truly we didn't."

"The concert was my idea, father," said Faith, afraid that Mr. Meredith might blame Jerry too much. "You know the Methodists themselves had a sacred concert in their church three Sunday nights ago. I thought it would be good fun to get one up in imitation of it. Only they had prayers at theirs, and we left that part out, because we heard that people thought it awful for us to pray in a graveyard. *You* were sitting in here all the time," she added, "and never said a word to us."

"I did not notice what you were doing. That is no excuse for me, of course. I am more to blame than you,—I realize that. But why did you sing that foolish song at the end?"

"We didn't think," muttered Jerry, feeling that it was a very lame excuse, seeing that he had lectured Faith so strongly in the Good-Conduct Club sessions for her lack of thought. "We're sorry, father,—truly, we are. Pitch into us hard—we deserve a regular combing down."

But Mr. Meredith did no combing down or pitching into. He sat down and gathered his small culprits close to him and talked a little to them, tenderly and wisely. They were overcome with remorse and shame, and felt that they could never be so silly and thoughtless again.

"We've just got to punish ourselves good and hard for this," whispered Jerry as they crept upstairs. "We'll have a session of the Club first thing to-morrow and decide how we'll do it. I never saw father so cut up. But I wish to goodness the Methodists would stick to one night for their prayer meeting and not wander all over the week."

"Any how, I'm glad it wasn't what I was afraid it was," murmured Una to herself.

Behind them, in the study, Mr. Meredith had sat down at his desk and buried his face in his arms.

"God help me!" he said. "I'm a poor sort of a father. Oh, Rosemary! If you had only cared!"

CHAPTER XXVIII

A Fast Day

THE Good-Conduct Club had a special session the next morning before school. After various suggestions, it was decided that a fast day would be an appropriate punishment.

"We won't eat a single thing for a whole day," said Jerry. "I'm kind of curious to see what fasting is like, anyhow. This will be a good chance to find out."

"What day will we choose for it?" asked Una, who thought it would be quite an easy punishment and rather wondered that Jerry and Faith had not devised something harder.

"Let's pick Monday," said Faith. "We mostly have a pretty *filling* dinner on Sundays, and Mondays' meals never amount to much anyhow."

"But that's just the point," exclaimed Jerry. "We mustn't take the easiest day to fast, but the hardest—and that's Sunday, because, as you say, we mostly have roast beef that day instead of cold ditto. It wouldn't be much punishment to fast from ditto. Let's take next Sunday. It will be a good day, for father is going to exchange for the morning service with the Upper Lowbridge minister. Father will be away till evening. If Aunt Martha wonders what's got into us, we'll tell her right up that we're fasting for the good of our souls, and it is in the Bible and she is not to interfere, and I guess she won't."

Aunt Martha did not. She merely said in her fretful, mumbling way, "What foolishness are you young rips up to now?" and thought no more about it. Mr. Meredith had gone away early in the morning before any one was up. He went without his breakfast, too, but that was, of course, of common occurrence. Half of the time he forgot it and there was no one to remind him of it. Breakfast—Aunt Martha's breakfast—was not a hard meal to miss. Even the hungry "young rips" did not feel it any great deprivation to abstain from the "lumpy porridge and blue milk" which had aroused the scorn of Mary Vance. But it was different at dinner time. They were furiously hungry then, and the odour of roast beef which pervaded the manse, and which was wholly delightful in spite of the fact that the roast beef itself was badly underdone, was almost more than they could stand. In desperation they rushed to the graveyard where they couldn't smell it. But Una could not keep her eyes from the dining room window, through which the Upper Lowbridge minister could be seen, placidly eating.

"If I could only have just a weeny, teeny piece," she sighed.

"Now, you stop that," commanded Jerry. "Of course it's hard—but that's the punishment of it. I could eat a graven image this very minute, but am I complaining? Let's think of something else. We've just got to rise above our stomachs."

At supper time they did not feel the pangs of hunger which they had suffered earlier in the day.

"I suppose we're getting used to it," said Faith. "I feel an awfully queer all-gone sort of feeling, but I can't say I'm hungry."

"My head is funny," said Una. "It goes round and round sometimes."

But she went gamely to church with the others. If Mr. Meredith had not been so wholly wrapped up in and carried away with his subject he might have noticed the pale little face and hollow eyes in the manse pew beneath. But he noticed nothing and his sermon was something longer than usual. Then, just before he gave out the final hymn, Una Meredith tumbled off the seat of the manse pew and lay in a dead faint on the floor.

Mrs. Elder Clow was the first to reach her. She caught the thin little body from the arms of white-faced, terrified Faith and carried it into the vestry. Mr. Meredith forgot the hymn and everything else and rushed madly after her. The congregation dismissed itself as best it could.

"Oh, Mrs. Clow," gasped Faith, "is Una dead? Have we killed her?"

"What is the matter with my child?" demanded the pale father.

"She has just fainted, I think," said Mrs. Clow. "Oh, here's the doctor, thank goodness."

Gilbert did not find it a very easy thing to bring Una back to consciousness. He worked over her for a long time before her eyes opened. Then he carried her over to the manse, followed by Faith, sobbing hysterically in her relief.

"She is just hungry, you know—she didn't eat a thing to-day—none of us did—we were all fasting."

"Fasting!" said Mr. Meredith, and "Fasting?" said the doctor.

"Yes—to punish ourselves for singing *Polly Wolly* in the graveyard," sobbed Faith.

"My child, I don't want you to punish yourselves for that," said Mr. Meredith in distress. "I gave you your little scolding—and you were all penitent—and I forgave you."

"Yes, but we had to be punished," explained Faith. "It's our rule—in our Good-Conduct Club, you know—if we do anything wrong, or anything that is likely to hurt father in the congregation, we *have* to punish ourselves. We are bringing ourselves up, you know, because there is nobody to do it."

Mr. Meredith groaned, but the doctor got up from Una's side with an air of relief.

"Then this child simply fainted from lack of food and all she needs is a good square meal," he said. "Mrs. Clow, will you be kind enough to see she gets it? And I think from Faith's story that they all would be the better of something to eat, or we shall have more faintings,"

"I suppose we shouldn't have made Una fast," said Faith remorsefully. "When I think of it, only Jerry and I should have been punished. *We* got up the concert and we were the oldest."

"I sang *Polly Wolly* just the same as the rest of you," said Una's weak little voice, "so I had to be punished, too."

Mrs. Clow came with a glass of milk, Faith and Jerry and Carl sneaked off to the pantry, and John Meredith went into his study, where he sat in the darkness for a long time, along with his bitter thoughts. So his children were bringing themselves up because there was "nobody to do it"—struggling along amid their little perplexities without a hand to guide or a voice to counsel. Faith's innocently uttered phrase rankled in her father's mind like a barbed shaft. There was "nobody" to look after them—to comfort their little souls and care for their little bodies. How frail Una had looked, lying there on the vestry sofa in that long faint! How thin were her tiny hands, how pallid her little face! She looked as if she might slip away from him in a breath—sweet little Una, of whom Cecilia had begged him to take such special care. Since his wife's death he had not felt such an agony of dread as when he had hung over his little girl in her unconsciousness. He must do something—but what? Should he ask Elizabeth Kirk to marry him?

She was a good woman—she would be kind to his children. He might bring himself to do it if it were not for his love of Rosemary West. But until he had crushed that out he could not seek another woman in marriage. And he could not crush it out—he had tried and he could not. Rosemary had been in church that evening, for the first time since her return from Kingsport. He had caught a glimpse of her face in the back of the crowded church, just as he had finished his sermon. His heart had given a fierce throb. He sat while the choir sang the "collection piece," with his bent head and tingling pulses. He had not seen her since the evening upon which he had asked her to marry him. When he had risen to give out the hymn his hands were trembling and his pale face was flushed. Then Una's fainting spell had banished everything from his mind for a time. Now, in the darkness and solitude of the study it rushed back. Rosemary was the only woman in the world for him. It was of no use for him to think of marrying any other. He could not commit such a sacrilege even for his children's sake. He must take up his burden alone—he must try to be a better, a more watchful father—he must tell his children not to be afraid to come to him with all their little problems. Then he lighted his lamp and took up a bulky new book which was setting the theological world by the ears. He would read just one chapter to compose his mind. Five minutes later he was lost to the world and the troubles of the world.

CHAPTER XXIX

A Weird Tale

ON an early June evening Rainbow Valley was an entirely delightful place and the children felt it to be so, as they sat in the open glade where the bells rang elfishly on the Tree Lovers, and the White Lady shook her green tresses. The wind was laughing and whistling about them like a leal, glad-hearted comrade. The young ferns were spicy in the hollow. The wild cherry trees scattered over the valley, among the dark firs, were mistily white. The robins were whistling over in the maples behind Ingleside. Beyond, on the slopes of the Glen, were blossoming orchards, sweet and mystic and wonderful, veiled in dusk. It was spring, and young things *must* be glad in spring. Everybody was glad in Rainbow Valley that evening—until Mary Vance froze their blood with the story of Henry Warren's ghost.

Jem was not there. Jem spent his evenings now studying for his entrance examination in the Ingleside garret. Jerry was down near the pond, trouting. Walter had been reading Longfellow's sea poems to the others and they were steeped in the beauty and mystery of the ships. Then they talked of what they would do when they were grown up—where they would travel—the far, fair shores they would see. Nan and Di meant to go to Europe. Walter longed for the Nile moaning past its Egyptian sands, and a glimpse of the sphinx. Faith opined rather dismally that she supposed she would have to be a missionary—old Mrs. Taylor had told her she ought to be—and then she would at least see India or China, those mysterious lands of the Orient. Carl's heart was set on African jungles. Una said nothing. She thought she would just like to stay at home. It was prettier here than anywhere else. It would be dreadful when they were all grown up and had to scatter over the world. The very idea made Una feel lonesome and homesick. But the others dreamed on delightedly until Mary Vance arrived and banished poesy and dreams at one fell swoop.

"Laws, but I'm out of puff," she exclaimed. "I've run down that hill like sixty. I got an awful scare up there at the old Bailey place."

"What frightened you?" asked Di.

"I dunno. I was poking about under them lilacs in the old garden, trying to see if there was any lilies-of-the-valley out yet. It was dark as a pocket there—and all at once I seen something stirring and rustling round at the other side of the garden, in those cherry bushes. It was *white.* I tell you I didn't stop for a second look. I flew over the dyke quicker than quick. I was sure it was Henry Warren's ghost."

"Who was Henry Warren?" asked Di.

"And why should he have a ghost?" asked Nan.

"Laws, did you never hear the story? And you brought up in the Glen. Well, wait a minute till I get my breath all back and I'll tell you."

Walter shivered delightsomely. He loved ghost stories. Their mystery, their dramatic climaxes, their eeriness gave him a fearful, exquisite pleasure. Longfellow instantly grew tame and commonplace. He threw the book aside and stretched himself out, propped upon his elbows to listen whole-heartedly, fixing his great luminous eyes on Mary's face. Mary wished he wouldn't look at her so. She felt she could make a far better job of the ghost story if Walter were not looking at her. She could put on several frills and invent a few artistic details to enhance the horror. As it was, she had to stick to the bare truth—or what had been told her for truth.

"Well," she began, "you know old Tom Bailey and his wife used to live in that house up there thirty years ago. He was an awful old rip, they say, and his wife wasn't much better. They'd no children of their own, but a sister of old Tom's died and left a little boy—this Henry Warren—and they took him. He was about twelve when he came to them, and kind of undersized and delicate. They say Tom and his wife used him awful from the start—whipped him and starved him. Folks said they wanted him to die so's they could get the little bit of money his mother had left for him.

Henry didn't die right off, but he begun having fits—epileps, they called 'em—and he grew up kind of simple, till he was about eighteen. His uncle used to thrash him in that garden up there, 'cause it was back of the house where no one could see him. But folks could hear and they say it was awful sometimes hearing poor Henry plead with his uncle not to kill him. But nobody dared interfere 'cause old Tom was such a reprobate he'd have been sure to get square with 'em some way. He burned the barns of a man at Harbour Head who offended him. At last Henry died and his uncle and aunt give out he died in one of his fits and that was all anybody ever knowed, but everybody said Tom had just up and killed him for keeps at last. And it wasn't long till it got round that Henry *walked*. That old garden was *ha'nted*. He was heard there at nights, moaning and crying. Old Tom and his wife got out—went out West and never come back. The place got such a bad name nobody'd buy or rent it. That's why it's all gone to ruin. That was thirty years ago, but Henry Warren's ghost ha'nts it yet."

"Do you believe that?" asked Nan scornfully. "*I* don't."

"Well, *good* people have seen him—and heard him," retorted Mary. "They say he appears and grovels on the ground and holds you by the legs and gibbers and moans like he did when he was alive. I thought of that as soon as I seen that white thing in the bushes and thought if it caught me like that and moaned I'd drop down dead on the spot. So I cut and run. It *mightn't* have been his ghost, but I wasn't going to take any chances with a ha'nt."

"It was likely old Mrs. Stimson's white calf," laughed Di. "It pastures in that garden—I've seen it."

"Maybe so. But *I'm* not going home through the Bailey garden any more. Here's Jerry with a big string of trout and it's my turn to cook them. Jem and Jerry both say I'm the best cook in the Glen. And Cornelia told me I could bring up this batch of cookies. I all but dropped them when I saw Henry's ghost."

Jerry hooted when he heard the ghost story—which Mary repeated as she fried the fish, touching it up a trifle or so, since Walter had gone to help Faith set the table. It made no impression on Jerry, but Faith and Una and Carl had been secretly much frightened, though they would never have given in to it. It was all right as long as the others were with them in the valley; but when the feast was over and the shadows fell they quaked with remembrance. Jerry went up to Ingleside with the Blythes to see Jem about something, and Mary Vance went around that way home. So Faith and Una and Carl had to go back to the manse alone. They walked very close together and gave the old Bailey garden a wide berth. They did not believe that it was haunted, of course, but they would not go near it for all that.

CHAPTER XXX

The Ghost on the Dyke

SOMEHOW, Faith and Carl and Una could not shake off the hold which the story of Henry Warren's ghost had taken upon their imaginations. They had never believed in ghosts. Ghost tales they had heard a-plenty—Mary Vance had told some far more blood-curdling than this; but those tales were all of places and people and spooks far away and unknown. After the first half-awful, half-pleasant thrill of awe and terror they thought of them no more. But this story came home to them. The old Bailey garden was almost at their very door—almost in their beloved Rainbow Valley. They had passed and repassed it constantly; they had hunted for flowers in it; they had made short cuts through it when they wished to go straight from the village to the valley. But never again! After the night when Mary Vance told them its gruesome tale they would not have gone through or near it on pain of death. Death! What was death compared to the unearthly possibility of falling into the clutches of Henry Warren's grovelling ghost?

One warm July evening the three of them were sitting under the Tree Lovers, feeling a little lonely.

Nobody else had come near the valley that evening. Jem Blythe was away in Charlottetown, writing on his entrance examinations. Jerry and Walter Blythe were off for a sail on the harbour with old Captain Crawford. Nan and Di and Rilla and Shirley had gone down the harbour road to visit Kenneth and Persis Ford, who had come with their parents for a flying visit to the little old House of Dreams. Nan had asked Faith to go with them, but Faith had declined. She would never have admitted it, but she felt a little secret jealousy of Persis Ford, concerning whose wonderful beauty and city glamour she had heard a great deal. No, she wasn't going to go down there and play second fiddle to anybody. She and Una took their story books to Rainbow Valley and read, while Carl investigated bugs along the banks of the brook, and all three were happy until they suddenly realized that it was twilight and that the old Bailey garden was uncomfortably near by. Carl came and sat down close to the girls. They all wished they had gone home a little sooner, but nobody said anything.

Great, velvety, purple clouds heaped up in the west and spread over the valley. There was no wind and everything was suddenly, strangely, dreadfully still. The marsh was full of thousands of fireflies. Surely some fairy parliament was being convened that night. Altogether, Rainbow Valley was not a canny place just then.

Faith looked fearfully up the valley to the old Bailey

garden. Then, if anybody's blood ever did freeze, Faith Meredith's certainly froze at that moment. The eyes of Carl and Una followed her entranced gaze and chills began gallopading up and down their spines also. For there, under the big tamarack tree on the tumble-down, grass-grown dyke of the Bailey garden, was a something white—shapelessly white in the gathering gloom. The three Merediths sat and gazed as if turned to stone.

"It's—it's the—calf," whispered Una at last.

"It's—too—big—for the calf," whispered Faith. Her mouth and lips were so dry she could hardly articulate the words.

Suddenly Carl gasped,

"It's coming here."

The girls gave one last agonized glance. Yes, it was creeping down over the dyke, as no calf ever did or could creep. Reason fled before sudden, over-mastering panic. For the moment every one of the trio was firmly convinced that what they saw was Henry Warren's ghost. Carl sprang to his feet and bolted blindly. With a simultaneous shriek the girls followed him. Like mad creatures they tore up the hill, across the road and into the manse. They had left Aunt Martha sewing in the kitchen. She was not there. They rushed to the study. It was dark and tenantless. As with one impulse, they swung around and made for Ingleside—but not across Rainbow Valley. Down the hill and through the Glen street they flew on the wings of their wild terror, Carl in the lead, Una bringing up the rear. Nobody tried to stop them, though everybody who saw them wondered what fresh devilment those manse youngsters were up to now. But at the gate of Ingleside they ran into Rosemary West, who had just been in for a moment to return some borrowed books.

She saw their ghastly faces and staring eyes. She realized that their poor little souls were wrung with some awful and real fear, whatever its cause. She caught Carl with one arm and Faith with the other. Una stumbled against her and held on desperately.

"Children, dear, what has happened?" she said. "What has frightened you?"

"Henry Warren's ghost," answered Carl, through his chattering teeth.

"Henry—Warren's—ghost!" said amazed Rosemary, who had never heard the story.

"Yes," sobbed Faith hysterically. "It's there—on the Bailey dyke—we saw it—and it started to—chase us."

Rosemary herded the three distracted creatures to the Ingleside veranda. Gilbert and Anne were both away, having also gone to the House of Dreams, but Susan appeared in the doorway, gaunt and practical and unghostlike.

"What is all this rumpus about?" she inquired.

Again the children gasped out their awful tale, while Rosemary held them close to her and soothed them with wordless comfort.

"Likely it was an owl," said Susan, unstirred.

An owl! The Meredith children never had any opinion of Susan's intelligence after that!

"It was bigger than a million owls," said Carl, sobbing—oh, how ashamed Carl was of that sobbing in after days—"and it—it *grovelled* just as Mary said—and it was crawling down over the dyke to get at us. Do owls *crawl?*"

Rosemary looked at Susan.

"They must have seen something to frighten them so," she said.

"I will go and see," said Susan coolly. "Now, children, calm yourselves. Whatever you have seen, it was not a ghost. As for poor Henry Warren, I feel sure he would be only too glad to rest quietly in his peaceful grave once he got there. No fear of *him* venturing back, and that you may tie to. If you can make them see reason, Miss West, I will find out the truth of the matter."

Susan departed for Rainbow Valley, valiantly grasping a pitchfork which she found leaning against the back fence where the doctor had been working in his little hay-field. A pitchfork might not be of much use against "ha'nts," but it was a comforting sort of weapon. There was nothing to be seen in Rainbow Valley when Susan reached it. No white visitants appeared to be lurking in the shadowy, tangled old Bailey garden. Susan marched boldly through it and beyond it, and rapped with her pitchfork on the door of the little cottage on the other side, where Mrs. Stimson lived with her two daughters.

Back at Ingleside Rosemary had succeeded in calming the children. They still sobbed a little from shock, but they were beginning to feel a lurking and salutary suspicion that they had made dreadful geese of themselves. This suspicion became a certainty when Susan finally returned.

"I have found out what your ghost was," she said, with a grim smile, sitting down on a rocker and fanning herself. "Old Mrs. Stimson has had a pair of factory cotton sheets bleaching in the Bailey garden for a week. She spread them on the dyke under the tamarack tree because the grass was clean and short there. This evening she went out to take them in. She had her knitting in her hands so she flung the sheets over her shoulders by way of carrying them. And then she must drop one of her needles and find it she could not and has not yet. But she went down on her knees and crept about to hunt for it, and she was at that when she heard awful yells down in the valley and saw the three children tearing up the hill past her. She thought they had been bit by something and it gave her poor old heart such a turn that she could not move or speak, but just crouched there till they disappeared. Then she staggered back home and they have been applying stimulants to her ever since, and her heart is in a terrible condition and she says she will not get over this fright all summer."

The Merediths sat, crimson with a shame that even Rosemary's understanding sympathy could not remove. They sneaked off home, met Jerry at the manse gate and made remorseful confession. A session of the Good-Conduct Club was arranged for next morning.

"Wasn't Miss West sweet to us to-night?" whispered Faith in bed.

"Yes," admitted Una. "It is such a pity it changes people so much to be made stepmothers."

"I don't believe it does," said Faith loyally.

CHAPTER XXXI

Carl Does Penance

"I DON'T see why we should be punished at all," said Faith, rather sulkily. "We didn't do anything wrong. We couldn't help being frightened. And it won't do father any harm. It was just an accident."

"You were cowards," said Jerry with judicial scorn, "and you gave way to your cowardice. That is why you should be punished. Everybody will laugh at you about this, and that is a disgrace to the family."

"If you knew how awful the whole thing was," said Faith with a shiver, "you would think we had been punished enough already. I wouldn't go through it again for anything in the whole world."

"I believe you'd have run yourself if you'd been there," muttered Carl.

"From an old woman in a cotton sheet," mocked Jerry. "Ho, ho, ho!"

"It didn't look a bit like an old woman," cried Faith. "It was just a great, big, white thing crawling about in the grass just as Mary Vance said Henry Warren did. It's all very fine for you to laugh, Jerry Meredith, but you'd have laughed on the other side of your mouth if you'd been there. And how are we to be punished? *I* don't think it's fair, but let's know what we have to do, Judge Meredith!"

"The way I look at it," said Jerry, frowning, "is that Carl was the most to blame. He bolted first, as I understand it. Besides, he was a boy, so he should have stood his ground to protect you girls, whatever the danger was. You know that Carl, don't you?"

"I s'pose so," growled Carl shamefacedly.

"Very well. This is to be your punishment. To-night you'll sit on Mr. Hezekiah Pollock's tombstone in the graveyard alone, until twelve o'clock."

Carl gave a little shudder. The graveyard was not so very far from the old Bailey garden. It would be a trying ordeal. But Carl was anxious to wipe out his disgrace and prove that he was not a coward after all.

"All right," he said sturdily. "But how'll I know when it is twelve?"

"The study windows are open and you'll hear the clock striking. And mind that you are not to budge out of that graveyard until the last stroke. As for you girls, you've got to go without jam at supper for a week."

Faith and Una looked rather blank. They were inclined to think that even Carl's comparatively short though sharp agony was lighter punishment than this long drawn-out ordeal. A whole week of soggy bread without the saving grace of jam! But no shirking was permitted in the club. The girls accepted their lot with such philosophy as they could summon up.

That night they all went to bed at nine, except Carl, who was already keeping vigil on the tombstone. Una slipped in to bid him good night. Her tender heart was wrung with sympathy.

"Oh, Carl, are you much scared?" she whispered.

"Not a bit," said Carl airily.

"I won't sleep a wink till after twelve," said Una. "If you get lonesome just look up at our window and remember that I'm inside, awake, and thinking about you. That will be a little company, won't it?"

"I'll be all right. Don't you worry about me," said Carl.

But in spite of his dauntless words Carl was a pretty lonely boy when the lights went out in the manse. He had hoped his father would be in the study as he so often was. He would not feel alone then. But that night Mr. Meredith had been summoned to the fishing village at the harbour mouth to see a dying man. He would not likely be back until after midnight. Carl must dree his weird alone.

A Glen man went past carrying a lantern. The mysterious shadows caused by the lantern-light went hurtling madly over the graveyard like a dance of demons or witches. Then they passed and darkness fell again. One by one the lights in the Glen went out. It was a very dark night, with a cloudy sky, and a raw east wind that was cold in spite of the calendar. Far away on the horizon was the low dim lustre of the Charlottetown lights. The wind wailed and sighed in the old fir trees. Mr. Alec Davis' tall monument gleamed whitely through the gloom. The willow beside it tossed long, writhing arms spectrally. At times, the gyrations of its boughs made it seem as if the monument were moving, too.

Carl curled himself up on the tombstone with his legs tucked under him. It wasn't precisely pleasant to hang them over the edge of the stone. Just suppose—just suppose—bony hands should reach up out of Mr. Pollock's grave under it and clutch him by the ankles. That had been one of Mary Vance's cheerful speculations one time when they had all been sitting there. It returned to haunt Carl now. He didn't believe those things; he didn't even really believe in Henry Warren's ghost. As for Mr. Pollock, he had been dead for sixty years, so it wasn't likely he cared who sat on his tombstone now. But there is something very strange and terrible in being awake when all the rest of the world is asleep. You are alone then with nothing but your own feeble personality to pit against the mighty principalities and powers of darkness. Carl was only ten and the dead were all around him—and he wished, oh, he wished that the clock would strike twelve. Would it *never* strike twelve? Surely Aunt Martha must have forgotten to wind it.

And then it struck eleven—only eleven! He must stay yet another hour in that grim place. If only there were a few friendly stars to be seen! The darkness was so thick it seemed to press against his face. There was a sound as of stealthy passing footsteps all over the graveyard. Carl shivered, partly with prickling terror, partly with real cold.

Then it began to rain—a chill, penetrating drizzle. Carl's thin little cotton blouse and shirt were soon wet through. He felt chilled to the bone. He forgot mental terrors in his physical discomfort. But he must stay there till twelve—he was punishing himself and he was on his honour. Nothing had been said about rain—but it did not make any difference. When the study clock finally struck twelve a drenched little figure crept stiffly down off Mr. Pollock's tombstone, made its way into the manse and upstairs to bed. Carl's teeth were chattering. He thought he could never get warm again.

He was warm enough when morning came. Jerry gave one startled look at his crimson face and then rushed to call his father. Mr. Meredith came hurriedly, his own face ivory white from the pallor of his long night vigil by a death bed. He had not got home until daylight. He bent over his little lad anxiously.

"Carl, are you sick?" he said.

"That—tombstone—over there," said Carl, "it's—moving—about—it's coming—at—me—keep it—away—please."

Mr. Meredith rushed to the telephone. In ten minutes Dr. Blythe was at the manse. Half an hour later a wire was sent to town for a trained nurse, and all the Glen knew that Carl Meredith was very ill with pneumonia and that Dr. Blythe had been seen to shake his head.

Gilbert shook his head more than once in the fortnight that followed. Carl developed double pneumonia. There was one night when Mr. Meredith paced his study floor, and Faith and Una huddled in their bedroom and cried, and Jerry, wild with remorse, refused to budge from the floor of the hall outside Carl's door. Dr. Blythe and the nurse never left the bedside. They fought death gallantly until the red dawn and they won the victory. Carl rallied and passed the crisis in safety. The news was phoned about the waiting Glen and people found out how much they really loved their minister and his children.

"I haven't had one decent night's sleep since I heard the child was sick," Miss Cornelia told Anne, "and Mary Vance has cried until those queer eyes of hers looked like burnt holes in a blanket. Is it true that Carl got pneumonia from staying out in the graveyard that wet night for a dare?"

"No. He was staying there to punish himself for cowardice in that affair of the Warren ghost. It seems they have a club for bringing themselves up, and they punish themselves when they do wrong. Jerry told Mr. Meredith all about it."

"The poor little souls," said Miss Cornelia.

Carl got better rapidly, for the congregation took

enough nourishing things to the manse to furnish forth a hospital. Norman Douglas drove up every evening with a dozen fresh eggs and a jar of Jersey cream. Sometimes he stayed an hour and bellowed arguments on predestination with Mr. Meredith in the study; oftener he drove on up to the hill that overlooked the Glen.

On the day when Carl was able to come downstairs Mr. Meredith called all his children into the library and told them that they were to inflict no more punishments on themselves without first consulting him.

"But Aunt Martha is always warning us that we mustn't disturb you," said Faith.

"Never mind that. You must remember what I say, darlings. Your little club is all right in principle. But henceforth I am to be the judge who passes sentence."

When Carl was able to go again to Rainbow Valley they had a special feast in his honour and the doctor came down and helped them with the fireworks. Mary Vance was there, too, but she did not tell any ghost stories. Miss Cornelia had given her a talking to on that subject which Mary would not forget in a hurry.

CHAPTER XXXII

Two Stubborn People

ROSEMARY WEST, on her way home from a music lesson at Ingleside, turned aside to the hidden spring in Rainbow Valley. She had not been there all summer; the beautiful little spot had no longer any allurement for her. The spirit of her young lover never came to the tryst now; and the memories connected with John Meredith were too painful and poignant. But she had happened to glance backward up the valley and had seen Norman Douglas vaulting as airily as a stripling over the old stone dyke of the Bailey garden and thought he was on his way up the hill. If he overtook her she would have to walk home with him and she was not going to do that. So she slipped at once behind the maples of the spring, hoping he had not seen her and would pass on.

But Norman had seen her and, what was more, was in pursuit of her. He had been wanting for some time to have a talk with Rosemary, but she had always, so it seemed, avoided him. Rosemary had never, at any time, liked Norman Douglas very well. His bluster, his temper, his noisy hilarity, had always antagonized her. Long ago she had often wondered how

Ellen could possibly be attracted to him. Norman Douglas was perfectly aware of her dislike and he chuckled over it. It never worried Norman if people did not like him. It did not even make him dislike them in return, for he took it as a kind of extorted compliment. He thought Rosemary a fine girl, and he meant to be an excellent, generous brother-in-law to her. But before he could be her brother-in-law he had to have a talk with her, so, having seen her leaving Ingleside as he stood in the doorway of a Glen store, he had straightway plunged into the valley to overtake her.

Rosemary was sitting pensively on the maple seat where John Meredith had been sitting on that evening nearly a year ago. The tiny spring shimmered and dimpled under its fringe of ferns. Ruby-red gleams of sunset fell through the arching boughs. A tall clump of perfect asters grew at her side. The little spot was as dreamy and witching and evasive as any retreat of fairies or dryads in ancient forests. Into it Norman Douglas bounced, scattering and annihilating its charm in a moment. His personality seemed to swallow the place up. There was simply nothing there but Norman Douglas, big, red-bearded, complacent.

"Good evening," said Rosemary coldly, standing up.

"'Evening, girl. Sit down again—sit down again. I want to have a talk with you. Bless the girl, what's she looking at me like that for? I don't want to eat you—I've had my supper. Sit down and be civil."

"I can hear what you have to say quite as well here," said Rosemary.

"So you can, girl, if you use your ears. I only wanted you to be comfortable. You look so durned uncomfortable, standing there. Well, *I'll* sit anyway."

Norman accordingly sat down in the very place John Meredith had once sat. The contrast was so ludicrous that Rosemary was afraid she would go off into a peal of hysterical laughter over it. Norman cast his hat aside, placed his huge, red hands on his knees, and looked up at her with his eyes a-twinkle.

"Come, girl, don't be so stiff," he said, ingratiatingly. When he liked he could be very ingratiating. "Let's have a reasonable, sensible, friendly chat. There's something I want to ask you. Ellen says *she* won't, so it's up to me to do it."

Rosemary looked down at the spring, which seemed to have shrunk to the size of a dewdrop. Norman gazed at her in despair.

"Durn it all, you might help a fellow out a bit," he burst forth.

"What is it you want me to help you say?" asked Rosemary scornfully.

"You know as well as I do, girl. Don't be putting on your tragedy airs. No wonder Ellen was scared to ask you. Look here, girl, Ellen and I want to marry each other. That's plain English, isn't it? Got that? And Ellen says she can't unless you give her back some tom-fool promise she made. Come now, will you do it? Will you do it?"

"Yes," said Rosemary.

Norman bounced up and seized her reluctant hand.

"Good! I knew you would—I told Ellen you would. I knew it would only take a minute. Now, girl, you go home and tell Ellen, and we'll have the wedding in a fortnight and you'll come and live with us. We shan't leave you to roost on that hill-top like a lonely crow—don't you worry. I know you hate me, but, Lord, it'll be great fun living with some one that hates me. Life'll have some spice in it after this. Ellen will roast me and you'll freeze me. I won't have a dull moment."

Rosemary did not condescend to tell him that nothing would ever induce her to live in his house. She let him go striding back to the Glen, oozing delight and complacency, and she walked slowly up the hill home. She had known this was coming ever since she had returned from Kingsport, and found Norman Douglas established as a frequent evening caller. His name was never mentioned between her and Ellen, but the very avoidance of it was significant. It was not in Rosemary's nature to feel bitter, or she would have felt very bitter. She was coldly civil to Norman, and she made no difference in any way with Ellen. But Ellen had not found much comfort in her second courtship.

She was in the garden, attended by St. George, when Rosemary came home. The two sisters met in the dahlia walk. St. George sat down on the gravel walk between them and folded his glossy black tail gracefully around his white paws, with all the indifference of a well-fed, well-bred, well-groomed cat.

"Did you ever see such dahlias?" demanded Ellen proudly. "They are just the finest we've ever had."

Rosemary had never cared for dahlias. Their presence in the garden was her concession to Ellen's taste. She noticed one huge mottled one of crimson and yellow that lorded it over all the others.

"That dahlia," she said, pointing to it, "is exactly like Norman Douglas. It might easily be his twin brother."

Ellen's dark-browed face flushed. She admired the dahlia in question, but she knew Rosemary did not, and that no compliment was intended. But she dared not resent Rosemary's speech—poor Ellen dared not resent anything just then. And it was the first time Rosemary had ever mentioned Norman's name to her. She felt that this portended something.

"I met Norman Douglas in the valley," said Rosemary, looking straight at her sister, "and he told me you and he wanted to be married—if I would give you permission."

"Yes? What did you say?" asked Ellen, trying to speak naturally and off-handedly, and failing completely. She could not meet Rosemary's eyes. She looked down at St. George's sleek back and felt horribly afraid. Rosemary had either said she would or she wouldn't. If she would Ellen would feel so ashamed and remorseful that she would be a very uncomfortable bride-elect; and if she wouldn't—well, Ellen had once learned to live without Norman Douglas, but she had forgotten the lesson and felt that she could never learn it again.

"I said that as far as I was concerned you were at full liberty to marry each other as soon as you liked," said Rosemary.

"Thank you," said Ellen, still looking at St. George.

Rosemary's face softened.

"I hope you'll be happy, Ellen," she said gently.

"Oh, Rosemary," Ellen looked up in distress, "I'm so ashamed—I don't deserve it—after all I said to you"—

"We won't speak about that," said Rosemary hurriedly and decidedly.

"But—but," persisted Ellen, "you are free now, too—and it's not too late—John Meredith"—

"Ellen West!" Rosemary had a little spark of temper under all her sweetness and it flashed forth now in her blue eyes. "Have you quite lost your senses in *every* respect? Do you suppose for an instant that *I* am going to go to John Meredith and say meekly, 'Please, sir, I've changed my mind and please, sir, I hope you haven't changed yours.' Is that what you want me to do?"

"No—no—but a little—encouragement—he would come back"—

"Never. He despises me—and rightly. No more of this, Ellen. I bear you no grudge—marry whom you like. But no meddling in my affairs."

"Then you must come and live with me," said Ellen. "I shall not leave you here alone."

"Do you really think that I would go and live in Norman Douglas' house?"

"Why not?" cried Ellen, half angrily, despite her humiliation.

Rosemary began to laugh.

"Ellen, I thought you had a sense of humour. Can you *see* me doing it?"

"I don't see why you wouldn't. His house is big enough—you'd have your share of it to yourself—he wouldn't interfere."

"Ellen, the thing is not to be thought of. Don't bring this up again."

"Then," said Ellen coldly, and determinedly, "I shall not marry him. I shall not leave you here alone. That is all there is to be said about it."

"Nonsense, Ellen."

"It is not nonsense. It is my firm decision. It would be absurd for you to think of living here by yourself—a mile from any other house. If you won't come with me I'll stay with you. Now, we won't argue the matter, so don't try."

"I shall leave Norman to do the arguing," said Rosemary.

"*I*'ll deal with Norman. I can manage *him.* I would never have asked you to give me back my promise—never—but I had to tell Norman why I couldn't marry him and he said *he* would ask you. I couldn't prevent him. You need not suppose you are the only person in the world who possesses self-respect. I never dreamed of marrying and leaving you here alone. And you'll find I can be as determined as yourself."

Rosemary turned away and went into the house, with shrug of her shoulders. Ellen looked down at St. George, who had never blinked an eyelash or stirred a whisker during the whole interview.

"St. George, this world would be a dull place without the men, I'll admit, but I'm almost tempted to wish there wasn't one of 'em in it. Look at the trouble and bother they've made right here, George,—torn our happy old life completely up by the roots, Saint. John Meredith began it and Norman Douglas has finished it. And now both of them have to go into limbo. Norman is the only man I ever met who agrees with me that the Kaiser of Germany is the most dangerous creature alive on this earth—and I can't marry this sensible person because my sister is stubborn and I'm stubborner. Mark my words, St. George, the minister would come back if she raised her little finger. But she won't, George—she'll never do it—she won't even crook it—and I don't dare meddle, Saint. I won't sulk, George; Rosemary didn't sulk, so I'm determined I won't either, Saint; Norman will tear up the turf, but the long and short of it is, St. George, that all of us old fools must just stop thinking of marrying. Well, well, 'despair is a free man, hope is a slave,' Saint. So now come into the house, George, and I'll solace you with a saucerful of cream. Then there will be one happy and contented creature on this hill at least."

CHAPTER XXXIII

Carl Is—Not—Whipped

"THERE is something I think I ought to tell you," said Mary Vance mysteriously.

She and Faith and Una were walking arm in arm through the village, having foregathered at Mr. Flagg's store. Una and Faith exchanged looks which said, "*Now* something disagreeable is coming." When Mary Vance thought she ought to tell them things there was seldom much pleasure in the hearing. They often wondered why they kept on liking Mary Vance—for like her they did, in spite of everything. To be sure, she was generally a stimulating and agreeable companion. If only she would not have those convictions that it was her duty to tell them things!

"Do you know that Rosemary West won't marry your pa because she thinks you are such a wild lot? She's afraid she couldn't bring you up right and so she turned him down."

Una's heart thrilled with secret exultation. She was very glad to hear that Miss West would not marry her father. But Faith was rather disappointed.

"How do you know?" she asked.

"Oh, everybody's saying it. I heard Mrs. Elliott

talking it over with Mrs. Doctor. They thought I was too far away to hear, but I've got ears like a cat's. Mrs. Elliott said she hadn't a doubt that Rosemary was afraid to try stepmothering you because you'd got such a reputation. Your pa never goes up the hill now. Neither does Norman Douglas. Folks say Ellen has jilted him just to get square with him for jilting her ages ago. But Norman is going about declaring he'll get her yet. And I think you ought to know you've spoiled your pa's match and *I* think it's a pity, for he's bound to marry somebody before long, and Rosemary West would have been the best wife *I* know of for him."

"You told me all stepmothers were cruel and wicked," said Una.

"Oh—well," said Mary rather confusedly, "they're mostly awful cranky, I know. But Rosemary West couldn't be very mean to any one. I tell you if your pa turns round and marries Emmeline Drew you'll wish you'd behaved yourselves better and not frightened Rosemary out of it. It's awful that you've got such a reputation that no decent woman'll marry your pa on account of you. Of course, *I* know that half the yarns that are told about you ain't true. But give a dog a bad name. Why, some folks are saying that it was Jerry and Carl that threw the stones through Mrs. Stimson's window the other night when it was really them two Boyd boys. But I'm afraid it *was* Carl that put the eel in old Mrs. Carr's buggy, though

I said at first I wouldn't believe it until I'd better proof than old Kitty Alec's word. I told Mrs. Elliott so right to her face."

"What did Carl do?" cried Faith.

"Well, they say—now, mind, I'm only telling you what people say—so there's no use in your blaming me for it—that Carl and a lot of other boys were fishing eels over the bridge one evening last week. Mrs. Carr drove past in that old rattletrap buggy of hers with the open back. And Carl he just up and threw a big eel into the back. When poor old Mrs. Carr was driving up the hill by Ingleside that eel came squirming out between her feet. She thought it was a snake and she just give one awful screech and stood up and jumped out clean over the wheels. The horse bolted, but it went home and no damage was done. But Mrs. Carr jarred her legs most terrible, and has had nervous spasms ever since whenever she thinks of the eel. Say, it was a rotten trick to play on the poor old soul. She's a decent body, if she is as queer as Dick's hat band."

Faith and Una looked at each other again. This was a matter for the Good-Conduct Club. They would not talk it over with Mary.

"There goes your pa," said Mary as Mr. Meredith passed them, "and never seeing us no more'n if we weren't here. Well, I'm getting so's I don't mind it. But there are folks who do."

Mr. Meredith had not seen them, but he was not

walking along in his usual dreamy and abstracted fashion. He strode up the hill in agitation and distress. Mrs. Alec Davis had just told him the story of Carl and the eel. She had been very indignant about it. Old Mrs. Carr was her third cousin. Mr. Meredith was more than indignant. He was hurt and shocked. He had not thought Carl would do anything like this. He was not inclined to be hard on pranks of heedlessness or forgetfulness, but *this* was different. *This* had a nasty tang in it. When he reached home he found Carl on the lawn, patiently studying the habits and customs of a colony of wasps. Calling him into the study Mr. Meredith confronted him, with a sterner face than any of his children had ever seen before, and asked him if the story were true.

"Yes," said Carl, flushing, but meeting his father's eye bravely.

Mr. Meredith groaned. He had hoped that there had been at least exaggeration.

"Tell me the whole matter," he said.

"The boys were fishing for eels over the bridge," said Carl. "Link Drew had caught a whopper—I mean an awful big one—the biggest eel I ever saw. He caught it right at the start and it had been lying in his basket a long time, still as still. I thought it was dead, honest I did. Then old Mrs. Carr drove over the bridge and she called us all young varmints and told us to go home. And we hadn't said a word to her, father, truly. So when she drove back again, after going to the store, the boys dared me to put Link's eel in her buggy. I thought it was so dead it couldn't hurt her and I threw it in. Then the eel came to life on the hill and we heard her scream and saw her jump out. I was awful sorry. That's all, father."

It was not quite as bad as Mr. Meredith had feared, but it was quite bad enough. "I must punish you, Carl," he said sorrowfully.

"Yes, I know, father."

"I—I must whip you."

Carl winced. He had never been whipped. Then, seeing how badly his father felt, he said cheerfully,

"All right, father."

Mr. Meredith misunderstood his cheerfulness and thought him insensible. He told Carl to come to the study after supper, and when the boy had gone out he flung himself into his chair and groaned again. He dreaded the evening sevenfold more than Carl did. The poor minister did not even know what he should whip his boy with. What was used to whip boys? Rods? Canes? No, that would be too brutal. A limber switch, then? And he, John Meredith, must hie him to the woods and cut one. It was an abominable thought. Then a picture presented itself unbidden to his mind. He saw Mrs. Carr's wizened, nut-cracker little face at the appearance of that reviving eel—he saw her sailing witch-like over the buggy wheels. Before he could prevent himself the minister laughed. Then he was angry with himself and angrier still with Carl. He would get that switch at once—and it must not be too limber, after all.

Carl was talking the matter over in the graveyard with Faith and Una, who had just come home. They were horrified at the idea of his being whipped—and by father, who had never done such a thing! But they agreed soberly that it was just.

"You know it was a dreadful thing to do," sighed Faith. "And you never owned up in the club."

"I forgot," said Carl. "Besides, I didn't think any harm came of it. I didn't know she jarred her legs. But I'm to be whipped and that will make things square."

"Will it hurt—very much?" said Una, slipping her hand into Carl's.

"Oh, not so much, I guess," said Carl gamely. "Anyhow, I'm not going to cry, no matter how much it hurts. It would make father feel so bad, if I did. He's all cut up now. I wish I could whip myself hard enough and save him doing it."

After supper, at which Carl had eaten little and Mr. Meredith nothing at all, both went silently into the study. The switch lay on the table. Mr. Meredith had had a bad time getting a switch to suit him. He cut one, then felt it was too slender. Carl had done a really indefensible thing. Then he cut another—it was far too thick. After all, Carl had thought the eel was dead. The third one suited him better; but as he picked it up from the table it seemed very thick and heavy,—more like a stick than a switch.

"Hold out your hand," he said to Carl.

Carl threw back his head and held out his hand unflinchingly. But he was not very old and he could not quite keep a little fear out of his eyes. Mr. Meredith looked down into those eyes—why, they were Cecilia's eyes—her very eyes—and in them was the selfsame expression he had once seen in Cecilia's eyes when she had come to him to tell him something she had been a little afraid to tell him. Here were her eyes in Carl's little, white face—and six weeks ago he had thought, through one endless, terrible night, that his little lad was dying.

John Meredith threw down the switch.

"Go," he said, "I cannot whip you."

Carl fled to the graveyard, feeling that the look on his father's face was worse than any whipping.

"Is it over so soon?" asked Faith. She and Una had been holding hands and setting teeth on the Pollock tombstone.

"He—he didn't whip me at all," said Carl with a sob, "and—I wish he had—and he's in there, feeling just awful."

Una slipped away. Her heart yearned to comfort her father. As noiselessly as a little gray mouse she opened the study door and crept in. The room was dark with twilight. Her father was sitting at his desk. His back was towards her—his head was in his hands.

He was talking to himself—broken, anguished words—but Una heard—heard and understood, with the sudden illumination that comes to sensitive, unmothered children. As silently as she had come in she slipped out and closed the door. John Meredith went on talking out his pain in what he deemed his undisturbed solitude.

CHAPTER XXXIV

Una Visits the Hill

UNA went upstairs. Carl and Faith were already on their way through the early moonlight to Rainbow Valley, having heard therefrom the elfin lilt of Jerry's jews-harp and having guessed that the Blythes were there and fun afoot. Una had no wish to go. She sought her own room first where she sat down on her bed and had a little cry. She did not want anybody to come in her dear mother's place. She did not want a stepmother who would hate her and make her father hate her. But father was so desperately unhappy—and if she could do anything to make him happier she *must* do it. There was only one thing she could do—and she had known the moment she had left the study that she must do it. But it was a very hard thing to do.

After Una cried her heart out she wiped her eyes and went to the spare room. It was dark and rather musty, for the blind had not been drawn up nor the window opened for a long time. Aunt Martha was no fresh-air fiend. But as nobody ever thought of shutting a door in the manse this did not matter so much, save when some unfortunate minister came to stay all night and was compelled to breathe the spare room atmosphere.

There was a closet in the spare room and far back in the closet a gray silk dress was hanging. Una went into the closet and shut the door, went down on her knees and pressed her face against the soft silken folds. It had been her mother's wedding dress. It was still full of a sweet, faint, haunting perfume, like lingering love. Una always felt very close to her mother there—as if she were kneeling at her feet with head in her lap. She went there once in a long while when life was *too* hard.

"Mother," she whispered to the gray silk gown, "*I* will never forget you, mother, and I'll *always* love you best. But I have to do it, mother, because father is so very unhappy. I know you wouldn't want him to be unhappy. And I will be very good to her, mother, and try to love her, even if she is like Mary Vance said stepmothers always were."

Una carried some fine, spiritual strength away from her secret shrine. She slept peacefully that night with the tear stains still glistening on her sweet, serious, little face.

The next afternoon she put on her best dress and hat. They were shabby enough. Every other little girl in the Glen had new clothes that summer except Faith and Una. Mary Vance had a lovely dress of white embroidered lawn, with scarlet silk sash and shoulder bows. But to-day Una did not mind her shabbiness. She only wanted to be very neat. She washed her face carefully. She brushed her brown hair until it was as smooth as satin. She tied her shoelaces carefully, having first sewed up two runs in her one pair of good stockings. She would have liked to black her shoes, but she could not find any blacking. Finally, she slipped away from the manse, down through Rainbow Valley, up through the whispering woods, and out to the road that ran past the house on the hill. It was quite a long walk and Una was tired and warm when she got there.

She saw Rosemary West sitting under a tree in the garden and stole past the dahlia beds to her. Rosemary had a book in her lap, but she was gazing afar across the harbour and her thoughts were sorrowful enough. Life had not been pleasant lately in the house on the hill. Ellen had not sulked—Ellen had been a brick. But things can be felt that are never said and at times the silence between the two women was intolerably eloquent. All the many familiar things that had once made life sweet had a flavour of bitterness now. Norman Douglas made periodical irruptions also, bullying and coaxing Ellen by turns. It would end, Rosemary believed, by his dragging Ellen off with him some day, and Rosemary felt that she would be almost glad when it happened. Existence would be horribly lonely then, but it would be no longer charged with dynamite.

She was roused from her unpleasant reverie by a timid little touch on her shoulder. Turning, she saw Una Meredith.

"Why, Una, dear, did you walk up here in all this heat?"

"Yes," said Una, "I came to—I came to"—

But she found it very hard to say what she had come to do. Her voice failed—her eyes filled with tears.

"Why, Una, little girl, what is the trouble? Don't be afraid to tell me."

Rosemary put her arm around the thin little form and drew the child close to her. Her eyes were very beautiful—her touch so tender that Una found courage.

"I came—to ask you—to marry father," she gasped.

Rosemary was silent for a moment from sheer dumbfounderment. She stared at Una blankly.

"Oh, don't be angry, please, dear Miss West," said Una, pleadingly. "You see, everybody is saying that you wouldn't marry father because we are so bad. He is *very* unhappy about it. So I thought I would come and tell you that we are never bad *on purpose*. And if you will only marry father we will all try to be good and do just what you tell us. I'm *sure* you won't have any trouble with us. *Please*, Miss West."

Rosemary had been thinking rapidly. Gossipping surmise, she saw, had put this mistaken idea into

Una's mind. She must be perfectly frank and sincere with the child.

"Una, dear," she said softly. "It isn't because of you poor little souls that I cannot be your father's wife. I never thought of such a thing. You are not bad—I never supposed you were. There—there was another reason altogether, Una."

"Don't you like father?" asked Una, lifting reproachful eyes. "Oh, Miss West, you don't know how nice he is. I'm sure he'd make you a *good* husband."

Even in the midst of her perplexity and distress Rosemary couldn't help a twisted, little smile.

"Oh, don't laugh, Miss West," Una cried passionately. "Father feels *dreadful* about it."

"I think you're mistaken, dear," said Rosemary.

"I'm not. I'm *sure* I'm not. Oh, Miss West, father was going to whip Carl yesterday—Carl had been naughty—and father couldn't do it because you see he had no *practice* in whipping. So when Carl came out and told us father felt so bad, I slipped into the study to see if I could help him—he *likes* me to comfort him, Miss West—and he didn't hear me come in and I heard what he was saying. I'll tell you, Miss West, if you'll let me whisper it in your ear."

Una whispered earnestly. Rosemary's face turned crimson. So John Meredith still cared. *He* hadn't changed his mind. And he must care intensely if he had said that—care more than she had ever supposed he did. She sat still for a moment, stroking Una's hair. Then she said,

"Will you take a little letter from me to your father, Una?"

"Oh, are you going to marry him, Miss West?" asked Una eagerly.

"Perhaps—if he really wants me to," said Rosemary, blushing again.

"I'm glad—I'm glad," said Una bravely. Then she looked up, with quivering lips. "Oh, Miss West, you won't turn father against us—you won't make him hate us, will you?" she said beseechingly.

Rosemary stared again.

"Una Meredith! Do you think I would do such a thing? Whatever put such an idea into your head?"

"Mary Vance said stepmothers were all like that—and that they all hated their stepchildren and made their father hate them—she said they just couldn't help it—just being stepmothers made them like that"—

"You poor child! And yet you came up here and asked me to marry your father because you wanted to make him happy? You're a darling—a heroine—as Ellen would say, you're a brick. Now listen to me very closely, dearest. Mary Vance is a silly little girl who doesn't know very much and she is dreadfully mistaken about some things. I would never dream of trying to turn your father against you. I would love you all dearly. I don't want to take your own mother's place—she must always have that in your hearts. But neither have I any intention of being a stepmother. I want to be your friend and helper and *chum.* Don't you think that would be nice, Una—if you and Faith and Carl and Jerry could just think of me as a good jolly chum—a big older sister?"

"Oh, it would be lovely," cried Una, with a transfigured face. She flung her arms impulsively round Rosemary's neck. She was so happy that she felt as if she could fly on wings.

"Do the others—do Faith and the boys have the same idea you had about stepmothers?"

"No. Faith never believed Mary Vance. I was dreadfully foolish to believe her, either. Faith loves you already—she has loved you ever since poor Adam was eaten. And Jerry and Carl will think it is jolly. Oh, Miss West, when you come to live with us, will you—could you—teach me to cook—a little—and sew—and—and—and do things? I don't know anything. I won't be much trouble—I'll try to learn fast."

"Darling, I'll teach you and help you all I can. Now, you won't say a word to anybody about this, will you—not even to Faith, until your father himself tells you you may? And you'll stay and have tea with me?"

"Oh, thank you—but—but—I think I'd rather go right back and take the letter to father," faltered Una. "You see, he'll be glad that much *sooner,* Miss West."

"I see," said Rosemary. She went to the house, wrote a note and gave it to Una. When that small damsel had run off, a palpitating bundle of happiness,

Rosemary went to Ellen, who was shelling peas on the back porch.

"Ellen," she said, "Una Meredith has just been here to ask me to marry her father."

Ellen looked up and read her sister's face.

"And you're going to?" she said.

"It's quite likely."

Ellen went on shelling peas for a few minutes. Then she suddenly put her hands up to her own face. There were tears in her black-browed eyes.

"I—I hope we'll all be happy," she said between a sob and a laugh.

Down at the manse Una Meredith, warm, rosy, triumphant, marched boldly into her father's study and laid a letter on the desk before him. His pale face flushed as he saw the clear, fine, handwriting he knew so well. He opened the letter. It was very short—but he shed twenty years as he read it. Rosemary asked him if he could meet her that evening at sunset by the spring in Rainbow Valley.

CHAPTER XXXV

"Let the Piper Come"

"AND so," said Miss Cornelia, "the double wedding is to be sometime about the middle of this month."

There was a faint chill in the air of the early September evening, so Anne had lighted her ever ready fire of driftwood in the big living room, and she and Miss Cornelia basked in its fairy flicker.

"It is so delightful—especially in regard to Mr. Meredith and Rosemary," said Anne. "I'm as happy in the thought of it, as I was when I was getting married myself. I felt exactly like a bride again last evening when I was up on the hill seeing Rosemary's trousseau."

"They tell me her things are fine enough for a princess," said Susan from a shadowy corner where she was cuddling her brown boy. "I have been invited up to see them also and I intend to go some evening. I understand that Rosemary is to wear white silk and a veil, but Ellen is to be married in navy blue. I have no doubt, Mrs. Dr. dear, that that is very sensible of her, but for my own part I have always felt that if I were ever married *I* would prefer the white and the veil, as being more bride-like."

A vision of Susan in "white and a veil" presented itself before Anne's inner vision and was almost too much for her.

"As for Mr. Meredith," said Miss Cornelia, "even his engagement has made a different man of him. He isn't half so dreamy and absent-minded, believe *me.* I was so relieved when I heard that he had decided to close the manse and let the children visit round while he was away on his honeymoon. If he had left them and old Aunt Martha there alone for a month I should have expected to wake every morning and see the place burned down."

"Aunt Martha and Jerry are coming here," said Anne. "Carl is going to Elder Clow's. I haven't heard where the girls are going."

"Oh, I'm going to take them," said Miss Cornelia. "Of course I was glad to, but Mary would have given me no peace till I asked them any way. The Ladies' Aid is going to clean the manse from top to bottom before the bride and groom come back, and Norman Douglas has arranged to fill the cellar with vegetables. Nobody ever saw or heard anything quite like Norman Douglas these days, believe *me.* He's so tickled that he's going to marry Ellen West after wanting her all his life. If *I* was Ellen—but then, I'm not, and if she is satisfied I can very well be. I heard her say years ago when she was a schoolgirl that she didn't want a tame puppy for a husband. There's nothing tame about Norman, believe *me.*"

The sun was setting over Rainbow Valley. The pond was wearing a wonderful tissue of purple and gold and green and crimson. A faint blue haze rested on the eastern hill, over which a great, pale, round moon was just floating up like a silver bubble.

They were all there, squatted in the little open glade—Faith and Una, Jerry and Carl, Jem and Walter, Nan and Di, and Mary Vance. They had been having a special celebration, for it would be Jem's last evening in Rainbow Valley. On the morrow he would leave for Charlottetown to attend Queen's Academy. Their charmed circle would be broken; and, in spite of the jollity of their little festival, there was a hint of sorrow in every gay young heart.

"See—there is a great golden palace over there in the sunset," said Walter, pointing. "Look at the shining towers—and the crimson banners streaming from them. Perhaps a conqueror is riding home from battle—and they are hanging them out to do honour to him."

"Oh, I wish we had the old days back again," exclaimed Jem. "I'd love to be a soldier—a great, triumphant general. I'd give *everything* to see a big battle."

Well, Jem was to be a soldier and see a greater battle than had ever been fought in the world; but that was as yet far in the future; and the mother, whose first-born son he was, was wont to look on her boys and thank God that the "brave days of old," which

Jem longed for, were gone forever, and that never would it be necessary for the sons of Canada to ride forth to battle "for the ashes of their fathers and the temples of their gods."

The shadow of the Great Conflict had not yet made felt any forerunner of its chill. The lads who were to fight, and perhaps fall, on the fields of France and Flanders, Gallipoli and Palestine, were still roguish schoolboys with a fair life in prospect before them: the girls whose hearts were to be wrung were yet fair little maidens a-star with hopes and dreams.

Slowly the banners of the sunset city gave up their crimson and gold; slowly the conqueror's pageant faded out. Twilight crept over the valley and the little group grew silent. Walter had been reading again that day in his beloved book of myths and he remembered how he had once fancied the Pied Piper coming down the valley on an evening just like this.

He began to speak dreamily, partly because he wanted to thrill his companions a little, partly because something apart from him seemed to be speaking through his lips.

"The Piper is coming nearer," he said, "he is nearer than he was that evening I saw him before. His long, shadowy cloak is blowing around him. He pipes—he pipes—and we must follow—Jem and Carl and Jerry and I—round and round the world. Listen—listen—can't you hear his wild music?"

The girls shivered.

"You know you're only pretending," protested Mary Vance, "and I wish you wouldn't. You make it too real. I hate that old Piper of yours."

But Jem sprang up with a gay laugh. He stood on a little hillock, tall and splendid, with his open brow and his fearless eyes. There were thousands like him all over the land of the maple.

"Let the Piper come and welcome," he cried, waving his hand. "*I'll* follow him gladly round and round the world."

THE END